Here's wha
Cathe

BOOKS BY CATHERINE BRUNS

Cookies & Chance Mysteries:
Tastes Like Murder
Baked to Death
Burned to a Crisp
Frosted with Revenge
Silenced by Sugar
Crumbled to Pieces
A Spot of Murder (short story in the Killer Beach Reads collection)
A Drizzle Before Dying (short story in the Pushing Up Daisies collection)

Cindy York Mysteries:
Killer Transaction
Priced to Kill
For Sale by Killer

Aloha Lagoon Mysteries:
Death of the Big Kahuna
Death of the Kona Man

CRUMBLED TO PIECES

a Cookies & Chance mystery

Catherine Bruns

Acknowledgements

Special thanks to Retired Troy Police Captain Terrance Buchanan, who always gives so generously of his time and knowledge. I so appreciate Kim Davis and Carmen Story sharing their delicious recipes with me for everyone to enjoy. Constance Atwater is an exceptional beta reader and always comes through when I need her. As always, special thanks to publisher Gemma Halliday and her editing team, especially Danielle Kuhns.

And to all who enjoy reading about Sally's adventures, please know how much I appreciate you as well.

May you always have good fortune.

CHAPTER ONE

——————

A shiver of excitement slid down my spine as I stared at the piece of paper between my hands. Printed on the slim strip were words I had wanted to hear for a long time. Sure, it was only a piece of paper and I shouldn't make too much out of it. But for the last few days I'd suspected I might be in this condition, and this message only served to confirm my belief. *Yes.* My biggest dream was about to become a reality.

A new blessing will be born to your family soon.

It was early afternoon on an oppressively humid July day, and I was thankful for the cool air that blew through the air conditioner's vents in my cookie shop, Sally's Samples. At the moment, I was alone in the storefront. My best friend and baker, Josie Sullivan, was in the kitchen taking cookies out of the oven, and the smell of cinnamon and butter blended together as they drifted toward me in a warm haze. Ah, snickerdoodles. We made over twenty different varieties of cookies, and I was proud to say I could recognize almost every flavor by their smell.

My heart raced with excitement. I reached for my cell to call my husband, Mike, then stopped myself. *Don't, Sal. He'll think you're being silly.*

If the fortune cookie message proved true, this would be the most beautiful gift to share with him. Our first wedding anniversary was a week from next Sunday, and by then I'd know for certain if I was pregnant. Given how tired I'd been feeling the last week and my recent weight gain, I had a premonition that we were indeed expecting a baby.

When I celebrated my thirtieth birthday a couple of weeks ago and blew out the candles on my cake, I silently wished for a child. This was nothing new. I'd wanted a baby for as long as I could remember. During my first marriage, I'd hoped in vain for a family, even though Colin, my ex-husband who was now also deceased, had told me from the beginning it was never going to happen. He didn't want kids and said he didn't even like them. For five years I had foolishly thought he'd change his mind someday. Then I'd found him in bed with my high school nemesis, Amanda Gregorio, and my dreams had melted faster than an ice cream cone on a hot summer's day.

"What are you smiling about?"

I jumped at the sound of Josie's voice. She stood in the doorway of the back room, hands on her hips, watching me with suspicious blue eyes.

I started to stammer, something I always did when nervous. "Um…nothing."

She glanced down at the broken fortune cookie on the counter, and a smile quivered at the corners of her mouth. "Sally Muccio Donovan, I thought you were done believing in those ridiculous strips of paper."

"Yes, I am." The homemade fortune cookies and their messages had been both a curse and a blessing to the shop in our two years of operation. The messages always seemed to come true in some shape or form, whether good or bad. On our honeymoon last year, Mike and I had had a long talk, and he'd said I was taking them too seriously. I'd agreed with him. Slowly the messages had started to become more positive in nature, and if today's was any indication, I'd just hit the jackpot, so to speak.

Josie put out her hand. "Okay, let's have it."

"Don't be silly." I started to tuck the message away into my jeans pocket, but Josie was too quick and snatched it out of my hands.

"Come on, Jos, give it back!" My face burned with embarrassment—we might as well be back in middle school. Josie and I had been best friends since the age of eight. She'd always been the leader while I'd dutifully followed along, despite the trouble she'd sometimes gotten me into.

Josie held the message up to the front window, the brilliant sunlight from outside streaming through the paper. Her saucy grin quickly changed to an expression of wonder. "Sal," she whispered. "Is it true?"

My tone was giddy as I snatched the paper and placed it back in my pocket for safekeeping. "I don't know for sure yet. But within a week I will."

Josie's face lit up like a Christmas tree, and she reached out to hug me. A loose tendril from her rich auburn hair, which had been tied back in a ponytail, brushed against my cheek. "I'm sorry I teased you. This is so awesome. I know how much you've always wanted a baby."

"Okay, go ahead and say what you're thinking."

Her face was puzzled. "What am I thinking?"

I turned away from her and started to place the rest of the fortune cookies on a tray inside the display case. "No, I didn't open it on purpose. The cookie cracked open in my hand. It wasn't planned."

"So maybe it's fate—and the message really is true." Her eyes gleamed with excitement. "Wouldn't that be the best anniversary gift ever for you and Mike?"

My lower lip started to tremble. "I shouldn't get my hopes up." I'd gone through a major disappointment a couple of months back and been so depressed that I'd told Josie I was sick and stayed home for a day—something I never did. "It means so much to me. Gosh, I've dreamed about saying those words for so long."

She must have heard the quiver in my voice, because she put an arm around my shoulders. "Aw, Sal. It's only been a year. That's not very long. It's nothing to worry about."

"Says the woman who got pregnant every time her husband looked at her in a funny way," I retorted.

Josie laughed. She had four boys who ranged in age from two to eleven years old. She and her husband Rob had gotten married right out of high school when she became pregnant with their first child. "Hey, what can I tell you? I was just born lucky, I guess. But everyone's different. Who knows? Maybe your first baby will end up as twins, and then you can retire from baby-making."

I shook my head. "Nope. I want at least four, like you."

"You have no idea what you're in for," she teased, then hesitated for a moment. "Did you and Mike go see a specialist? I remember you talked about it once, but I didn't want to pry."

"No. I mentioned it, but Mike shot the idea right down. He's not exactly a fan and said we should let nature take its course."

"He was probably right," Josie agreed.

A distinct babble of voices could be heard from above. Josie craned her neck toward the ceiling and lifted an eyebrow at me. "I can't believe you're letting that friend of Nicoletta's rent space over the shop."

"Why not?" I placed a tray of cooled snickerdoodles inside the case, tempted to snitch one but then forced myself not to. They smelled like a little piece of heaven. "The apartment's been sitting there empty and useless since Gianna moved out, and Mike and I can use the extra money."

My baby sister had moved in with her boyfriend, Johnny Gavelli, a few months ago when he'd purchased a house. I'd thought about advertising the apartment in the local Colwestern paper, but Nicoletta Gavelli, Johnny's grandmother, had assured me her friend Allegra Fiato was interested. She was still living with Nicoletta and only running her business out of the apartment—for now.

Allegra was new to the town of Colwestern. She'd moved here from Italy, where she and her husband Felipo had resided for the past several years. Although she'd been Nicoletta's houseguest the past few months, I'd only met her once before they'd approached me last month about Allegra renting the place. Nicoletta had brought her into the bakery to view the apartment, and she'd immediately signed a standard lease agreement. Gianna, who was an attorney, had been instrumental in helping me put the document together. Allegra had already paid me first and last month's rent in advance plus a security deposit. She hadn't even balked at the price I'd asked for. Everything had fallen into place, and been too good of an opportunity for me to pass up.

Josie snorted. "I don't trust that old lady. Plus, we have no idea what she's doing up there. She said she's selling candy, but maybe it's drugs for all we know."

I waved my hand in a dismissive manner. "You know how Mrs. Gavelli feels about drugs. The idea is just ridiculous."

"Well, they've both been very secretive about the so-called business venture since Allegra signed the lease," Josie declared. "I'm afraid her selling homemade candy won't be good for the bakery. Too much competition."

"Actually, it might bring in new customers for us," I said thoughtfully. "She's only planning to be open four days a week. So, if you need a candy fix and the store isn't open, why not get cookies instead?"

I had to admit my first impression of Allegra had not been a favorable one. She was rude and interrupted me constantly, even while I was on the phone. She'd come downstairs this morning to ask about having one of the outlets replaced while Josie and I had been waiting on a room full of customers. When Allegra started complaining, Josie ordered her back upstairs, and we hadn't seen her since. Her voice now rumbled through the ceiling like an impending storm.

Footsteps sounded on the wooden stairs, and both Nicoletta and Allegra came into view. I tried my best to get along with Nicoletta, but she didn't make it easy some days. It looked like Johnny might propose to Gianna soon, and I pitied my sister having to call the woman grandmother-in-law someday. Nicoletta couldn't hold a candle to our own grandmother. Grandma Rosa, my mom's mother, was as close to perfection as one could get. Still, I pitied Nicoletta. Her life had not been an easy one. Sophia, her only child, had died of a drug overdose when Johnny was five, and Nicoletta had been left to raise him.

Nicoletta was in her late seventies, close to my grandmother's age, and had been in remission from bone cancer for about a year. Except for her short white hair, the rest of her was outfitted in her usual drab black outfit, which consisted of a housecoat, stockings, and sturdy Birkenstock shoes. On the current ninety-degree day, I thought I might melt from just looking at her.

Allegra was a few years younger than Nicoletta but dressed in a similar fashion. Her gray housecoat dress was ill-fitting, and she wore black leather sandals instead of shoes. Allegra's cropped hairdo may have been the same ebony color as mine, but hers undoubtedly came out of a bottle. While Nicoletta's face was worn and leathery in appearance, Allegra's was covered with liver spots, and deep crow's feet outlined snappish black eyes, which surveyed me coldly.

"Hi, ladies," I greeted them. "Is everything all set for your grand opening tomorrow, Mrs. Fiato?"

Allegra gave me an appraising glance up and down. "No, it not okay," she grunted. "The faucet in the kitchen leak. Very bad. When your man come to fix?"

Cripes. Mike owned a small one-man construction company, and he'd already made two visits to Allegra's apartment while she'd been setting up this week. He had so many jobs piled up during the summertime, his busiest season, that I hated to bug him about minor things like this. Still, Allegra was a paying tenant, and she had to be taken care of.

"I thought Mike looked at it the other day," I said. "Didn't he install a new faucet for you?"

"Is no good," Allegra spat out between yellowed, crooked teeth. "It still leak. He better come fix today, or I not be happy."

I had news for this woman—she was never going to be happy. As my grandmother often said, there were some people on this earth who could never be pleased. I counted to five in my head before answering. "Okay. Let me know if he can stop by later. You don't have to be here."

Neither woman answered me as they turned to go back upstairs together. "What I tell you?" Allegra said to her friend in a low, disgusted tone.

"I know," Nicoletta replied. "She a problem. That missy been up to no good ever since she lure my Johnny into garage. And he only eight years old."

I gritted my teeth together in annoyance as I waited for Mike to answer his phone. How I hated it when Nicoletta rehashed that tired old story. In the first place, I'd only been six, and Johnny had lured *me* in there, saying he had ice cream. What he'd really wanted to do was play doctor—I'd been the innocent patient when Nicoletta discovered us, and she'd almost died from the shame.

After four rings, Mike picked up, sounding busy and distracted. "Yeah, baby, what is it?"

"Allegra—err, Mrs. Fiato is complaining about her

faucet again," I said. "She said it's still leaking."

He muttered a curse word under his breath. "That's impossible. I tested it. There's no way it's leaking."

I shut my eyes tight. "Is there any way you can come out this afternoon and take a look at it?"

His response was an audible sigh that sounded almost like a hiss. "Princess, I'm right in the middle of a roofing job. I can't just jump off and rush over to fix something for that old woman every time she calls. She's going to have to wait."

"Maybe tonight then?" I tried to keep the desperation out of my voice, but it was difficult. "Honey, she's threatening to make trouble."

There was a loud crash in the background, and Mike hollered, "Hey, watch it with those boards! You want to kill someone?" His voice became calmer when he spoke into the phone. "Baby, I can't talk right now. Tell her I'll stop on my way home tonight, okay? Maybe around nine. That's the best I can do. To be honest, I'm starting to wish you'd never rented to that woman. She's been nothing but trouble."

"You're right." It was my turn to sigh. "Maybe once she opens her store and gets preoccupied with everything, she'll leave us alone. But we can use the money if I'm going to add on to the shop this coming winter. It's going to be a big expense, remember, even with my talented, handsome husband performing all the work."

He chuckled. "Resorting to flattery now, are we?"

"Well, you *are* talented, and in more ways than one," I teased.

"Tell me more," Mike laughed, and then there was another loud noise in the background. "Damn it," he growled. "Gotta go. I'll see you about ten o'clock at this rate, and that's if I'm lucky. Love you." He clicked off before I could respond.

Josie gave me a sly wink. "Let me guess. Hubby's sorry you rented to the spawn of Satan, same as me."

I winced. "Shh. What if they're at the top of the stairs listening? And for your information, he didn't call her that."

"Whatever. It fits," Josie insisted. "That woman is going to be nothing but trouble for us, Sal. Mark my words."

* * *

I planned to wait up for Mike to get home and was snuggled in my cozy bed by nine o'clock, with Spike, our black-and-white Shih-Tzu, curled up at the foot, sound asleep. I flipped through the television channels aimlessly until I found an episode of *48 Hours*. I didn't especially like crime shows since my life often resembled one, but this one caught my immediate attention. It was about a woman who owned a restaurant and had found a dead body outside of it one day.

Yikes. That one hit too close to home. I shuddered and immediately switched the channel. A rerun of *Dexter* was on Showtime. *Good grief.* Yeah, I knew a serial killer—or ten. Art was imitating my life here. I clicked the channel again and found an episode *of Scooby Doo. Ah, this is good.* Safe, predictable, and no violence. I yawned, snuggled farther under the covers, and in no time was sound asleep.

A soft kiss awakened me. I slowly opened my eyes to see Mike sitting on the side of our bed, a steaming cup of coffee in hand. "Morning, princess."

"What time is it?" I asked groggily.

"Five thirty," he said and kissed me again. "I missed you last night."

"You should have woken me when you got in."

He handed me the cup and softly stroked my cheek. "You were sleeping so pretty that I didn't have the heart to."

I swallowed a huge sip of the beverage. "You look awfully tired."

He took the cup from me and placed it on the nightstand, then wove his hands through my hair. Mike's own black hair curled at the ends and needed a cut. It was past the nape of his neck, but I loved running my hands through the silky strands. His midnight blue eyes were full of love as he kissed me again— long and hard this time. Desire stirred in the pit of my stomach.

"I'll try to get home earlier tonight," he promised. "It's nice to have plenty of work—and money—coming in, but not worth all the time I'm spending away from my beautiful wife. I'm planning to clear a couple of days so we can go away for our anniversary."

I ran my finger over the stubble gathered on his chin. "We don't have to go anywhere special. I just want to be alone with you." Then I hesitated. "Uh, I hate to spoil the moment, but did you ever make it over to Allegra's last night?"

He stiffened slightly against me. "Yeah, I was there."

Uh-oh. If anything, I knew my husband, and Mike's attitude indicated to me that something had not gone as planned. "Was everything all right?"

"Yeah." He frowned then let out a deep breath. "Actually, no."

What was going on? "You couldn't fix the faucet?"

Mike's jaw hardened. "Well, you see, that's the problem. There was nothing wrong with the faucet."

My brow furrowed, and I stared at him in confusion. "I don't understand. Why would she say it was broken then?"

His face reddened with obvious discomfort. "Sal, I don't know how to tell you this, but—that woman—I think you should try to get her out of there, if it's possible."

He was starting to frighten me. "What did she do? Break it on purpose?"

Mike shook his head and swallowed hard. "Nothing like that. She—she asked me if I wanted to spend the night. With *her.*"

My jaw almost hit the floor. "Excuse me?"

"I couldn't quite believe it myself," he admitted. "She answered the door in a see-through nightgown." He shut his eyes as if trying to block out the vision. "It was one of the most embarrassing moments of my life."

"Oh my God." Now I was livid. "That old woman made a pass at you? You're like—what— forty years younger than her! Are you sure you didn't imagine it?"

Before he even responded, I had to admit to myself it was a possibility. I'd overheard Allegra say something to Nicoletta about "that bakery girl's husband" after I'd shown her the apartment while Mike had been there as well. At the time, I'd just thought it had related to repairs, but perhaps not. "I don't believe this. What else did she say?"

He stared down at the bed, unable to meet my eyes. "Sal, let's not talk about it anymore, okay?"

I lifted his chin with my fingertips and forced him to look into my eyes. "Tell me."

He blew out a ragged breath. "It's not so much what she said but what she did."

"Okay, you're really scaring me. What did she do?"

"She…" Mike stared down at the bed again. "When I was under the sink, on my knees, she came up behind me and…" He practically squirmed. "She copped a feel."

"She did *what?*" I pushed the covers and Mike back angrily, surprised at my sudden strength. I hurried across the room to the closet and threw on a pair of jeans. "Why, that dirty old woman. There's no way I'll put up with her groping my husband, and I'm going to tell her so—right now."

"Sal!" He grabbed my arm and whirled me around to face him. "Please. I don't want anyone to know about this. Good God, it's embarrassing enough that I had to tell you."

"But she had no right to do that! It's…sexual harassment! What about the whole 'me too' movement? It applies to men as well, doesn't it?"

He scrunched up his face as if in acute pain. "I'd rather just forget about the whole thing."

"What did you do after it happened?" I asked.

Mike's face was stoic. "Well, I was a little shocked but managed to get up from under the sink and calmly told her everything was fine. Then I said the next time it acted up, someone else would be coming out to have a look. I picked up my tools and left. I think she got the message."

Poor Mike. From the expression he wore, it looked like he'd lost his best friend. It was almost comical, except this was no laughing matter. That woman—despite her age—had made it clear she wanted my husband. Mike had never had a shortage of admirers, and women always stared or checked him out whenever we went somewhere together. This was a new one, though. To think this woman—close to my own grandmother's age—would do something of that caliber made my blood boil. It was obvious to me now why Allegra kept needing repairs at the apartment.

"Please, Sal." His face and neck were both a beet red color. "Promise me you won't tell anyone. Not even Josie."

"Fine," I sighed. "If that's what you really want, then I won't say anything. I still think we should confront Allegra together, though."

He shook his head furiously. "She'd only deny it. I would rather let this go away on its own. By the way, do you happen to know what kind of business she's running? There's a display case almost identical to yours. It was the only piece of equipment I saw in the place."

"Josie and I saw the case being delivered yesterday," I said. "Nicoletta's selling homemade candy and varieties of gourmet nuts, I believe. It may end up bringing in some new customers for my shop as well."

Mike traced a finger down the side of my face but looked unconvinced. "Well, that would be one way to look on the bright side, I guess."

Puzzled, I stared up into his handsome tanned face. "What does that mean?"

His dark blue eyes were troubled as he spoke the same words Josie had the day before. "It means this woman is going to be nothing but trouble for us, Sal. You can pretty much count on that."

CHAPTER TWO

———

Josie raised her slim hand and pointed at the sign that was attached to our front door, held in place with black electrical tape. "Did she even ask you before she put it up?"

I raised an eyebrow in warning, then gave the elderly man I was waiting on his little pink box filled with jelly thumbprint cookies and Josie's newest creation, double chocolate chili cookies. They had a delicious spicy bite to them without being overpowering. "Thanks so much. Have a great day."

After the man had departed, I joined Josie at the door. "No, she didn't ask. I thought she was going to put a sign by the stairs. But let's not talk ill of our tenant while customers are in the shop, okay?"

She made a face. "Why not? There's nothing positive to say about the old bat, that's for damn sure. She makes Mrs. Gavelli look like Mother Theresa. Her grand opening is only causing more work for us. Did you see the dirt she tracked in by our front door this morning? *I* had to sweep it up."

We paused as the door opened, the string of silver bells on it jingling away merrily, and two middle-aged women nodded politely at us before ascending the stairs. "Yeah, I know. Gee, Allegra's already getting a steady stream of customers, so whatever she's doing up there, she's doing it well. She also took out a half-page ad in the Colwestern Times. That had to cost a small fortune."

Josie shook her head and walked into the back room. "Figures. I was kind of hoping she'd go bankrupt on her first day. There's something else I wanted to mention. I'm pretty sure she used our ovens this morning."

I grabbed a mitt and removed a tray of vanilla cookies

from the oven. Josie placed another tray of the cookies that had already cooled in front of her on the wood block table and began to ice them with her creamy fudge frosting. "Are you serious?"

She nodded, her thin lips twisting into a frown. "There was debris on the bottom of a couple, and I just cleaned them yesterday. Two of them were still warm when I arrived to open the bakery, and she was already upstairs."

"That's strange. Allegra has a stove up there." Cripes. I hoped hers wasn't on the blink. She'd want Mike to come fix it, and as far as I was concerned, that was no longer an option.

"Hey, Sal!" a male voice yelled from the storefront. "Where are you?"

Josie peered out the doorway. "What's your father doing here?"

"He probably needs to lay in to a fresh supply of fortune cookies. Maybe he's mentioning them in his blog today." One never knew with my father. I went out to greet him with Josie following.

Domenic Muccio was seated at one of the little white tables by my front window and was in the process of setting up his laptop. *Oh boy.* "Hi, Dad. What are you doing here?"

"I need some peace and quiet to work on my book," he grumbled. "Your mother has got some of those flighty real estate agent friends of hers at the house for brunch. All their yacking was giving me a headache."

Josie struggled to keep a straight face. My mother had a real estate license, but as far as I knew, she'd never made a single sale. She changed careers as often as some people changed their socks. Her latest venture consisted of assisting my father with his death blog, which he wrote faithfully every day. She would proofread his comments and make suggestions. Based on the success of the blog, he had decided to write a book, which consisted of past posts, long-winded narratives about the deaths of famous people he admired, and rambling, uneven observations attributed to the entire death process. He even kept two coffins in the house—one in the living room and the other in my old bedroom. They helped with his thought process, or so he said.

I couldn't very well ask my father to leave but was afraid he'd stop customers on the way in and ask about their plans for the hereafter. While I didn't want to be mean, we couldn't afford to lose customers. As I thought about how to phrase my words, Dad strolled casually behind the display case and helped himself to a cup of coffee from my Keurig on the counter. I took in his outfit and winced. My mother was known for dressing like a teenager, even though she was over fifty. Dad was the complete opposite and openly embraced his age.

"Nice legs, Domenic." Josie grinned. He was dressed in a faded Mets T-shirt, beige cargo shorts, and white socks paired with brown leather sandals.

He raised one leg in the air proudly. "Thanks, Josie. I've worked hard on these gams, let me tell you." At the age of sixty-seven, he was rapidly losing his hair and gaining a girth to his stomach. The doctor had warned him to take off a few pounds, especially after the minor stroke he'd had last year, but my father always said life was meant to be enjoyed. He paired the concept with plenty of delicious, rich Italian food. It didn't help matters that my grandmother was a fantastic cook.

"Dad, you're welcome to stay as long as you promise not to talk about the blog to our customers," I said. "They're here to buy cookies, not plan their funerals."

He gave me a thumbs-up and sat back down. "No problem. Just get your old man a couple of fortune cookies and some of Josie's genettis, and you won't hear another peep out of me. I'll be as quiet as a corpse in a funeral parlor."

Jeez Louise. "Dad, please. You'll scare customers away if you talk like that."

He made a motion of locking his lips and throwing away the key. "No worries, baby girl. I'll be good."

"Yeah, right," Josie mumbled in a disbelieving tone.

Resigned, I went behind the counter to grab a piece of waxed paper then placed three fortune cookies and two genettis together on a paper plate. The Italian glazed cookies with colorful nonpareils looked inviting, and again, I had to force myself from indulging. Lately all I seemed to think about was food.

As I was setting the plate in front of my father, the two women who had come in a few minutes ago descended the stairs, each carrying a little white box. They nodded politely at us and opened the front door as a woman with two little girls bounded in and right up the stairs.

Dad watched them, a genetti poised against his lips. "What's your new tenant selling, Sal?"

I opened the display case to make room for a tray of jelly cookies. "Some varieties of homemade candy. I believe she's selling gourmet nuts too."

His brow wrinkled as he watched me. "But you don't know for certain? What if she's dealing drugs?"

What was it with everyone and this drug theory? "Dad, there's no way Allegra is dealing drugs. Mrs. Gavelli is upstairs with her."

He gave a loud harrumph and cracked open a fortune cookie. "Well, I wouldn't put anything past anyone these days, especially that old broad. I still can't believe she's taken the woman in to live with her. Allegra is causing nothing but trouble in our neighborhood."

Josie grabbed the back of the chair next to my father and clutched it between her hands. "Why? What's going on?"

"She called the cops on the Gardners across the street," my father explained. "They had a party the other night, and Allegra complained that they were making way too much noise."

It seemed Allegra was busy making new friends everywhere.

Dad crunched the cookie around in his mouth and watched as two more women came in, nodded to us, and then went upstairs. "I may have to go see what all the fuss is about." He stared down at the message in his hands. "Hey, check this out. I got one that says, 'You should write a book!' I knew there was something to these babies when you first decided to make them. Wait a second." He scratched his head thoughtfully. "Aren't you printing your own messages now?"

"Sometimes," I admitted. "But we still buy them from the novelty store once in a while."

He put the message in his shorts pocket. "This is a good omen. Now if only Steve Steadman would answer my emails, I'd be all set."

"Who's Steve Steadman?" Josie asked before I could poke her in the ribs. It sounded like it was related to his book, and everyone in the family was tired of hearing about it.

My father chewed on another cookie as we waited for him to respond. "He's a big-time literary agent who lives in Nevada. He has a passion for books about death, and he's made some huge deals for his clients. For some reason he doesn't seem to be getting my emails, though."

Josie turned away in an attempt to hide the smile on her face. Somehow, I suspected Mr. Steadman was getting his emails okay. He sounded like a smart guy to me. If he ever responded to one of my father's notes, Steve would be doomed because my father would never leave him alone again. Dad was a bit like a stray dog at times. Once you fed him, he stayed.

"Make yourself comfortable, Dad. Josie and I have some cookies to frost in the back room."

He rose to his feet. "I think I'm going to take a little trip upstairs and see exactly what they're selling. Be right back."

We left him lumbering up the stairs and went into the back room. I started to cover the vanilla cookies with fudge frosting while Josie peered into one of the plastic storage bins we used to store the extra fortune cookies.

"I baked five dozen fortune cookies yesterday, but there's only about a dozen in here. Did you use them, Sal?"

I shook my head. "I noticed that too. I thought maybe someone requested them for a party and you forgot to tell me about it."

Josie's mouth formed a thin hard line. "I bet the old lady upstairs stole them."

"Will you stop? You can't go around accusing people like that."

She removed her apron and flung it on the counter. "I want to see what's going on up there too. And if I spot any fortune cookies lying around, you can bet there's going to be hell to pay."

She started for the doorway but was interrupted by my father's presence. He stared from me to Josie, and I noticed the color had disappeared from his usually ruddy cheeks.

"Dad, what's wrong?"

He opened the white paper bag in his hand and drew out three jelly cookies and a fortune cookie. "Sal, are you aware that

Allegra's running a bakery upstairs?"

My chest tightened with discomfort. "What are you talking about? She's selling homemade candy."

My father gave me a sympathetic look and handed us each a jelly cookie. "No, baby girl. She's got some candy and nuts up there, but she's also selling cookies, and they're just like yours. Hers are cheaper too. A *lot* cheaper."

Josie's face suffused with anger. "What exactly is going on here?" She bit into the cookie that my father had handed her, and then swore. "This is my *exact* recipe. That old lady is a thief!"

"I can't believe this." Not knowing what else to do, I walked into the front room and sank down in the chair next to my father's laptop. "Why would she do such a thing?"

"Because she's evil," Josie spat out. "What mystifies me is how she ever expected to get away with it."

I raised my hand in the air. "Calm down. We've got to think this through rationally and not do anything stupid. The woman has a lease, and she's got rights. Let me get Gianna on the phone. The first thing we need to do is find out how we can legally remove her from the building."

"You mean throw her bony butt out of here," Josie snapped. "Well, I have no problem hurling it into the street."

"Stop it," I said with exasperation. "We could get into big trouble if we lay so much as a finger on her."

My father nodded wisely, his mouth full of jelly cookie. "Sal's right, Josie."

Josie's nostrils flared. "Then I'm going upstairs to have a talk with little miss copycat baker. She can't use *my* recipes without *my* permission! She must have lifted the fortune cookies *and* my recipes from the back room. The nerve!"

She started for the stairs, but I was quick to stop her. "Wait a minute. I'm just as upset as you are, but it's not going to do any good to get into a fight with the woman, especially when she has customers upstairs." Who were probably *our* former customers, come to think of it.

Josie scowled, and her cheeks flushed a bright red. "Then what do you suggest?"

I turned to my father. "Dad, would you please go

upstairs and ask Allegra to come down here for a minute? Don't tell her why, though."

"Sure thing, baby girl." He started back up the stairs, whistling under his breath, and took another bite of jelly cookie. "Hey, these might even be better than yours, Josie."

"What the hell!" Josie screeched and bounded for the stairs again.

It took all my strength to keep her in place. "Listen to me! We're not going upstairs to make a scene. When she comes down here, we'll have a calm, cool, and rational talk with her."

Josie folded her arms over her chest. "I don't think that's possible. But if it is, then what?"

Then I hurl her bony butt into the street. How I wished it was that simple. Frustrated, I blew out a long breath. "I'll have to check with Gianna." My sister was a public defender, but she'd at least know what type of steps I should take or could refer me to someone. "I think sometimes that tenants have more rights than the landlord. Maybe if I tell Allegra it's not working out and give her time to find another place—plus a partial refund—she'll leave graciously."

Josie barked out a laugh. "I didn't know you still believed in fairy tales, Sal."

What a mess. It didn't help matters that Nicoletta was also upstairs, and if someone—aka Josie—said the wrong thing, this might turn into a full-fledged battle. "Maybe you should wait in the back room."

Her mouth fell open in surprise. "No way! She's going to walk all over you if I'm not here."

I placed my hands on my hips. "Would you please give me a little credit? I'm not going to lie down on the floor and let her step on me, nor am I going to start a war. But I'd prefer that you don't put her face through the wall, okay?"

Footsteps clattered on the stairs, and Allegra appeared, followed by my father. Her skinny frame was sickly looking and almost sticklike, especially when positioned next to my father's well rounded one. Dad was nibbling away at something that resembled a truffle—a new chocolate stain was visible on the Mets T-shirt stretched tightly over his protruding stomach. Allegra must have been feeding the enemy's father upstairs.

Well, at least it wasn't another cookie.

"Why you bother me?" Her eyes, black as coal, narrowed in on my face and then moved to take in Josie. "I have successful business to run and no time for likes of *you*."

I shot Josie a glance in warning then took a step toward the elderly woman. "Allegra, I need to ask you about those cookies you're selling upstairs. Where did you get the recipes from?"

She shrugged. "My daughter—she give. She excellent cook. She own bakery in Las Vegas."

"How about we get her on the phone?" Josie suggested angrily. "Then we'll ask her to recite the recipe, ingredient by ingredient, for the jelly cookies?"

"Jos, please." I turned back to Allegra. "Someone used our ovens without permission this morning. We also have a large number of fortune cookies missing from our back room. Do you know anything about it?"

Allegra's bushy white eyebrows formed a thick caterpillar as she frowned. "So what? You have plenty, and I take. You give free one to customer, so why not give me too? I pay you rent."

Apparently I wasn't getting through to the woman. "We give out a free one to each person," I explained patiently. "Not three dozen."

"That's thirty dollars you owe us," Josie huffed.

Allegra gave Josie an icy stare. "Don't mess with me, little hussy. I know your type well."

Josie muttered a swear word under her breath and started toward the woman. Horrified, I held her back. "I can handle this. Why don't you go in the back room and finish frosting those fudgy delight cookies?"

Before I could say anything further, Allegra stuck her hand into the front pocket of her dress and waved a fortune cookie at me. "My customers—they like these. I think I bake them too. I think I run you out of business. Your grandmama say you smart detective—that you solve many murders. I should have known she wrong. She make up lies so I *think* you smart. But you just some dumb lamb that I pull wool over eyes."

Her sharp and vicious tongue rendered me speechless for

a moment. I was glad when Josie stepped in to say what I couldn't.

"Why, you miserable old sourpuss," Josie said bitterly. "You're not going to get away with this. Sal's sister is a lawyer. We'll toss your scrawny butt out into the street."

Nicoletta appeared on the stairs and glared down at us. "You need to shut up. Customers can hear." She said something in Italian that sounded like "troublemakers," to which Allegra nodded her head vigorously.

"Mrs. Gavelli, would you come down here, please?" This was what hurt me the most. Although Nicoletta and I didn't always have an ideal relationship, it pained me to think that she knew what Allegra had planned all along, and she'd actually helped the woman sell cookies and steal from me in the process.

Her black Birkenstocks thunked on the stairs as she made her way over to us. Nicoletta gave me a deer in the headlights look, and suddenly I wondered if it was all part of an act. Her dark eyes peered out at me from underneath a green polka-dotted kerchief wrapped around her head. "What you want?"

Josie interrupted. "How could you do this to Sal and me, Nicoletta? You're also hurting your own grandson in the process. He's practically engaged to Gianna, you know. How could you help this woman sell the same cookies we make down here and at a cheaper price to boot?"

She scowled, the lines deepening further in her leathery-looking face. "I no help with nothing. That Allegra's idea. I only help make candy. What else she do is her own business."

Allegra gave me a cool, superior smile. "Tell your husband my faucet—it broke again. He need to get under the sink." She licked her lips. "I like when he do that."

"What's she talking about?" Josie whispered.

"Nothing." I'd told Mike that I wouldn't reveal what Allegra had done to him last night, and I fully intended to keep my promise. There must have been steam pouring out of my ears, and I struggled to control my temper. If poor Mike knew what was happening, he would want to die.

I'd had the misfortune of meeting several rotten individuals during the course of my life. Still, I liked to believe the majority of people on this earth were good at heart. But it had quickly become apparent to me that Allegra Fiato's was carved out of stone.

I exhaled sharply and turned to Allegra. "I will give you a complete refund of your rent money, but in return I want you to vacate the building as soon as possible." I'd text Gianna and ask her to recommend an attorney for me to consult with.

"Witch!" Allegra cried. "You cannot do that. I no leave."

"Forget about that, Sal." Josie gave Allegra a small push toward the door. "Satan can leave now and take her partner in crime with her." She glared at Nicoletta.

Oh, Josie, don't touch her! The woman was a lawsuit waiting to happen.

"You be sorry you mess with us!" Nicoletta exploded and then turned to me. "I knew you no good ever since you drag my Johnny into that garage."

"Wow." My father leaned forward excitedly from his seat at the table. "This is better than binge-watching *Forensic Files.*"

I stared at him in disbelief. "Please, Dad."

"Sorry, I couldn't help myself." He grinned at me sheepishly then popped another cookie into his mouth.

Allegra spat on the floor and swore, then shook her finger in my face. "Oh, you gonna be sorry. I make you *very* sorry." She started toward the stairs, but Josie blocked her exit. "What you think you do, tramp?"

"Get out of here now," Josie hissed, her arms spread out on either side. "Get in your car and drive away. *Far* away."

Allegra said something in Italian that sounded like a swear word—or several. "I go get police. You not do this to me." She pushed my front door open with such a vengeance I half expected it to fly off the hinges.

Nicoletta slapped Josie's hand away. "I need to go upstairs and see about customers. Look what you do. You make Allegra so mad now I have to take care of everything. She so angry maybe she never come back."

"Oh, she'll be back," Josie muttered. "I'm positive of that. She's a sure thing, like death or six feet of snow in Buffalo during the winter."

An ear-piercing thud sounded from outside. Josie and I exchanged mystified glances while Mrs. Gavelli hurried back upstairs.

"Is that Mr. Barton working on his roof again? I thought he said yesterday that he was all done." Josie cocked her head in the direction of the street.

My father went to the front door, pushed it open, and then peered out into the road. "Oh boy. You'd better call 9-1-1, Sal." He popped another jelly cookie into his mouth.

An uneasy tingle crept down my spine. "Why? What's wrong?" I didn't wait for him to answer and went to stand next to him. Then I gasped out loud.

Allegra was lying on the side of the road, facedown, the breezy summer wind blowing through the skirt of her cotton housedress. Even from this distance, I could tell that both her legs were broken and her body was lifeless and still. Josie and I both shrieked and ran toward her.

"Oh God," I whispered as we reached Allegra's side, my heart hammering against the wall of my chest.

"Is she breathing?" Josie asked anxiously.

I bent over Allegra and gently turned her face to the side, staring down at it. Dark eyes were wide open and stared blankly into space. Abrasions covered her bare arms, and her face was a mess of scratches from the fall.

"Allegra?" I spoke softly and held her hand between mine. "Allegra, can you hear me?"

There was no response. The elderly woman's face was as white as powdered sugar. I reached down to take her pulse.

"Sal," Josie said grimly as we sat together on the side of the dusty road. "She's not—"

With a sigh, I released Allegra's hand. "Yes. She's dead."

CHAPTER THREE

———

"Murderer," Nicoletta growled at Josie and me as dribbles of spittle collected in the corners of her mouth. "You kill my friend out of spite. You no get away with this, I tell you!"

"Stop it, *pazza*," Grandma Rosa scolded. "It was an accident. They had nothing to do with Allegra's death."

The four of us stood next to the front bay window of my bakery and watched as Allegra's body was loaded into the coroner's van. After recovering from the initial shock, my first call had been to 9-1-1, and then I had notified my grandmother. She and Nicoletta had been friends ever since Grandma Rosa came to live with my parents. That was 27 years ago, after my grandfather died. Grandma Rosa had gotten to know Allegra well through her friendship with Nicoletta these past few months. I remembered her telling me a few weeks back that Allegra and her husband Felipo had lived in New Jersey before returning to Sicily several years ago.

Grandma Rosa had arrived at my home to live with us shortly after Gianna was born. She was a fabulous cook but an even better person. She gave sound advice, never judged, and made the world's best ricotta cheesecake. For some reason, I secretly suspected she was not a big fan of Allegra's, but my grandmother never said a cross word about anyone and didn't have a mean bone in her body.

"You no call me crazy," Nicoletta huffed. "Your granddaughter—she jealous of Allegra's business. They fight—I see with my own two eyes! Allegra run outside, and car mow her down."

"It wasn't like that at all," I protested as we continued to stare out the window. A crowd of interested spectators watched curiously as the vehicle carrying Allegra's body got ready to depart. Two police cars with flashing lights were stationed at the curb in addition to a van that bore the name of a local television station. I stifled a groan. More bad publicity that I didn't need for my bakery.

A very good-looking cop with dirty blond hair was chatting earnestly with an EMT. After the medic got in his van and drove off, the cop said something to another officer and then started walking toward the bakery. Our eyes met and held. He shook his head at me in apparent disbelief.

Great. Now I was really in trouble.

Josie saw our exchange and nudged me in the ribs. "Get ready for your lecture."

Brian Jenkins was a Colwestern police officer whom I'd met two years earlier, after returning to my hometown in the Buffalo region when I'd divorced Colin Brown. He had been the first cop to arrive at the bakery for a homicide investigation when Amanda, my former high school nemesis and Colin's mistress, had dropped dead on my front porch.

Brian and I had become fast friends, and he'd made it clear from the beginning that he wanted to be something more as well. Even though Mike and I had been apart for ten years back then, I hadn't stopped loving him, and we'd resumed dating as if we'd never been apart. A few months after I returned home, we moved in together and Mike began proposing to me. The scars from Colin's infidelity and verbal abuse had been fresh and raw in my mind, so it had been difficult to commit at first. After almost losing my life in a confrontation with Colin's killer, I'd decided we'd wasted enough time and accepted Mike's proposal.

Although Brian had been upset about my decision, he had fully recovered and was currently dating another high school classmate of mine, Ally Tetrault. They'd been together for about a year. She was a nurse at Colwestern Hospital, and from what I'd seen, they were very happy together.

The bells on my front door jingled as Brian entered, his green eyes shining in the bright sunlight that filtered through the window. He placed his hands on his slim hips and scowled at me, Greek god-like face stern. "Again, Sally? This is starting to feel like some type of conspiracy toward me."

"But I had nothing to do with it," I protested. "She was killed by a hit-and-run driver."

"It *all* your fault!" Nicoletta shrieked. She grabbed Brian by the sleeve of his dark blue uniform shirt. "My friend run into the road after these two hussies upset her." She shook her finger menacingly at Josie. "This one a bad lot—you can tell by her red hair. Demon."

Josie glared at the woman. "Now hang on a second, old lady. Your so-called friend was stealing my recipes and selling the cookies upstairs. She had no business—"

"Who you call 'old lady'?" Nicoletta shouted and shoved Josie backward.

"Game on!" Josie stretched her hands out in front of her, as if she was going for Nicoletta's throat. I stepped in front of my friend, half-afraid she might sucker-punch the elderly woman in the jaw.

"All right, ladies," Brian said wearily. "Let's try to stay calm here." He smiled politely and tipped his hat at Nicoletta. "Would you mind letting me talk to Sally alone for a minute?"

Nicoletta gave a loud harrumph. "You better take them to jail, that all I know. Come, Rosa. I need speak to you." She shot us all a surly look and then started up the stairs, her heavy black shoes pounding away on the wooden boards.

My grandmother gave me a wan smile of encouragement as she started to follow Nicoletta. "I will be with the crazy one if you need me, *cara mia*." She squeezed my hand. "Do not worry. I shall try to talk some sense in her."

"Rosa!" Mrs. Gavelli jumped on the stairs like a two-year-old, and for a moment, I was afraid she might topple over. "I need you!"

Grandma Rosa sighed wearily as she climbed the staircase. "That woman—she tries my patience some days. All right, every day."

Brian watched her depart then slumped down into the chair she had vacated. "Sally, I'm convinced you are disaster prone. I've lost track of how many homicides you've been involved in."

To be honest, so had I. "Jeez, Brian, you act like I go around looking for dead bodies."

He stared at me thoughtfully. "I'm starting to wonder. Tell me what happened right before Mrs. Fiato got run over."

"Look," Josie said miserably, "I feel terrible about this, Brian, really I do. When Allegra came down the stairs, I picked a fight with her. I was so angry that I wasn't thinking straight."

Brian's mouth twitched slightly at the corners. "Was she really operating another bakery upstairs?"

"We were told it was a candy store." Defensiveness crept into my tone, and I realized how this must have sounded to him—like I was some type of an imbecile who didn't even know what was going on underneath my own roof. "She stole some of Josie's recipes plus a few trays of fortune cookies without asking. Allegra even used our ovens to do her baking. It was the first day she'd been open, so we *definitely* would have found out before long. My father went upstairs to check the place out and told us what was going on."

"I think she wanted us to find out," Josie said bitterly. "Maybe she hoped we'd start a fight, try to kick her out, and then she could sue us. Like that old movie with Michael Keaton where he was the psycho tenant."

"*Pacific Heights.*" At least Josie hadn't beaten our tenant up, like in the movie, but given more time, she might have tried. "Brian, I'm so sorry she's dead, but give us a break here. This shouldn't be put on our heads. I was charging her a very fair rent because she was Mrs. Gavelli's friend. I would have even let her use the ovens if she'd only asked me first."

"Well, I wouldn't have," Josie declared.

I groaned in response. "You're not helping. But it does feel like Allegra was biting the hand that fed her."

"She would have bitten your head off if she could," Josie added. "The woman was nuts, but I never thought she'd be so upset that she'd run out in front of a moving vehicle."

Brian removed a small notepad from the breast pocket of his uniform. "Did either one of you see what happened? We're trying to find an eyewitness but haven't had any luck yet."

Josie and I both shook our heads.

"We were talking and not watching the street. All of a sudden, we heard a loud thud," I said. "My father went to the front door and spotted Allegra lying on the side of the road. I called 9-1-1 right away."

Brian looked around the shop. "By the way, where is your father? I thought I saw him when I first arrived."

This was embarrassing. "He...uh...went to hang out at the morgue."

Brian cocked a fine blond eyebrow at me. "Excuse me?"

Go ahead and say it, Sal. "He was kind of hoping he could see the autopsy performed on Allegra's body."

"What the hell," Brian sputtered. "Sally, they'll never allow your father in there! Isn't it about time he gave up this weird hobby of his?"

"It's not a hobby," Josie insisted. "It's an obsession. He's almost done writing his book about it too."

"Does he actually think it will sell?" Disbelief registered in Brian's eyes.

He did indeed. "Dad's cautiously optimistic," I said. "He wants to see an autopsy performed so he can do a future blog about it."

Brian stared at me as though I had two heads. "Okay, this is too much for me to absorb right now. Can we get back to the hit-and-run incident?"

"By all means." I was relieved to let the topic drop. My father had gone from planning his own funeral to driving a hearse, studying to become an undertaker, and currently running his own blog where he called himself "Father Death." To everyone's surprise, it was making money from funeral homes that paid to advertise there. Gianna had confided to me that she'd prayed the book would stay unpublished for a long time, perhaps forever.

"So all you two heard was a thud? No tires squealing?"

Josie and I looked at one another. "Not me. How about you?" I asked.

She frowned and shook her head. "Nothing like that. Just a thud."

Brian took off his hat and scratched his head. "Strange. That makes me think the car didn't even attempt to stop."

I didn't like what he was implying. "Is there a way to determine who might have done this? Could some type of test be done on Allegra's body?"

Brian placed the pad back inside his pocket. "An autopsy will be done on Mrs. Fiato right away, of course." He narrowed his eyes at me. "And without your father being present. Her clothes will be removed and placed in a bag, and then they'll be sent to a police lab where they're checked for DNA."

I scrunched my face into a frown, not entirely understanding. "DNA? But Allegra wasn't attacked."

He shook his head. "It's not about her DNA. I meant the car's DNA—well, in theory. We should find paint chips on Mrs. Fiato's body to help us discover the make and model of the vehicle. We might not be able to determine the exact year but can usually come close. Then we can run a check through the DMV for cars like that in our area and expand it if necessary. Hopefully we'll find it based on the information, though."

"Wow, that's fascinating," Josie breathed and then glanced over at me. "What's wrong, Sal?"

"I'm not sure," I stammered. "What you said, Brian, about not hearing the car's brakes. Is it possible…that someone might have done this…on purpose?"

A muscle ticked in Brian's jaw. "Sally, it happened right in front of *your* bakery. The woman had one of *your* fortune cookies in her hand. I've never been superstitious before in my life, but—in answer to your question—yeah, I'd say it's a definite possibility."

CHAPTER FOUR

———

"Why can't we wait outside?" Josie wanted to know. "I hate these things. Look, I'm sorry the woman is dead, but I feel like a phony being here. I couldn't stand the sight of her."

In panic, I glanced around the inside of the funeral home, hoping no one had heard. "Shh. I already told you, my grandmother asked me if I would pick her up. Mrs. G's going to ride with Allegra's niece back to her office. You can go ahead and leave now if you want, and I'll drive Grandma's car back to her house. Mike can pick me up there."

"Never mind," Josie sighed as she signed the guest registry. "I'll stay."

I helped myself to a Mass card. It was three days after the fatal accident, a muggy and humid Tuesday evening. Even though the air conditioner hummed away at a comfortable level, sweat had started to pool on my forehead. I'd have never admitted it out loud, but I felt the same way as Josie. I didn't want to be here and wasn't looking forward to seeing Nicoletta. The feeling was probably mutual. We'd closed the shop an hour early so we could arrive before the viewing ended at seven o'clock.

Nicoletta had shut the doors forever on Allegra's candy and rip-off cookie shop immediately after her death. I'd never known of a business that had closed the same day as it opened before. She'd also been the one to arrange the funeral, which I thought was a bit strange since Allegra had three children. Two of them, Anna and Enzo, only lived a few hours away in New Jersey. From what Grandma Rosa had told me the other day, Allegra and her husband had come from Sicily to America when they were newlyweds and barely out of their teens. They'd settled in Jersey and raised their family then had returned to Italy when their children were grown. Violet, daughter and alleged baker, lived in what Nicoletta declared was the Devil's favorite city, Las Vegas.

"I can't believe Allegra's other daughter isn't coming," Josie said, almost as if she could read my thoughts as we looked at pictures of Allegra and her family displayed on an easel next to the podium. "Who doesn't go to their own mother's funeral?"

"It's awful." My own mother was something short of a nutcase, but I still loved her dearly. Such uncaring behavior was beyond my comprehension. Then again, I didn't know the entire story. Maybe Violet had another reason for not coming. I couldn't bear to think about losing my parents or my beloved grandmother. Sure, we had our differences and argued, but family always came first with us. Violet had told Nicoletta on the phone that she didn't like to fly and New York was too long of a distance for her to travel right now.

I studied the Mass card in my hands. A young, exotic-looking Allegra stared back at me with dark, calculating eyes—the same eyes that had glared at me menacingly the other day when she'd cursed and spat on my floor. The black-and-white photo depicted her at about 30-years-old, my present age. Her long dark hair cascaded down her back as she stared at the camera, unsmiling, of course. Not much had changed. I shivered and turned my attention to the caption underneath the photo, which consisted of a Bible verse.

Although I wasn't much of a churchgoer these days, Grandma Rosa had made sure I faithfully attended Sunday school as a child, and this had been one of my favorite verses. From the Book of John: *I am the light of the world. He who follows me will not walk in darkness.*

Josie wasn't very religious, less so than me, but she read the verse with apparent interest from over my shoulder. "Get a load of this. Isn't it a hoot? They're comparing Allegra to Jesus now?"

"I'm not sure that's the intent," I said quietly.

"Well, I can't think of two people more different," she declared. "Perhaps they should have written: 'Allegra is the darkness of the night. Those who follow her will wallow in intense heat—forever.'"

I glanced up at her, startled. "Jos! That's a terrible thing to say about the woman. She's dead, remember."

Maybe we were at fault. Maybe if Allegra had been paying attention and wasn't so distracted by our argument, she would have seen the car approach. Then I remembered our discussion with Brian. *Had it really been an accident?*

Josie snorted. "I'm sorry, Sal. Perhaps that was a little cold. But something tells me that even though the woman is dead, she's still going to continue to annoy us like a bunch of mosquitoes on a hot summer day."

Secretly I was afraid that she might be right. The plague had already started in the form of the media. Allegra's death had generated a lot of local attention, especially when word got out she had perished in front of my bakery with one of my cryptic fortune cookies in her hand. The media always had a field day at my expense. They'd even announced on the news last night what her fortune cookie had said. *Your luck will completely change today.* Good grief.

On more than one previous occasion, the newspaper had mentioned Sally's Samples was famous for its original fortune cookies—and unlucky ones. It had served to make customers even more curious about them so that necessarily hadn't been a bad thing. Even though we'd switched locations a year ago because of a fire, the weird messages had followed us. A high school nemesis had dropped dead on my front porch, and then, later on, the building had burned down. At our present location, someone had tried to shoot me, and I'd also ended up locked in the freezer.

Perhaps the newspaper had taken all this into consideration when they'd proposed a new name for my bakery in yesterday's edition. Sally's Samples was now being referred to as Sally's Shambles.

"It sounds awful to refer to Allegra like that," I said. "You're lucky my grandmother didn't hear you. She'd say it was blasphemous."

"There she is now," Josie announced as Grandma Rosa came through the double-wide doorway from the adjoining viewing room. She was dressed in a black skirt and long-sleeved gray blouse. I was sweltering just looking at her, but she appeared as cool and sweet as the iced tea I'd sipped on my way over.

I never ceased to marvel at the woman. She'd stayed with Nicoletta last night and was doing everything possible to comfort her friend at such a sad time. If I'd been forced to spend an evening with Nicoletta, I might have jumped from the nearest bridge.

"*Cara mia*. Hello, Josie." She gave us each a kiss on the cheek. "Thank you for coming to get me. I know you would rather not be here."

"Did Gianna and Johnny come?" I asked.

Grandma Rosa nodded. "They were here when the service first started. Gianna had to go back to her office tonight, and there was an orientation at Johnny's school." Johnny was a history teacher.

I noted the sudden pursing of her lips. "What's wrong?"

My grandmother glanced around, as if worried someone might overhear us, but we were alone by the podium. "I am worried about Nicoletta. She seems to think there is something more to Allegra's accident."

I thought of the brake-squealing comment again. "Like what, exactly?"

"She believes Allegra's death was intentional. When I asked Nicoletta how she knows, she shrimped up. This worries me," Grandma Rosa confessed.

Baffled, Josie and I looked at each other, and then it slowly dawned on us.

"The expression is clammed up, Rosa," Josie said.

She shrugged. "Whatever. I like shrimp."

"Why would she say something like that?" Josie scoffed. "Who would have a reason to kill dear, sweet Allegra? Except everyone in town, that is."

"Jos," I warned.

Grandma Rosa ignored Josie's outburst and pinned me with her somber gaze. "If Nicoletta is correct, she wants me to help her find out who did this. But we are not good detectives like you and Josie. Would you both want to help us?"

"I'm not sure we'd be much help," I said. If anything, we

might make things worse. It had happened before.

"If anyone can find the truth, it is you," she said simply. "You are a very good sloth."

I assumed my grandmother didn't really believe that I was lazy and shiftless—at least I hoped not. "You mean sleuth, Grandma."

She shrugged. "That is good too."

"Excuse me, Rosa." A tall, slender woman with jet black hair styled in a bob gently touched her arm. "Nicoletta is looking for you."

The look of weariness was apparent in my grandmother's face. She was going to be 77 years old on my wedding anniversary and, at this moment, looked her age. For the past three days, Mrs. Gavelli had clung to my grandmother like she was a life preserver. Seventy-two hours with that woman had to be torture for anyone, even my long-suffering grandmother.

Grandma Rosa gestured toward me. "This is my granddaughter, Sally Donovan, and her friend, Josie Sullivan. Girls, this is Allegra's daughter, Anna."

Anna nodded cordially at us. Her dark eyes were bloodshot and her thin, angular face expressionless. She wore a maroon-colored blouse with black slacks and matching kitten-heeled sandals. Anna was close to six feet in height and towered over my petite five-foot three-inch stature.

"Nice to meet you." Her face flushed suddenly, and her deep voice was reminiscent of someone who smoked three packs a day. "You're the one who owns the bakery, right? The same building my mother was running hers out of?"

Now it was my turn to flush. Her tone was sarcastic, as if she intended to mock me. "Uh, yes. That's right. I'm sorry about your mother." Now I was curious what else she might have heard about us from Nicoletta or, possibly, Allegra. I waited to see if Anna might burst out laughing or break down sobbing in my arms.

Neither one of those scenarios happened. Anna clicked her tongue against the roof of her mouth and shook her head at us. "Boy, you should have run the other way when you saw my mother coming. Why would anyone want to rent to the Devil herself?" Instead of waiting for our response, she made the sign of the cross on her chest, turned on her heel, then crossed into the viewing room.

The three of us were speechless for a moment. Finally, Josie found her voice. "What the heck was that all about?"

Grandma Rosa's face was grim. "There was no love lost between Allegra and her children. Of course, I do not know all the details of their relationship but find it very disrespectful she would say such a thing—and at her own mother's service. It is not right."

"That was disturbing." I shifted my handbag on my shoulder. "I guess we should go pay our respects now."

"You can meet Allegra's son, Enzo, and say hello to Nicoletta if you like," Grandma Rosa said. "The priest will be giving a talk in a few minutes. Remember, there is no body."

"Excuse me?" I asked in surprise.

My grandmother closed her eyes for a second. "There is no body. Allegra is still with the coroner. They are running tests and trying to determine more information about the hit-and-run."

Confused, Josie stared at her. "How can they hold a wake without her body? It doesn't make any sense."

"That is what Allegra asked for," Grandma Rosa said. "We are not certain how long it will be until they release her body. In her will she stated she wished to be cremated when her time came. Allegra did not want to be laid out for everyone to see. Her son is leaving for Italy sometime next week, so they decided to hold the service now." She nodded at me. "Perhaps you could ask your officer friend how long her body will have to remain."

"Uh, that might not be a good idea." Brian was probably sick and tired of me showing up at every single crime scene he investigated. But there was no way I could ever refuse my grandmother anything. "Dad's already been bugging him. He tried to sneak into the morgue the other night. I think Brian's had it with our family—forever."

Grandma Rosa studied me for a second. "Perhaps, yes, with most of the family. But there is one person he will never tire of."

Her words shocked me. Sure, Brian had been interested in me at one point and very persistent, even when I made it clear that I only wanted Mike, but that was ancient history now. Brian was living with Ally and very happy. "What exactly are you trying to say?"

Her mouth twitched slightly. "He is a friend, no?"

"Yes," I said evenly. "And that's all he will ever be."

Grandma Rosa patted me on the arm. "Of course that is how *you* feel, *cara mia*. But remember, we cannot change other people's feelings." She walked toward the viewing room and gestured for us to follow. "Come now."

Josie raised an eyebrow in questioning at me, but I didn't want to get into it. Was my grandmother trying to say Brian was still attracted to me? I was in love with my husband and only my husband. This would make things very awkward between Brian and me. I treasured his friendship and didn't want to lose it. Grandma Rosa had to be wrong about something eventually, and I hoped she'd missed the mark on this one.

The front door of the funeral parlor opened, and my mother and father stepped into the hallway. I should have expected they would be here. Besides my father's insatiable love of wakes, Nicoletta had been their neighbor for many years, and they'd met Allegra a few times. Perhaps a teeny part of me had hoped they wouldn't show, because wherever they went, bedlam was certain to follow.

"Hi, sweetheart," my mother crooned and reached over to give me a kiss. She was wearing a strapless, black satin dress that came to about mid-thigh. As usual, she looked spectacular. My mother was always dressed to kill. With her size four figure and lovely face, every man between the ages of 20 and 90 always stopped to look at her. It made me uncomfortable, but my father took it all in stride. On some level, I think he even enjoyed it. He and my mother loved each other deeply, so instead of acting jealous, he proudly showed her off every chance he got.

No insecurities were present in my parents' 32-year marriage. There was too much weirdness instead. They did as they pleased, marched to the beat of their own drummer, and enjoyed life to its fullest. Sure, they were nuts on some level. Maybe in the grand scheme of life, everyone else was doing things wrong while they were doing it right. Some days I just didn't know anymore.

My mother beamed at Josie. "Hello, dear. How are the kids?"

Josie gave her a peck on the cheek. "They're all great, Maria. Thanks for sending over the water guns and the bubble mower. They're having a blast with them."

"Our pleasure." My mother looked wistful. "I can't wait to do the same thing for my grandchildren. *If* I ever have any."

She cast a hopeful sideways glance at me. Normally I would have been upset by her admission. My mother had been putting the baby pressure on me since the first day of my marriage. However, I had a strong premonition that in a week or so, I'd be telling her some news that would put her over the moon. I'd already bought the pregnancy test and only needed to take it. The test might work now, but I wanted to wait a few days to be on the safe side.

My father rubbed his hands together in gleeful satisfaction. He loved wakes and anything with a death theme. "We didn't miss anything, did we?"

"As for you," Grandma Rosa scolded him, "I will not have you upsetting Nicoletta and Allegra's children by asking about the cremation process. You save that stuff for the *pazzas* who follow you on the *stupido* blog of yours."

"Hey," my father protested. "It's not stupid. When I get hold of Steve Steadman, he's going to publish my book. I've got to track that guy down sooner rather than later. I've even been thinking about flying out to see him. Then Stephen King and I will be sharing space together on Amazon."

Nicoletta was standing next to a small round oak table, which held a portrait of Allegra on it. It was the same photo featured on the mass cards. Nicoletta was flanked by Anna on one side and a bearded, dark-haired man on the other.

"That is Enzo," my grandmother murmured in my ear. "A bad lot, I am afraid."

"Does he hate his mother too?" Josie asked.

Grandma Rosa snorted. "The man is—what do you say—useless. He plays the ponies all the time. His wife divorced him last year because he could not hold down a steady job. He is always being fired. Nicoletta said he was up at Saratoga the other day—you know, the horse-racing town. He has friends there he stays with. All he thinks about is the gambling."

"Speaking of gambling, what's the real reason Vegas Violet didn't come?" I asked in a low tone. "It sounds like none of Allegra's kids liked her."

My grandmother's face was somber. "Yes, I am sorry to say you are right, my dear. It is a very sad situation. I have never met Violet, so I cannot tell you much about her."

"Aw, it can't be that bad," my father protested as his brown eyes surveyed the room. "She doesn't have a big turnout, though. Of course, when my time comes, they'll be lined up down the block."

My grandmother said something in Italian that sounded like whacko, but I didn't ask for details. As we approached the people at the front of the room, Nicoletta's gaze stayed focused on Josie and me. Her pupils grew in size and threatened to bulge out of her head.

"Why do murderers come here?" she demanded in a loud voice that caused heads near us to turn. "You have no shame."

"Hush, fool," my grandmother grunted. "Do not make a scene. You know the girls are not responsible for her death."

Nicoletta folded her arms across her chest. "I do *not* know. You defend her 'cause she your granddaughter."

"Hi there." Enzo reached forward and clasped my hand. "I'm Enzo Fiato, the deceased's son."

"Sally Donovan." His hand was moist and clammy, and I quickly drew mine back in repulsion. "I'm Rosa's granddaughter, and this is my friend, Josie Sullivan."

He nodded to Josie, but his gaze didn't waver from my face. "My, you're lovely. Are you married?"

Ew. I nodded. "Yes, and very happily."

"Bummer." His eyes widened in delight. "Well, if you ever want a one-night stand, let me know."

Dear God. What was wrong with this family? "Uh, thanks, but no thanks." My teeth clenched together in annoyance. "I happen to love my husband."

He blew out a sigh. "Love doesn't last forever, baby. Only death, taxes, and my mother's ominous presence are sure things. You can bet that cute little face of yours that she's hovering over this room right now like the black plague. Well, gotta go. Nice talking to you." Enzo hurried over to a pretty blonde in a short black dress who had stopped to talk to Anna.

"What a terrible thing to say about your own mother," I whispered to Josie.

She glared at Enzo, but he wasn't paying attention to us anymore. "That guy is definitely on the prowl. And the thought of Allegra floating above us in the air kind of gives me the willies."

I shuddered. "Well, if she is, you can bet she's also spitting down on us right about now."

"That boy needs a good smack upside his head," Grandma Rosa declared. "It is as if he is here to look for a girlfriend instead of pay his respects."

An attractive woman in a dark gray suit approached us. "Hello, Rosa." She stuck her hand out. "We've never met, but Allegra told me all about you. I'm Lena Ambrose."

My grandmother nodded and took her hand. "Of course. It is very nice to meet you. I know Allegra thought very highly of you." She turned to me. "This is my granddaughter, Sally, and her friend Josie. This is Allegra's niece, Lena."

"Nice to meet you," we both said simultaneously.

She smiled politely and brushed back her brown curly hair from her oval-shaped face. "Likewise. Allegra spoke of you a few times."

Oh, I bet she did. It was on the tip of my tongue to ask what she might have said, but I probably didn't want to know.

"We're going back to my office afterward for the official reading of the will. Do you need a ride?" Lena asked.

My grandmother looked confused. "Sally is taking me home. The reading is for family, and I do not wish to interfere. Unless Nicoletta would like for me to be there, then I will go."

"Don't you have to wait until all the children are together to read it?" Josie asked Lena.

Lena shook her head. "Allegra already informed her kids what was being left to them. She also requested that the document be read immediately after her service. The will hasn't gone through probate yet, but she had no outstanding debts, didn't own any real estate, and the process shouldn't take very long. Rosa, Aunt Allegra left you a little something as well, so you should be there. She always said how much she enjoyed talking to you, especially over the past few months. She liked to hear about your family, especially your granddaughters."

Yikes. The woman had also enjoyed bullying me, but I wisely kept that comment to myself. Even though Allegra had been entirely disagreeable, it didn't surprise me to learn she had been taken with my grandmother's charm. Everyone loved her— it was impossible not to.

Lena gestured at me. "Sally and Josie are welcome to come as well. It won't take long." She stared over my head and waved at someone. "I'm sorry, but would you excuse me for a minute? There's a friend of mine I'd like to talk to." She didn't wait for our response as she crossed the room and hastily enveloped a burly looking man in an embrace.

Grandma Rosa studied me carefully. "You do not have to go, *cara mia.* I am certain you would like to get home to your husband. Josie too."

"It's okay," I reassured her. "Mike's working late tonight. He's doing a complete renovation on a house over on Sandberg Avenue. New walls, kitchen cabinets, bathroom—the works. It has to be done by this weekend, so I won't be seeing much of him until then."

"Rob's off tonight," Josie put in. "He's at home with the kids, so I can come too."

Grandma Rosa nodded her approval. "That is good. I would like you both to be there. I have a bad feeling about this."

"About the will?" I asked.

She glanced around and then lowered her voice. "I do not like to speak ill of the dead, but Allegra was the type of person who—how do you say—enjoyed rubbing sugar into a person's wounds."

"As a baker, I love that analogy." Josie grinned. "And I'm not even going to bother to correct you this time, Rosa."

CHAPTER FIVE

———

Lena's office was located in Gateway Tower, an impressive 13-floor building on the border of Colwestern near the neighboring town of Colgate. Gianna had mentioned the firm Ambrose & Whitaker, which occupied most of the building, a couple of times in passing before. Besides estate law, they also practiced criminal law like Gianna, who was a public defender. The firm had a reputation for taking on high-profile cases.

Lena's office was on the tenth floor, modern and bright and done in neutral tones with a hand-carved mahogany bookcase that ran the entire length of one wall. Oriental rugs covered the highly polished wooden floors, and a floor-to-ceiling window located behind an expensive mahogany desk. The window treated us to a spectacular view of the sun setting amongst a beautiful array of orange and yellow hues.

"Can I get anyone some coffee while we wait for Anna and Enzo to arrive?" Lena asked. There was a Keurig perched on a small, white-tiled breakfast bar in the far corner of her office. A microwave and small fridge were also in plain view. With the comfortable furniture, stunning view of a nearby lake, and the 70-inch flat screen television on the wall, this would make a great place to crash for a while.

"None for me, thank you," my grandmother said as Josie and I both shook our heads.

Nicoletta's scowl changed to a broad smile as she regarded Lena. "I adore some coffee, if not too much trouble. Thank you, my dear."

I blinked, not sure if I'd heard the old woman right. This was a first—to see Nicoletta speak graciously to another person. It was obvious Lena was held in high regard, while someone like me was forever destined to be the gum on the bottom of Nicoletta's Birkenstocks.

As if she'd read my mind, Nicoletta leaned across the arm of the chic, white leather sofa and pinched my hand. "Lena—she married to Senator Ambrose. You have heard of him, no?"

"Yes, of course," I said, impressed by the revelation. Martin Ambrose occupied the Democratic seat in the Senate and had been in office for several years. He was also the owner of the law firm.

Although I knew next to nothing about political figures, Martin had a high approval rating and was up for reelection this coming November. Everyone said he was a shoo-in to win again.

"Wow." Josie's blue eyes went wide with awe. "Why is she working as an attorney, then?"

Nicoletta thrust her chest forward. "Lena always want to be attorney, Allegra say. She work for Martin as intern before. Then she go to law school and pass exam, like Gianna. But she make more money than your sister. *Lots* more," she added proudly.

Ouch. How I pitied my sister. Gianna and Johnny had been dating for about a year now and seemed very happy together. It was no secret he'd been in love with her for a long time, and I suspected he planned to ask her to marry him soon. Johnny was a great guy, and my family adored him. The downside to all this? Nicoletta would be cemented into my sister's world for many years to come.

Lena must have overheard our mumblings, because she smiled modestly as she handed Nicoletta her coffee in a pink china cup. "I hope you can meet Martin soon," she said. "He's in New York City this week. With the election coming up, he's busier than ever." She heaved a small sigh. "I feel like I never see him anymore. He passed the bar himself several years ago and then opened the firm, but he hasn't practiced since gaining the Senate seat. Martin has been my biggest mentor and always knew law was my true passion. I owe him so much."

"How long have you been married?" I asked.

"Almost two years." She beamed at me. "I guess we have something in common. I heard you're a newlywed too.

Allegra showed me your wedding picture from the newspaper a few weeks back and said you were Rosa's granddaughter."

"Yes, it will be a year for us next week." Allegra had saved a picture of me? That seemed strange. Then again, maybe *I* wasn't the person in the picture she'd been interested in looking at.

Lena laughed. "She said something about how your husband was very attractive. No arguments there. Ah, my aunt, she always liked them young."

Yeah, no kidding. "Right," I murmured, not knowing what else to say. Heat rose inside me like an inferno at the thought of Allegra touching Mike in such a suggestive manner. Okay, I needed to stop with the resentment. The woman was dead, and there was a good chance someone might have killed her. Who else had she ticked off?

The office door opened, and Enzo and Anna sauntered in. Anna glanced around the room before her bloodshot eyes focused on Josie and me in apparent surprise. No introductions were made. Perhaps Lena knew we'd seen them at the service, but it still felt awkward, and the atmosphere became tense. They both nodded at Lena and stood awkwardly next to the sofa.

Enzo gave me a suggestive wink as his gaze slowly traveled down my body. *Ick.* The man was disgusting, and made me long for a cleansing hot shower.

"Would you two like a chair?" Lena asked politely.

"Cut the so-called niceties, Lena," Enzo snapped. "Let's get this over with, okay? Go ahead and tell everyone how the old witch has done her children wrong—once again." His eyes shifted to me. "I don't even know why *some* people are here. Did dear sweet Mom leave her money to them instead of us?"

Oh boy. Looks like someone was holding a bit of a grudge.

There was an awkward silence in the room as Nicoletta set her coffee cup down on the glass coffee table and rose to her unintimidating four-foot-eleven-inch stature. She shook a bony finger menacingly at Enzo. "You have no respect. That is why your mama not leave you anything. You no care about her."

Anna's face flushed. "How dare you speak that way to my brother. We're her flesh and blood, not *you*."

I couldn't help but notice how Anna had slurred the word flesh. Her listless expression and the bloodshot eyes made me wonder if she'd been drinking.

"You only want her money," Nicoletta insisted. "At least I care about your mama. And she tell me other things."

"What things?" Anna asked in a shrill voice.

Lena clapped her hands. "Okay, this needs to stop. We're all adults here, so let's start acting like it."

"Easy for you to say, sweet cuz." Enzo folded both arms over his bony frame of a chest. "You've got yourself a nice little nest egg with your rich and powerful husband. We've always had to hear about the great Lena. 'Lena should have been my child, not my sister's. Lena married so well. Why can't you be more like your cousin?'"

My grandmother, like Josie and myself, remained silent throughout the bickering. She must have felt it wasn't her place to interfere, but she did reach a hand up and placed it firmly on Nicoletta's arm. Grandma Rosa then patted the seat next to her. Mrs. Gavelli muttered under her breath but sat back down on the sofa.

With a sigh, Lena removed a folded document from an envelope. "I know your mother sent you each a note about her new intentions a few weeks back," she said.

"Why'd she change the will?" Enzo asked suspiciously.

Lena shrugged. "It may have had something to do with your father's recent death. She didn't tell me."

"How convenient for you," Anna said, sarcasm evident in her slurred speech. "You just became a licensed estate attorney, and Mom hires you to draw up her will. How much did she secretly leave *you*? Oh, that's right. You don't need the money because you're the only one in the family who married well. The rest of us are losers."

"Wow," Josie whispered under her breath to me. "And I thought your family was nuts."

Sure, my parents were half-baked at times, but these people were filled with rage and resentment. Plus, their mother had just been killed. It didn't make for a very good combination.

Lena's mouth formed a thin, tight line. "Please don't make me privy to your disagreements with your mother," she said. "For the record, she left me nothing, and you'll see that for yourselves when you read the entire will."

"Maybe not in the document itself," Enzo put in. "But who's to say she didn't leave you some jewelry or slip you something on the sly without our knowledge?"

There hadn't been much to like about Allegra, but it was terrible to see how her own children were acting after her death. A bunch of two-year-olds would have behaved better. They should have been grieving, especially since their father had died recently too. Instead, their only concern seemed to be who got what from her estate and which child could cry the loudest about being cheated.

"I won't partake in this mudslinging anymore," Lena announced. "I'm going ahead with the official reading. Remember, I am only here to honor her wishes." She removed her eyeglasses from the top of her head and perched them on the end of her pert nose before she began to read. "'I, Allegra Ricci Fiato, being of sound mind and memory—'"

Enzo laughed. "Sound mind? Please. The woman was nuts."

"Disrespect!" Nicoletta yelled. "You rot in hell for saying that."

"Okay, I really don't want to be here," Josie muttered in my ear.

"You and me both," I said.

Lena's hazel eyes regarded Enzo with obvious contempt. "Do not interrupt me again, understand?" She continued to read. "'I hereby revoke all Wills and Codicils heretofore made by me at any time.'"

"Cockatiel?" Nicoletta mused out loud. "Allegra no have bird. She no like them."

With a pained look at her, Lena went on. "'I direct my Executor, hereinafter named, to pay all of my debts and funeral expenses as soon as practical after my death.'"

Anna pointed a French-manicured fingernail at her cousin. "That's you, I assume."

Lena gave a little toss of her head. "Actually, it's Nicoletta. But she has already asked for my help."

"Well, isn't that sweet," Enzo snickered.

"You shut up, boy!" Nicoletta told him angrily.

Lena ignored them and continued. "'To my dear friend Nicoletta Gavelli, the one person besides my beloved departed husband, Felipo, who has always been there for me, I leave my jewelry collection, with the exception of my gold locket. I will the necklace to Rosa Belgacci, who I am proud to call a friend since my return to America. May it be the key to her health when she wears it.'"

"I remember that necklace," Enzo mused. "Didn't it have a skull on it? She always liked hideous things."

"Then she must have liked him too," Josie whispered to me.

Anna wrinkled her brow. "My mother couldn't write her name in the snow. Are you sure these are her own words? Or did you write that line for her, Lena?"

"No," Lena snapped. "Now may I finish, please? 'All the rest, residue, and remainder of my Estate, or whatsoever kind that I give, devise, and bequeath to my daughter Violet Fiato, to be hers absolutely and forever. With the exception of the sum of five dollars apiece to both my son, Enzo Fiato, and my daughter, Anna Fiato Sheldon, for reasons that are well known to them.'"

"That mean old witch," Anna slurred. "I knew she wasn't leaving me anything, but to give it all to Violet? Pure spite. What about homeless cats and dogs instead? God, what the hell was that evil woman thinking? All because I told her she couldn't come and live with me, so she cuts her own daughter out of her will. Why would I have wanted that hideous woman around in the first place? All she did was judge me and complain that I smoke and drank too much. Boy, did we get robbed."

Even Nicoletta was silent, perhaps from shock.

Anna looked around at all of us as if trying to guess what we were thinking. "She may have been my mother, but she certainly didn't act like one. We never had a warm and fuzzy type of relationship. When Violet turned eighteen, she and my father went back to Italy to live. It was good riddance to all of us. Hey, we've raised you, and now you're on your own. I got pregnant, and she did nothing to help me. So I did what I was supposed to. I married the loser, and it ended in divorce. My mother and father never gave me a dime. Then after Dad died,

Mommy Dearest wants to live with me? Sorry, but no way."

I forgot my previous vow to keep silent. "Why didn't she go live with Violet in Vegas?" Especially if Violet was her favorite, as she appeared to be. "Maybe she could have worked in Violet's bakery." And left mine alone.

Anna choked back a laugh. "What? Who's been telling you bedtime stories? My sister doesn't have a bakery. Far from it. You know why my dear, sweet baby sister didn't come to New York? Not because of a fear of flying. It's because she doesn't care. She has her own little secret life out in Vegas. Now that she's inherited everything, she's going to live happily ever after."

Lena interrupted. "It's not that much money, Anna. Violet will still have to work. In answer to your question, Sally, Allegra didn't like the hot dry climate out there. She preferred a colder one."

"Yeah," Enzo agreed. "Freezing, like her heart."

Anna cocked her head in her brother's direction. "It appears we're done here." Her gaze came back to Lena. "I'll be waiting on that five-dollar check with bated breath." She started toward the door and stumbled slightly on a rug. Enzo caught his sister's arm and opened the door for her. They left without another word.

Lena put the will back in the envelope and closed her eyes for a second. "I'm very sorry you all had to witness that."

Nicoletta rose to her feet. "You good girl to do this. You pick out piece of Allegra's jewelry that you want, and I give."

Lena's face flushed with pleasure. She gave Nicoletta's hand a warm squeeze. "That's so sweet of you, but it won't be necessary. Aunt Allegra wanted you to have it all. She mentioned you already had the jewelry, but don't sell any of it until the will goes through probate, okay?"

Mrs. Gavelli frowned. "I no sell. Ever. I keep. Maybe someday I have great-grandchildren, and I give some to them. Or Johnny's bride." She stared at me with menacing black eyes. "*If* I like her."

Ouch. My poor sister.

"Is the locket Aunt Allegra spoke of in your possession as well?" Lena asked. "The one that is supposed to go to Rosa?"

Nicoletta shook her head. "I no see locket. No idea

where it is."

Lena's lips pursed into a slight frown. "That's strange. Why would she gift it to Rosa if no one knows where it is?"

"Do not worry," Grandma Rosa assured Lena. "Remember the saying. It will turn up like a bad nickel."

Josie and I both attempted to hide our smiles. "That's penny, Grandma."

She nodded. "I like that too."

CHAPTER SIX

———

The heat from the bright sun overhead was intense as Mike and I relaxed poolside at the Paris Hotel in Vegas. Drunk on love, I let him carry me up fifteen flights of stairs to our anniversary suite. Damn. The man wasn't even out of breath either. His blue eyes were wild with passion as he laid me down on the bed and kissed me so intently I thought I might burst into flames.

Then, at that wonderful moment, I spoke those two glorious words in his ear. "I'm pregnant."

I had only seen Mike cry a couple of times during my entire life, but the tears rolled down his cheeks like water gushing from a stream. As we both hugged each other in rapturous joy, the slot machine in our suite rumbled, its colorful lights blinking on and off as coins started to shoot out across the room. Everything was so perfect that I wanted to stay like this forever. A low humming started from the recesses of the machine, gradually becoming louder and louder, threatening to ruin our moment of happiness.

"Honey, make it stop," I pleaded to Mike, but he didn't answer. The noise continued, growing louder and more intense until I couldn't stand it anymore.

I opened my eyes. The room was dark, and Mike was snoring softly, one bare arm draped protectively around my chest. The red digits of the clock on the nightstand stood out against the blackness and alerted me to the fact that it was five o'clock. No Vegas, slot machines, or luxurious pool to speak of. With a sigh, I rolled over onto my back. I was exhausted, but at least we didn't have to get up for another hour.

As I started to snuggle closer to Mike, the humming

noise from my dream began again. My cell phone. Panic rose inside me. Who the heck was calling me at this ungodly hour? One thing was for certain—it couldn't be good. My stomach muscles clenched as I reached onto the nightstand to turn the lamp on. In the process, I managed to knock my phone onto the floor.

Mike opened one eye as I got back into bed with the phone. "Who died this time?" he asked sleepily.

"Very funny," I said dryly, but his words filled me with uneasiness. "Hello?"

"*Cara mia.*" My grandmother's voice floated through the phone and sounded a bit shaky.

I sat upright in bed. "Grandma, are you all right?"

"Yes, I am fine," she assured me. "But I need your help. Someone broke into Nicoletta's house."

"Is she okay?" I asked.

"Nicoletta is not hurt. She just called me. She heard a noise and went downstairs to check. The kitchen door slammed, and she saw the outline of someone running down the street in the dark. The contents of her desk were spilled out all over the floor."

I sucked in a deep breath. "It sounds like they were looking for something. Did she say if anything was missing?"

"What's wrong?" Mike switched on the lamp next to him and rubbed sleep from his eyes.

"She does not think so," Grandma Rosa said slowly.

I detected a note of hesitation in her voice. Why did I get the feeling my grandmother was hiding something from me? "She needs to call the police, Grandma. They might be able to find fingerprints."

"Nicoletta said she did not want to call them—yet. Believe me, I tried to get her to call too, *cara mia*. She says why bother? They will not catch the person."

"Is your grandmother okay?" Mike whispered.

I put a finger to my lips and nodded. "Grandma, she has to call them. What's really going on here?"

Grandma Rosa cleared her throat. "Nicoletta received a terrible note in the mail yesterday."

A knot formed in the pit of my stomach. "What did it

say?"

"Do you have time to stop by the house before you go to work this morning?" Grandma Rosa asked. "I would rather tell you about this in person. Have Mike come too. I will make breakfast."

"Of course." I hadn't gone to bed until midnight and was exhausted. My stomach felt a bit queasy as well, but this excited me. Every day I became more and more convinced that I was pregnant but didn't want to say anything until I knew for sure. "I have to open the shop this morning, so I can't stay very long."

"That is fine."

Mike leaned over and kissed me on the shoulder before he got out of bed. He was wearing blue plaid boxer shorts and nothing else, the unshaven stubble of his beard and his tousled hair making him look even more sexy than usual.

"Do you want to come to Grandma's with me for breakfast?" I asked.

He pushed a strand of dark hair off his forehead. "No time, princess. I'm way behind on this job. Tell her thanks for the early wakeup call though—it will help me catch up. I'm going to grab a quick shower and then hit the road." He tossed me a sexy teasing smile over his shoulder. "But there's always room for one more. Join me?"

My face grew warm, and I covered the phone with my hand, praying my grandmother hadn't heard. Then again, Grandma Rosa always seemed to know everything anyway. I nodded to my husband and uncovered my hand from the phone. "Grandma, I'll be there within the hour. Is there anything you need?"

My grandmother sighed. "Yes. Some new friends. The old ones are wearing me out. *Ciao, bella.*" With that, she clicked off.

* * *

An hour and a half later, I was sitting at the small, round table in my parents' kitchen as Grandma Rosa reached for my empty coffee cup. My earlier morning nausea has subsided once I got a whiff of her famous breakfast casserole. With layers of salami, cheese, and eggs baked inside her tender and flaky homemade piecrust, it had been easy for my appetite to make a return.

"More coffee?" she asked.

I placed a hand over the cup. "You don't happen to have any decaf, do you?"

She stared at me in surprise. "You never drink decaf. But I believe there is a box of those K-circles in the cupboard."

I pushed back my chair. "K-cups. I'll grab them. That quiche was amazing, by the way." Everything she made always was.

"Would you like more?" she asked.

"No, thanks. I'm starting to put on a few pounds." I couldn't keep the smile off my face as I hunted in the overhead oak cabinets and found the box of decaf K-cups she'd referred to. As I stuck one into the machine, I noticed her glancing at me curiously. "What?" I asked.

"It is nothing." She adjusted the gold watch on her wrist. "I wonder what is keeping Nicoletta."

The words had barely left her mouth when Nicoletta slammed open the kitchen door without even knocking. I almost did a double take when I saw her. Her short white hair was sticking up all over her head, and the housecoat she wore was wrinkled. Nicoletta looked as if she hadn't slept in about a week. She thrust a bony finger in my face.

"All right, missy hot shot detective. What you gonna do about this one, huh?"

Confused, I stared at her as Grandma Rosa scowled. "I have not told her anything yet, Nicoletta. Sally just finished her breakfast."

"She can eat anytime. She gettin' fat anyhow," Nicoletta growled.

I threw my napkin on the table. "Wow. That's a pretty rotten thing to say."

"Whatever," she grunted. "You help me or no?"

It was difficult to think about helping someone when the urge to choke them flashed through your brain. "Grandma said you received a threatening message in the mail. Do you have it with you?"

Nicoletta thrust her hand into the pocket of the drab gray housecoat and produced a folded piece of paper. "Here, I show you." She handed it to me.

Instinctively I reached for a napkin to grab hold of it.

Nicoletta's lips formed a sneer. "What the matter? I got cooties now?"

Good grief. "You'll have to show it to the police. There's a chance they might be able to lift fingerprints off the paper, so I don't want to touch it. You shouldn't have either. You'll also need to tell them that someone broke into your house."

"Bah." She sat down in the chair next to mine as Grandma Rosa set a cup of coffee in front of her. "This person too smart for that. Cops no find fingerprints."

I studied the note in front of me. The message had been printed from a computer onto an 8 by 11–inch piece of white copy paper in bold, capital letters. It was only one line long but terrifying enough to stop my heart for a few seconds.

Hand them over, old lady, or you're next.

"Holy cow." I glanced up at Nicoletta, who seemed pleased by my startled reaction. "Hand what over?"

She shrugged. "That what I want to know."

I paused to think for a moment. "Is there any chance this note was meant for Allegra and not you?"

Again, Nicoletta shook her head. "No. It addressed to me."

"Do you have the envelope with you?" It was doubtful I'd find any clues, but still worth a shot.

She produced the envelope from her pocket. Why she hadn't bothered to hand it to me with the letter, I had no idea, but that was Nicoletta for you. If she could further complicate the process, she was only too happy to oblige.

To my disappointment, the envelope had also been printed by a computer. A stamp was attached with no return address. The postmark said it had been mailed from New Jersey, which I found interesting since two of Allegra's children lived there. "When did you receive this?"

"The day after Allegra died," she said.

"And you have no idea what they're referring to?"

Her dark eyes surveyed me coldly. "If I know, you think

I ask *you?* Your grandmama say you excellent detective. She brag to Allegra before she die. So you tell *me*, missy."

"I'm not a fortune-teller, Mrs. Gavelli." I carefully placed the note back into the envelope. "We need to show this to Brian."

Nicoletta shook her head. "No. He not real cop."

I drew my eyebrows together. "What does that mean?"

"He too good-looking to be a cop," she insisted. "He like the fake ones on TV. I need to think this through first. Allegra's death no accident. She murdered."

I glanced up at my grandmother, who was standing against the kitchen counter with a dish towel in hand. "Is that what you think too?"

My grandmother looked from me to Nicoletta and then slowly nodded her head. "Yes, I do. I have thought this all along."

A chill crept down my spine as the non-squealing brakes came to mind again. "Who could have wanted her dead, and why?"

"Besides Josie, you mean." Nicoletta's tone was filled with contempt.

My patience was wearing thin. "Mrs. Gavelli, you know that Josie didn't have anything to do with this. They had an argument. Josie didn't push her out into the street or drive over her."

The kitchen door burst open at that moment, and my sister and Johnny both rushed in. "What's going on?" Gianna cried.

Johnny put an arm around Nicoletta's skinny shoulders and then knelt down beside her. "Gram, are you hurt?"

She patted Johnny on the head like he was a dog. "I tell you on the phone I okay. No need to make fuss."

"You scared us half to death," he muttered. Johnny had classic Italian good looks that consisted of wavy black hair and dark eyes that were usually brimming with some type of mischief. At the moment, they were full of concern as he stared at his grandmother. "Looks like everyone else beat us here. Why didn't you call me as soon as it happened?"

Nicoletta gave a loud harrumph. "I decide to go through Allegra's things and see if I find something robber want. *I* pretty good detective too."

Johnny rolled his eyes at this declaration then pointed a finger at me. "She wants to solve a mystery like you have."

Uh-oh. I wasn't sure if I was ready for Nicoletta as a potential sidekick. Then again, it might work. She could definitely scare a killer to death.

Nicoletta addressed my grandmother. "I no find locket either."

"What locket?" Gianna asked.

"It is nothing," Grandma Rosa assured her. "Allegra left me a gold locket in her will. We were at the reading last night—Nicoletta, your sister, Josie, and me."

Gianna looked baffled by this revelation. My baby sister was my pride and joy, and I was proud of the conscientious attorney she had become. She was always so perfect and well put together—until now. She still looked beautiful, but something seemed off about her. Gianna's face was thinner than usual, and there were pronounced circles under her eyes.

I knew that Gianna's caseload as a public defender had increased as of late and suspected that was the cause for her weariness—unless she and Johnny were having problems. She was dressed for a day at the office in a gray pencil skirt, white silk blouse, and black heels. Her lovely chestnut-colored hair that always fell so perfectly around her shoulders was windblown and the delicate blouse wrinkled. She wore no makeup and never needed any, but her face was devoid of color.

"Let me get this straight," Gianna said. "There was a memorial held last night without a body. Then you all traipsed over to her niece's office for a reading of the will? What's Lena's number? I'd like to talk to her. This sounds unethical."

"What you know," Nicoletta growled and punctuated her speech with a loud harrumph. "Allegra write all this down. That the way she want it done, and Lena only follow her orders. Lena a smart one. She going to be partner at the firm soon. Unlike *some* people."

Annoyance crept into Johnny's face. "Gram, stop comparing her to Gianna. They practice entirely different types of law. And everyone in this state knows that even though Martin Ambrose doesn't practice law, he owns the firm. Call me crazy, but maybe that's why his wife, who just passed the bar earlier this year, is already up for a partnership."

How interesting. Maybe everyone had known that—except me, that is. "Why don't we get back to the situation at hand." I looked at Johnny. "Your grandmother doesn't want the police to know someone broke into her house or that she received a threatening note. It said to 'hand them over or she was next.'"

Johnny was thunderstruck. "What the hell, Gram? You have to call the police."

"No cuss." Mrs. Gavelli tapped a finger to the side of her head. "Sally help me find out who did this."

So now she'd decided she wanted my help. I couldn't keep track. "Let's think for a minute. Is there anyone who might know what this person was looking for?"

Mrs. Gavelli paused to consider. "Maybe Violet."

"The daughter who lives in Vegas?" I asked.

She nodded. "She the only one that Allegra ever speak to. She talk to Violet on the phone same day she die."

"What did they say?" Gianna asked.

"How I know?" Nicoletta said angrily, "I no snoop."

Yeah, right.

"I think," Grandma Rosa said calmly, "that I should move in with Nicoletta for a while. I do not want her there by herself." She stared at Johnny. "Unless you were planning to."

Johnny's face was pained as he glanced from his grandmother to Gianna. "My best friend from college is getting married this weekend. I'm leaving this afternoon for California, and I won't be back until late Monday. But Gram is always welcome to stay with us." His eyes searched Gianna's face as if for confirmation. "Right, sweetheart?"

Gianna's head whipped around so fast I swore I felt a breeze in the room. The look she gave him might have stopped traffic. Oh, yeah, Johnny was definitely getting a tongue-lashing later.

"Aren't you going too?" I asked my sister. She hadn't mentioned the trip to me. Then again, I hadn't seen her in several days.

She shook her head. "No, my caseload is insane right

now." She dropped her gaze to the floor. "Too bad because I could really use a vacation."

Johnny kissed the top of her head. "You definitely could, my love. You're pushing yourself too hard."

My cell phone buzzed, and I glanced down at the screen. "Jos?"

"Yeah, it's me." Her voice was barely above a whisper. "I'm at the shop."

"Okay, I'm on my way over. What are you doing there so early? It was my turn to open."

Her voice sounded shaky. "I...uh, had to finish making a cake for Stephanie Stein's bridal shower. Sal, call Brian and have him meet you here."

Another nervous shiver slid down my spine. "Why? What's wrong?"

"Someone broke in and trashed the apartment over the bakery."

CHAPTER SEVEN

———

"You didn't touch anything, right?"

Josie gave Brian a disbelieving look. "We're not exactly new at this, Officer. Our shop has been broken into before, if you recall. Sal and I have pretty much seen it all by now."

A muscle twitched in Brian's jaw, but to his credit, he didn't say anything. Sure, we might have seen it all, but there was no doubt Brian had too. Although only a couple of years older than myself, some gray hairs had already started to mix in with his fine blond strands, and slight wrinkles were forming around his eyes. Being a police officer was a stressful job no doubt, but somehow, I sensed I was a contributing factor to his aging process.

"Why didn't the alarm go off?" Brian wanted to know.

"Nicoletta said she dropped by last night to get a few items left upstairs. She thinks she may have forgotten to turn it back on. Her friend Ronald was with her."

Brian narrowed his eyes. "Ronald Feathers? The old man who lives down your street and couldn't hear a train coming if it ran next to him?"

"The very same one." Ronald was Mrs. Gavelli's sometime boyfriend. He was eighty years old and hard of hearing, which might not be a bad thing where Nicoletta was concerned. "I didn't know Nicoletta still had the key to the building, but I politely asked for it back this morning."

He folded his arms across his chest. "Well, isn't that great. I should probably ask her if she has anything useful to add." Nicoletta and my grandmother were downstairs in the bakery. They had insisted on following us over when learning about the break-in.

Josie pursed her lips together. "It's not the first time this has happened since Allegra signed the lease. Those two witches forgot to turn the alarm on once before."

The three of us stood in the middle of the mess as we talked. Photos had already been taken, along with our statements. The bakery had been broken into and trashed once before, but fortunately nothing had been touched in it this time. Allegra's apartment was going to be a joy to clean up. She hadn't moved much furniture in, but the entire kitchen was in shambles. Contents of the drawers had been dumped out, and someone had even taken a hammer to the cash register, still perched on the folding table. The candies that remained in her display case had been removed and smashed onto the hardwood floors—from the looks of it, with someone's shoe. Chocolate smears covered the lace curtains as well.

The adjoining bedroom was empty, except for a small sofa Allegra had moved in there. She'd also hung a framed embroidered motto on the wall. The design was—of all things—a fortune cookie cracked open, and its message portrayed on a strip of paper read, "Your Fortune Looks Bright."

Josie laughed and pointed at the picture. "Hey, would you look at this. The old lady really did love her fortune cookies. Maybe that's why she decided to steal ours."

"What you say?" Nicoletta had appeared in the open doorway of the apartment. "Allegra make that with her own two hands. She steal nothing." She started toward Josie, only to be held back by my grandmother.

"Not again," Brian groaned. "Ladies, let's try to stay focused here. Mrs. Gavelli, when Sally called me about the break-in, she said you had an intruder in your house earlier this morning as well. It may have been the same person."

"Well, duh." Nicoletta rolled her eyes.

Brian blinked, and I did too. *Yeah, it's always good to disrespect a cop, Mrs. G.*

He let out a sigh and continued. "They were obviously looking for something. Any idea what?"

"It the same person who murder Allegra," Nicoletta declared.

Brian raised an eyebrow at her. "What makes you think

she was murdered?"

She looked at him like he was some type of imbecile. "Of course she murdered. What the matter? You not put two and two together here, sonny? Someone run Allegra over to get her out of way. Now they want what she have."

Brian bit into his lower lip as if he was trying to hold his temper. "And what does she have that they might want?"

She shook her head. "I dunno. But Allegra, she tell me something last week. Very strange. She say, 'Nicoletta, if something happen to me, you take care of things. Make sure justice served.'"

Her words made me uneasy. It sounded as if Allegra knew her life was in danger. "Did you find anything on Allegra's body after the car hit her?" I asked Brian.

Brian shook his head. "Only one of your fortune cookies in her hand, which you already knew." He hesitated then addressed Nicoletta and my grandmother. "Ladies, would you mind going downstairs to the bakery for a minute so I could speak with Sally alone?"

"Why?" Nicoletta demanded. "You want to make date with her? For shame. She married woman."

I rolled my eyes toward the ceiling. "Grandma, please get her out of here."

Brian glared at Nicoletta but said nothing further.

"We will go." Grandma Rosa took hold of Nicoletta by the arm.

Josie followed them out of the apartment. "I've got to get some more cookies in the oven, and since it's past nine, I'll open the shop." She winked at me. "But I'll come back up if we don't have any customers waiting."

As soon as Brian heard their feet on the stairs, he removed his hat and scratched the top of his head thoughtfully. "Sally, I don't want Mrs. Gavelli to know about this yet, but we have reason to believe she may be right. Allegra Fiato's death was no accident. We're going to be ruling it a homicide."

My mouth went dry. "What exactly did you find out?"

"We located an eyewitness," Brian explained. "A ten-year-old boy who lives down the street was riding his bike when the hit-and-run occurred. He saw the car coming, so he quickly rode his bike onto the sidewalk. When questioned, he told us that the car never even slowed down after it hit Allegra. He couldn't tell me anything about the make or model—only that it had two doors and was red. We got the paint chips back from the lab and have managed to narrow it down. The car that hit Allegra was a red Chevy Camaro, most likely a late-80s model."

"Wow." That impressed me. "It's amazing what you can find out these days."

He grinned. "Yep. It really is a fascinating process. We're trying to keep this quiet for now, but if Mrs. Gavelli finds out…" He blew out an exasperated breath. "Well, I'm afraid that she'll blab to everyone. If the person who ran Allegra over is still in town with the vehicle, we don't want them alerted."

"I won't breathe a word to her," I said. "Can I tell Josie at least though? And my grandmother? Neither one of them will say anything."

Brian threw up his hands in annoyance. "Hey, why not? What's two more people, right? Your grandmother probably has some idea of what's going on anyway. She always seems to be one step ahead of everyone else."

No kidding. Grandma Rosa was like my own personal fortune cookie, except that she only had kind and nice things to say.

"So now what?" I asked. "Obviously Mrs. Gavelli is in danger because of the note I showed you. Allegra must have had something incriminating on this person who ran her down, and it's obvious they will stop at nothing to get what they want. My grandmother has insisted on moving in with Mrs. Gavelli for the next few days. Brian, I'm terrified something might happen to her as well."

He nodded. "That's understandable. Knowing your grandmother, I doubt she'd leave her friend alone, though. What about Johnny? Would he be willing to move back in with his grandmother for a while?"

"Yes, but he's flying to California for a friend's wedding this afternoon."

There were footsteps on the stairs, and Nicoletta appeared again. "I no need my grandson to babysit me," she said in a bitter tone, obviously having overheard us. "I got baseball bat." She thrust a finger toward Brian. "You know who killer is?"

He smiled patiently as if she was a child. "Mrs. Gavelli, we aren't certain that your friend was murdered."

"You no give me that bull. I *know* she murdered." Nicoletta started to count on her hands. "Her children a bad lot. They could do this. And the people who live across the street from me, they no like her. She call police and tell them they smoke weed."

"The Gardners?" This surprised me. I didn't know the young couple well, since they'd only moved into the neighborhood last year. Rachel and Carl Gardner were a couple of years younger than Mike and me and had a baby daughter. From what my father had said, they liked to have barbecues on the weekends and invite friends over.

My father and mother had relayed the story to me last month of how the Gardners had gotten a little rowdy late one night, and Dad had gone over to ask them to keep it down. My mother had awakened at two in the morning to find herself alone in bed. She'd tracked Dad down across the street, where he'd been busy partying with the younger crowd. "They're good people," Dad told us later on. "And they love my blog."

"What does that have to do with anything?" Brian asked Nicoletta.

She narrowed her eyes at him. "They tell Allegra to mind her own business or she be sorry."

Brian sighed as he wrote something down on a pad of paper. "All right. Anyone else?"

Grandma Rosa waved her hand impatiently. "The Gardners are a nice young couple. They have a little girl. They do not bother anyone. Yes, they have many friends who come over on the weekend. So what? Allegra should not have been sticking her mouth where it did not belong."

"Nose, Grandma," I mumbled.

She nodded. "That works too."

Nicoletta gave my grandmother the evil eye. "Whatever." She turned her attention back to Brian. "Allegra's children no like her either. Her own flesh and blood! Disrespectful little maggots."

The woman always had such a way with words.

Brian checked his notes. "Are Anna and Enzo Fiato still in town?" he asked.

"Yes, they stay at hotel and then go home soon." Nicoletta clenched her jaw. "They no welcome in my house."

"What about Allegra's other daughter?" Brian turned a page. "Violet? No one's had any luck getting ahold of her?"

Nicoletta shook her head. "She no answer her phone. Anna tell her about service the other day, but she no come. After that, no answer phone anymore. Lena, Allegra's niece, call to tell her about the will and money, but she not hear back. I bet Violet send someone to break into my house."

Brian's expression was pained. "We don't have any proof that's what happened, Mrs. Gavelli."

Heels clacked on the wooden stairs, and Josie appeared. "What's going on?" she asked as she walked into the apartment.

Nicoletta tapped a finger to the side of her head. "Bologna. Violet a bad lot too. I get to the bottom of this. Someone kill my friend, and I find out who did it. Violet might know. So I go."

Brian raised an eyebrow in confusion. "You're going where?"

"I go to Vegas and talk to Violet myself." Nicoletta folded her arms triumphantly over her chest.

"Holy cow," Josie breathed. "Sin City will never be the same."

"Grandma," I pleaded. "Tell her to stay put. She'll listen to you." Nicoletta shouldn't be traveling by herself to Vegas. If Johnny came back home to find his grandmother gone, he would freak for sure. Plus, the woman might end up in jail while she was there.

Brian rocked back on his heels for a moment, and his mouth twitched at the corners. "Maybe that isn't such a bad idea."

I cocked my head to the side and studied him. "Okay, exactly how is this a *good* idea?"

Nicoletta grunted with apparent satisfaction. "I go now and make plane reservations. Rosa, you come to Vegas with me."

It was an order, and my grandmother did not take orders from anyone. She glanced from Nicoletta to me, over at Brian, and then back to me again. To my shock and surprise, she merely bobbed her head up and down. "Yes, I go."

"Good." Nicoletta crooked a finger at Josie. "I need fortune cookie to bring me luck. You get me some now."

"Forget it." Josie said stubbornly and refused to move.

"Please," I whispered in her ear. "Humor her for a moment while I find out what exactly is going on with my grandmother."

She exhaled sharply. "Okay, but I'd better get all the details." Josie turned to follow the elderly woman down the stairs. "And hurry up before I have a sudden urge to choke her."

I leaned against the display case. "Okay, Brian. Please explain how this is a good idea. My grandmother and Nicoletta Gavelli on a plane to Vegas? Perhaps Nicoletta would like to visit a strip club while she's there too."

Grandma Rosa's face broke into a smile. "Sally, my love, I can take care of myself and Nicoletta as well."

"It will keep them safe and out of harm's way until Johnny gets back." Brian turned to my grandmother. "That is, if you're planning on going right away."

My grandmother nodded. "Nicoletta first mentioned it after the break-in. She is very upset that Violet did not come and is suspicious of the girl. I cannot let her go there alone. We are thinking about leaving Friday morning. Nicoletta and I can stay at my daughter's house until then." Grandma Rosa's warm brown eyes fixated on me. "*Cara mia*, will you come to Vegas with us?"

The sudden request startled me. "Grandma, I have a business to run. I can't just pick up and leave anytime I want to."

She heaved a sigh. "I know this. But I would like for you to come, and Mike too, if possible. I did promise to take you both on a trip, remember? I will pay for the money you lose from the bakery."

I shook my head vehemently. "I'm not worried about that. But there's no way Mike will be able to go. He's in the middle of a job that has to be finished by this weekend."

"Well, perhaps Josie would like to go in his place, then."

This was all happening too fast. "We have orders to be delivered on Friday, so someone would have to be at the bakery for at least a little while. Plus, there are other things I have to consider too."

Grandma Rosa knitted her eyebrows together. "Like what?"

This was not the time or place to reveal my secret. Since my grandmother was a bit like a soothsayer at times, I had thought she might know, but she'd given no indication that she did. "Well, next weekend is also my first wedding anniversary, you know."

She chuckled under her breath. "We will be back in plenty of time for that. If we can get a flight Friday morning, it is my hope to return by Sunday night. I do not like to be away from home for long. As I said, I will pay for both you and Josie to go."

"Go where?" Josie walked back into the apartment. "Nicoletta's downstairs on her phone. I think she's calling Southwest Airlines about plane reservations. I've got to listen for the front door. If a customer comes in to buy cookies, she'll scare them away forever."

"How would you like to go to Las Vegas with Sally, me, and Nicoletta? It would be my treat," Grandma Rosa said.

Josie's mouth opened in amazement. "Are you serious? Aw hell, yes! I've always wanted to go to Vegas. The latter person excluded, but hey, no trip is perfect."

"It would only be for three days," Grandma Rosa explained. "We are hoping to leave on Friday and come back on Sunday. You would not be leaving Rob and the kids for too long."

Josie grinned. "Well, this might sound terrible, but I don't have a problem with that. I need a vacation *bad*. And any trip that doesn't include diapers or screaming kids is definitely a vacation. I'll have to make sure my mother-in-law can help out, but that shouldn't be a issue."

All three of them looked over at me expectantly. Now I was really torn. While Josie might have wanted a break from Rob and the kids, I hated leaving my husband. It would be the first time we'd been separated overnight since our wedding. A few months ago, I'd had to stay in the hospital for a night, and he'd stayed right by my side.

However, this meant so much to my grandmother, and there was no way I could deny her anything—she had done too much for me during my lifetime. Plus, it was an opportunity for poor Josie to have a well-deserved vacation, one she couldn't normally afford on her own. Grandma Rosa was worried about Nicoletta, and I in turn was worried about *her* safety if she stayed alone with the woman. Someone had already broken into Nicoletta's home once. What if they did it again? There was something of Allegra's that they wanted, but what was it?

Maybe Violet had the answer. When we returned, Johnny could watch over his grandmother until the person was apprehended. Then Grandma Rosa would be free to return home to the bosom of her own crazy family—my mother and father.

Having no choice, I relented. "Okay. I certainly don't want you two going alone but am not sure how I can help. I don't know Violet."

"You will be a great help," Grandma Rosa insisted. "You will get to the bottom of this and find Allegra's killer. It will be another chance for you to put your detective skills to work. Remember what I said. You are a very good sloth."

Brian's eyebrows shot up. "What did you call her?"

"I'll explain later," I told him.

CHAPTER EIGHT

———

"When are you coming back?" Mike wanted to know.

The remainder of Wednesday and Thursday had flown, and it was now Friday morning. Josie and I had rushed to fill orders for various parties and events happening this weekend. Josie had gone in early this morning to finish the baking. Gianna was stopping by for a couple of hours to help since she wasn't due in court until later today. On Saturday the shop would be closed, but our driver would make the rest of the deliveries.

I zipped my duffel bag shut. "Late Sunday night. Now, I have to hurry. I'm meeting the gang at the bakery, and we're leaving for the airport from there. Plus, I have to make sure Gianna has everything she needs. There's some of my grandmother's lasagna and sausage and peppers in the freezer if you get hungry."

He pulled me close. "The only thing I'll be hungry for is you. You know I hate sleeping alone. I'm going to miss you like crazy."

Mike placed his mouth over mine, and desire quickly consumed me. He'd just spent the last hour letting me know how much I'd be missed, but as far as I was concerned, it was never enough. He'd purposely started his workday late so that we could spend a little alone time together this morning.

"Take a later flight," he urged, moving his hands seductively underneath my shirt and grazing my skin gently with his fingertips.

"You do make it tough to say no to you, Mr. Donovan." I reached up to peck him on the lips again. "Unfortunately, that's not an option right now. I can't miss the flight." I tugged on the front of his T-shirt playfully. "If it was anyone else, I'd say no, but this means so much to Grandma."

Mike tucked a stray curl back behind my ear. "Your grandmother does so much for everyone else and asks for so little in return. I wouldn't want you to say no to her but confess I'm a bit selfish when it comes to sharing my princess. This is the first time we'll have been apart overnight since our wedding."

"I know. We'll have to make up for it when I get back. Besides, you have to finish the house renovation and won't be around much anyway. And if I remember correctly, there's a special event going on next weekend for just the two of us."

He nuzzled my hair with his face. "Have you thought about us going away somewhere for the weekend? We've got a lot to celebrate."

Do we ever. I couldn't keep the smile off my face. Josie was the only one who knew about the pregnancy. I'd decided to hold off on taking the test until Monday. I couldn't wait to see Mike's reaction. It would be nice if I could wait until our actual anniversary to deliver the news but wasn't sure I'd make it that long. "Surprise me."

"Oh, I'm full of surprises, princess. Wait until you see your present."

"Oh, yeah?" My eyes darted around the room with interest. "Where'd you hide it?"

He laughed and kissed me again. "You won't find it, so don't even try. Stick to the other kind of snooping you do best. You know, tracking down killers of old ladies."

I gave him a playful pout. "You're taking all the fun out of it."

His voice grew soft as he lifted my chin and cupped my face between his hands. "I want you to know that this has been the happiest year of my life, Sal. You mean more to me than anything else in this world."

Tears started to gather in the corners of my eyes. "I feel the same way about you. Life is only going to get better, sweetheart. Wait and see."

He placed the duffel in the back seat of my car and kissed me one more time before I got behind the wheel. "Call me when you land."

"I will. Love you."

"Love you too, princess. Good luck. I hope this woman has the information you're looking for."

"Me too." I waved to him and pulled out of the driveway. My thoughts turned to Violet as I drove, uneasiness washing over me like a tidal wave. Violet was Allegra's own flesh and blood. She'd received a nice inheritance but still hadn't bothered to come to her mother's service. Seriously, how dysfunctional was this family?

It was nine o'clock—opening time—when I arrived at the bakery. Josie's minivan was out front waiting to bring us all to the airport. Grandma Rosa and Nicoletta would be arriving within the hour. Our nonstop flight was scheduled to take off at one. We would land at six—or, according to Vegas time, three o'clock in the afternoon.

Josie was taking a tray of raspberry cheesecake cookies out of the oven. "I've been at it since six o'clock," she said. "I'm totally wired for this trip. I can't wait to hit the slots. By the way, Mickey said he could help Gianna behind the counter if she needs him."

Mickey was our part-time driver. "Gianna's only going to be here a couple of hours today, remember. I hate bothering her with this, especially now. Haven't you noticed how thin she looks? I think she's working too hard."

Josie arched an eyebrow at me. "With Johnny going away this weekend and her staying behind, I wonder if something's going on between them."

"Jeez, I hope not." But I'd wondered that too. Maybe her job was coming between them. My sister had wanted to be a lawyer ever since she was a little girl, and now that her career had finally started to take off, she planned to enjoy it for a while. Marriage and kids could wait—the kid part maybe indefinitely. We were very different in that aspect. It was also the main reason she and her previous boyfriend had broken up—he'd claimed Gianna was too obsessed with her career.

"When we get back, I think I'll take her out to lunch so that we can have a sisterly chat. I haven't seen much of her lately. By the way, thanks for finishing the cleanup in Allegra's apartment last night."

"No problem. I'm an expert at getting chocolate stains

out of everything. My boys have trained me well."

The bells on the front door jingled, and Grandma Rosa and Nicoletta walked in. Grandma Rosa carried one small suitcase while Mrs. Gavelli had three.

Josie scowled. "We're not going away for a month. Only two nights."

"What you know?" Nicoletta scowled. "I not leave my valuables behind. What if someone break in my house again?"

Personally, I didn't think Nicoletta had anything in her house that was of much value. She was a bit of a pack rat compared to my neat and orderly grandmother, but I wisely decided to keep my thoughts to myself. There was never any winning with the woman, so why bother? "Actually, the airline only allows you two bags plus your purse, so you'll have to leave one behind."

She gave me a cynical stare. "How many bags you take?"

"Only my duffel bag and my purse."

Nicoletta nodded. "Good. We all set, then. I use your extra one."

"Oh, fine." I gave in without a fight. Sure, Vegas was one place I'd always wanted to see, but something told me this trip wasn't going to be a laugh a minute.

Josie removed her apron and cap. "Are we ready to go?"

The bells sounded again, and my sister came in. She smiled at all of us, but it looked forced. Her hair was pulled back from her face in a ponytail, and again I noticed how pale and thin she was.

"The airlines always say to be there at least two hours before your plane takes off," Gianna said. "Don't wait till the last minute."

"You talk to Johnny?" Nicoletta demanded.

Gianna's smile faded. "Yes, he called me last night. He got in fine."

"Good." Nicoletta pointed a finger at her. "So I go to *his* house Sunday night?"

I noticed how Nicoletta didn't say *their* house. We all watched Gianna for her reaction.

She bit into her lower lip. "I'm sure my mother and

father won't mind you staying at their home for another night."
Grandma Rosa frowned. "They have gone away too."

This was news to me. "Where? They didn't say anything to me about it."

My grandmother shrugged. "Me neither. They never tell me anything, and I live there. It was all very last minute. They left a note yesterday that said they were leaving town. I imagine they are hunting for someone to buy that *pazza* book of your father's." She sighed in apparent disgust. "Nutsy cookies, they are."

"Your papa, he crazy, and not like a fox," Nicoletta agreed. "He want to show me casket in just my size. He trying to put me in the ground before my time."

Josie's mouth twitched at the corners, but mercifully she said nothing.

"Come," Grandma Rosa said. "We will go to the van." She gave Gianna a kiss, then drew back to examine her face. "Are you all right, my dear? You do not seem well."

Gianna glanced over at Nicoletta nervously then slowly nodded her head. "Yes, of course. Just a little tired."

"You are working too hard." Grandma Rosa patted her cheek. "You need a vacation."

My sister's cheeks flushed. "Yeah, don't I wish." She touched me lightly on the arm. "Can I talk to you for a sec? Alone?"

Josie grabbed her suitcase and opened the door for my grandmother and Nicoletta. "Let's go wait for Sal in my van, girls."

"I no girl," Nicoletta announced. "And I sit up front, not Sally."

"Lucky me." Josie's voice dripped with sarcasm. "This trip is already off to an awesome start."

It was going to be a very long plane ride. In resignation, I turned my attention back to my sister. Gianna was sitting at one of the little tables in front of the window, gripping the tablecloth Grandma Rosa had so lovingly made for me between her slim hands. Something was definitely wrong. I reached down and playfully tugged at her rich chestnut hair, which seemed rather limp today. Although she was still beautiful, something about her appearance triggered alarm in me. "Gi, what's wrong? And don't tell me nothing."

Gianna's large chocolate brown eyes stared into my own. "There's too much going on in my life lately."

She was really starting to worry me. "Is it Johnny? Or a case you're working on?" Her very first case as a licensed attorney had occurred about a year ago, and it had been a doozy. Gianna had defended a man accused of racketeering. After his dead body was found inside my shop, the police had turned their suspicions on her.

"Work is fine. Sure, it's stressful, but I knew to expect that. As for Johnny—yeah, living together has been a bit of a challenge."

"Did he ask you to marry him?" Johnny had been secretly in love with her for years, since we were kids, but a five-year age difference back then would have made any type of relationship between them inappropriate. While Johnny hadn't hesitated to throw my school books across the street or cajole me to follow him into a darkened garage, he'd always treated Gianna special, worshipping the ground she walked on. He'd bided his time for many years, until she'd broken up with her former boyfriend.

"Not yet, but I know it's coming." She swallowed hard and took a deep breath. "And I'm not ready. Sal, I can't believe I'm saying this, but—"

The horn on Josie's van sounded, and the noise continued, as if the horn were stuck. Startled, we glanced out the window to see Nicoletta riding shotgun to Josie, pressing on the wheel while Josie shouted at her. Nicoletta rolled down the window, pointed at her watch, and mouthed something at me that looked like *Move it.* Good grief. What had I gotten myself into?

"You'd better go." Gianna stood and put her arms around my shoulders, enveloping me in a tight hug. "We can talk when you get back. I'll stop over to see you on Monday. Oh, if you happen to talk to Johnny for any reason, please don't mention this conversation to him, okay?"

"Mention what? I don't even know what's going on!"

She grinned. "All the better, then. Come on. They're waiting."

I waved a hand dismissively in the van's direction. "Forget about that. I want to know what's bothering you."

The horn sounded again. Gianna heaved a long sigh and stared out the window at the offender. "Well, that's part of the problem right there. Look, it can wait a couple of days. Have a safe flight, and try to have a good time. That will be tough with Nicoletta along. I hope Violet has some information that will help."

"Gi—"

The horn sounded once again, and Gianna gave me a gentle shove toward the front door. "Sal, you know how much I love your fudgy delight cookies, right?"

"You're their number-one fan."

"Well, there aren't enough of them in this world to make me want to change places with you right now."

* * *

"For crying out loud," Josie grumbled. "If that old lady kicks my seat one more time, I'm going to let her have it."

"Shh," I said, although we needn't have worried. Nicoletta had earplugs in, claiming the noise of take-off and landing hurt her ears. She'd already upset everyone else on the plane, including the flight attendants. I suspected they would have cheerfully shoved her body, complete in its black housecoat, out the nearest window if they thought they could get away with it.

First the coffee had not been hot enough. She'd needed to use the restroom while they'd been serving beverages and complained the entire time how they were blocking her path. The in-house movie was *The Notebook*. She'd declared it filthy and yelled out loud that she didn't want to watch *39 Shades of Grey*. My grandmother, who was sitting in the seat next to Nicoletta, had busied herself with her crocheting and said very little. I suspected it was her attempt to keep calm. I checked my watch. If this plane didn't land soon, I might try to jump out of it.

"Never again," Josie said, as if echoing my thoughts. Then she looked at me sharply. "Did you take Dramamine? You look kind of green."

"Really?" I tried to hide the excitement in my voice. "It must be motion sickness." I'd been in such a rush I'd forgotten to take some before we'd left. Josie knew firsthand how motion sickness affected me. Once, as teenagers, we'd been on a boat outing with friends, and the rocking had made me so ill I'd thrown up all over the deck. I didn't mention the possibility again that I was pregnant. I'd already said too much the other day, and Mike should be the first one to hear the official news.

My thoughts were interrupted by the flight attendant's voice on the loudspeaker. She asked everyone to make sure their seatbelts were fastened and seats upright for our upcoming landing. Hallejuah.

"I can't believe we're finally here." Josie practically bounced in the seat with excitement. "I've always wanted to go to Vegas. We should see that Michael Jackson tribute show while we're here. And I definitely want to hit the casino. Remember the last time we went on vacation together?"

My eyebrows lifted. "How could I forget?" About a year and a half ago, Mike had been arrested for the murder of my ex-husband and then disappeared after he'd made bail. Josie and I had been scheduled to participate in a baking competition in Florida, where Colin was living before his death, so it seemed a good way to kill two birds with one stone—no pun intended. The competition had been draining without the added stress of worrying where Mike was every minute of the day. "That wasn't exactly a vacation."

Her face sobered. "I know. You were going through hell not knowing where Mike was, plus trying to figure out who'd framed him for killing your sleaze of an ex-husband. Oops." She grinned sheepishly. "I almost feel like I should cross myself for saying that because he's dead. Then again, I'm not Catholic."

"That's all right." Once I'd moved away and married Colin, I'd drifted away from religion. Mike was even worse than me. He'd been too busy trying to survive in a house with a drunken mother and abusive stepfather to give much thought to church. We only went at Christmas, although my parents and grandmother went faithfully most Sundays. My father had even offered to help assist the priest with funerals, but for some reason he'd declined his offer. "I want you to enjoy yourself and play slots to your heart's content. My only goal is to find Violet."

"Well, we do have an address," Josie pointed out. "Plus, Nicoletta has a picture of her, and we know she works at the MGM Grand Hotel. It shouldn't be that difficult to track her down."

But did Violet want to be found? "It's so weird. I mean, Allegra leaves her money, but she won't even come for her mother's service. There has to be more to it." This also did not make Violet look good in the eyes of the law. I'd promised to let Brian know when we found her.

"Why does there have to be more?" Josie wanted to know. "No one liked Allegra, that's for sure, except—" We both turned to look behind us in the space between our seats. Nicoletta was snoring loudly, so we were assured she couldn't hear us.

"The real mystery appears to be why. Her own children couldn't stand her. The neighbors disliked her. Why kill the woman now, though? She must have been hiding something." A sudden thought occurred to me. "What if she witnessed someone killing another person? Maybe she knew a secret—about one of her own kids? Hey, we know she wasn't exactly Mother of the Year material."

"My mother would never win any awards either," Josie reminded me. "One of Allegra's kids could have hated her enough to kill her. Especially if there was money at stake."

Although the thought was appalling, I had to admit there was some truth to it. If we could find out what Allegra had in her possession that someone might want badly enough to murder for, it might lead us straight to her killer.

CHAPTER NINE

———

We found our luggage at the baggage claim and then went to hail a cab. We were lucky enough to flag one down right away, since Nicoletta's hefty bags were proving to be a challenge. The driver, a Hispanic man of about fifty, loaded the luggage into his trunk. Somehow, he made it all fit. Nicoletta sat in the front seat with him while Josie, Grandma Rosa, and I deposited our weary bodies in the back.

"Destination?" he asked me.

"The Tropicana Hotel, please," I said.

"Is that where we're staying?" Josie asked. "I was hoping for the one shaped like the pyramid or even the castle."

"Those are the Luxor and Excalibur." I wouldn't have minded staying at one of those either. I'd looked at them online and thought their designs were fascinating. Then again, I wasn't paying, so it wasn't my decision.

"Has to be Tropicana," Nicoletta bellowed. "The owner Italian. He immigrate from Italy when a young man."

The driver turned his head to stare at her, confusion evident on his face. "A corporation owns that hotel, ma'am. You must be mistaken."

"No mistake," she declared. "He drink orange juice all day."

Josie laughed. "It's not owned by the same people who own the juice company, Tropicana. There's no relation."

"You wrong. They have same name. Is related," she insisted. She watched the traffic whizzing by. "Too much cars. What this—New York City?"

"Pretty damn close," the driver said with a grin.

She wagged a bony finger at him. "Watch your mouth.

No cuss."

The driver cocked one eyebrow at her before the light turned green. "So are you ladies in town to gamble or do some sightseeing?"

"Sightseeing," I said quickly.

"Gamble," Josie put in.

The driver looked in the rearview mirror at my grandmother, sandwiched in between Josie and myself. She merely shrugged. "I just follow the crowd."

"We here to find someone," Nicoletta announced. "Person who kill my friend."

Good grief. Did she always have to be so outspoken? "Um, Mrs. Gavelli, you shouldn't exaggerate like that." I gave a nervous little laugh as the driver's gaze met mine in the mirror. "She likes to tell stories."

"Sure," the cabbie said. "Hey, forget I asked. You know how the saying goes."

"What saying?" Nicoletta asked.

He laughed. "What happens in Vegas stays in Vegas."

Nicoletta frowned at him. "I do not understand. We no *happening*. We only here for visit."

He rolled his eyes but said nothing further as we pulled up in front of the hotel. Grandma Rosa paid the man as he helped us with our luggage.

"I'm tired," Josie complained as Grandma Rosa checked us in. "I'm still on Eastern time. For me that means seven o'clock and a dinner."

"A burger would hit the spot right about now." I was starving and hadn't been impressed with the meager snacks the airline had to offer.

The Tropicana Hotel was one of the oldest buildings on the Vegas Strip. Located on the northern end, it was not nearly as impressive-looking as some of the other hotels, namely the Paris with its Eiffel Tower ride or the New York-New York and its roller coaster. Even though the décor was older, the place had recently gone through a remodel and seemed clean enough. Plus, it had an enormous casino, which Josie eyed with interest as we got in the elevator and made our way up to the twelfth floor. We had rooms across the hall from each other. Once again, I marveled at my grandmother and her infinite patience. Being Nicoletta's roommate had to be the stuff nightmares were made of.

"What do you want to do first?" Grandma Rosa asked me as we unlocked our doors.

"We go find Violet," Nicoletta interrupted. "Then I no care what you all do. Go gamble, sin, whatever."

I blew out a sigh. It looked like hunger was going to have to wait. "All right. Why don't we meet in a half hour and take a cab to Violet's house?"

Grandma Rosa nodded her approval. "That is a good plan. Then we can stop and get you something to eat. You look hungry."

"How do you always know everything?" I asked in disbelief.

"I do not know everything," Grandma Rosa admitted. "But I do know you, *cara mia*. And *you* are definitely hungry."

Josie and I waited until they were safely in their room before we closed the door to ours and slid the lock in place. I tossed my duffel bag onto one of the queen-sized beds and drew out my cosmetic bag and a fresh change of clothing.

"If we find Violet right away, we can come back and eat, then go to the casino for drinks and gambling. I want to play the penny slots," Josie said as she changed her clothes.

"You and those slots," I teased as I threw on a pair of black shorts and a pink V-neck T-shirt. I was glad to have brought both sandals and sneakers with me. It had to be about 110 degrees outside, and even with the air conditioning on, I was sweltering.

Josie glanced around the room. "There's no fridge in here. What kind of hotel is this?"

"One with only the basics, I guess." There were two beds, a flat screen television, and a small wooden table and chairs, plus the adjoining bathroom. "We're only here for two nights. You can rough it."

Josie snorted. "Man, I don't mean to complain. Your grandmother is paying, so I feel like a heel for saying anything. But I do feel that I deserve to treat myself. If I win big, we're getting a suite, girlfriend." She plopped down on her bed. "Are there any male revue shows around here?"

I whipped my head around from the mirror where I was fixing my hair. "Josephine Sullivan, I am *not* going to any of those shows, and neither are you. You have a good-looking husband at home, not to mention four adorable little boys."

"Hey, I may be married, but I'm not dead," she protested. "There's no harm in looking."

I grabbed a pair of sunglasses from my bag. "Well, I have no desire to look. My man is all I want to look at."

"Ah, you're no fun," she complained. "Wait until you're an old married lady like me with a bunch of kids. Then you'll long for these kid-less opportunities."

"Nope." I grinned. "It's not gonna happen." My hair was already sticking to my face and neck because of the oppressive heat. As I pulled it into a ponytail, someone pounded on our door.

"We ready!" Nicoletta's voice boomed from the other side.

Josie clenched her fists. "Okay, as soon as we find Violet we can ditch the devil in her black dress for the rest of the trip, right?"

"You two need to behave." I opened the door and blinked, trying to adjust my eyes to the sight in front of me. Grandma Rosa stood next to Nicoletta in black slacks and a gray, short-sleeved cotton blouse. Nicoletta was still wearing the same black housecoat, stockings, and her Birkenstock shoes. Heat rose inside me like a sauna at the sight of her. "Mrs. Gavelli, you're going to fry in that outfit."

She waved her hand dismissively as we rode the elevator car down to the lobby. "I not show my body off around here. I no temptress."

"That's for sure," Josie mumbled. "Plus, you're used to hot places."

"Jos," I warned.

Nicoletta ignored the remark. "I hear stories about this city. It full of sluts. I set example for the younger generation."

"The younger generation does not care about you," my grandmother retorted. "There are other things far more interesting than you around here."

We hailed another cab, and Nicoletta gave the driver Violet's address.

The driver, a mustached man who was definitely wearing a hairpiece, raised a questioning eyebrow. "I believe that's a gated community, ladies. You do realize you won't be able to get in unless the owner is home?"

"Sure, we know," Nicoletta growled. Then she turned to me. "What he mean?"

"Violet's home must have security in place." It sounded a bit high-class to me. "Didn't you say she was a dealer in the casino?"

Nicoletta nodded. "That what her mama always tell me. Why?"

"Oh, no reason." Personally, I didn't think dealers made a lot of money, but heck, what did I know? Maybe Allegra sent Violet money. Perhaps her husband was wealthy—if she even had a husband.

When we reached the street where Violet's home was located, I looked past the iron gate, and my jaw dropped in amazement. These were not average-style houses like the small ranch where Mike and I lived. These were million-dollar homes with swimming pools and lavish lawns that thrived even in this godforsaken heat. Violet must be quite the dealer. Only, what was she dealing?

The cab stopped at a small booth to the left of the gate, and a bald, heavyset man slid the side window open and smiled at all of us. "Help you?"

"How's it going?" the cabbie asked before Nicoletta leaned across him and gave the guard Violet's information.

"Let me check and see if she's home." The guard, whose nametag identified him as Max, closed the window and picked up a phone. He stared into space for several seconds, then placed the phone down and reopened the window. "Miss Fiato isn't answering. Sorry."

"Do you know when she might be back?" I asked.

Max leaned in closer to get a look at me. "Sorry, but I can't give out any information about the owner's whereabouts. I suggest you call first next time. Have a great day."

"What a hummer," Grandma Rosa sighed.

"That's bummer, Rosa." Josie elbowed me in the side. "Now what do we do?"

"I'll have to proceed down this street and over to the next. It's one way," the driver told us.

There was a man in shorts and a white polo shirt on the lawn across the street from the security booth. He was busy adjusting one of the lawn sprinklers. *How do they stand this heat?* I leaned forward in the seat and spoke to the driver. "Can you pull up next to that man? I'd like to get out and talk to him for a minute."

"Sure thing," he said and placed the car in park.

I turned to Nicoletta. "Can I see that picture of Violet you have?"

She handed me a manila envelope, and I removed an 8 by 10 photograph. My eyes widened as I stared at the picture. Violet was gorgeous. Her heart-shaped face was surrounded by a black shimmering halo of curls and featured dark, almond-shaped eyes with long lashes, a pert nose, and full red, pouty lips. "Are you sure this is her?"

"What am I? Batty?" Nicoletta grunted. "Of course it her. She beautiful girl, no?"

Josie leaned over for a look. "She doesn't look like her brother or sister, that's for certain."

"She seems a lot younger too," I mused.

"Violet the baby," Nicoletta said. "About ten years younger than Anna."

The meter was running, so I opened the door and made my way over to the maintenance worker, a slim man in his forties.

He looked up and smiled. "Help you with something, miss?"

"Yes." A lie quickly took shape in my brain, and I held out the picture to him. "My sister, Violet Fiato, lives in the complex. I've been trying to reach her by phone, but she didn't answer. I wondered if you knew her."

The man took the photo from my hands and studied it. "Oh, sure. I don't remember her name, but there's no way I'd forget a face like that. She's only been here a few months, right?"

"Yes." It seemed like the right amount of time given

what I'd been told. My fibbing continued. "She came from New York. Uh, sis doesn't know I'm coming. It's a surprise, in case you happen to see her first."

"Gotcha." He removed his hat and scratched his straw-colored hair thoughtfully. "I always see her in the morning on her way home. She just left here—oh, about twenty minutes ago? She waved to me. Sorry you missed her."

Damn. "So she does work nights at the casino, then. I wondered if her schedule might have changed."

He shrugged. "Well, I have no idea where she works, but she's always dressed to kill. Driving that red Porsche doesn't exactly hurt her image either. Gorgeous lady. Good looks run in your family, if I may say so."

"Thank you," I said politely. "My sister is always so bad about answering her messages. I guess I'll have to stop by again in the morning."

He studied me, his broad forehead creasing into a frown. "None of my business, but that's a pretty long shift for working at a casino. I usually see her drive back home around eight or nine o'clock in the morning. If I were you, I wouldn't come back before then."

I nodded. "Will do. Thanks for all your help."

He tipped his cap and winked. "Anything for a pretty lady."

I returned to the cab, and four pairs of eyes fixated on me.

"What he say?" Nicoletta demanded.

"You can take us back to the hotel, please," I told the driver. "It looks like Violet works nights, and we just missed her. Let's grab something to eat and then go over to the MGM Grand to try to find her. If she's not there, we can come back here early tomorrow morning. The maintenance guy usually sees her around eight o'clock or so."

"That seems a very long shift to work," Grandma Rosa said, echoing his comment. "Perhaps she has a boyfriend and stays at his house."

Nicoletta drummed her fingers loudly against the glove compartment until the driver gave her a dirty look that suggested he wanted to cut them off. "I not sure. She have boyfriend in

New York before. I not know who, but Allegra say it end badly. This happen about the same time her papa die in Italy. So she come to Vegas. Allegra have to deal with this and Felipo's death—it all too much. Violet tell her mama she need to get away. Very upset she was."

As the cab drove away, I found myself more intrigued with this woman and wondered what the whole story was. Sure, I'd never met Violet, but it didn't take a mathematician to realize something was not adding up. Violet had come out here to live a few months ago and gotten herself an impressive job as a dealer. Somehow, she was already living in a million-dollar home and driving a Porsche.

What was the real deal with this supposed dealer? Where was all of this money coming from? With uneasiness, I wondered if it might have something to do with Violet's family—namely, her mother's murder.

CHAPTER TEN

———

An hour later, we were back inside one of the Tropicana's restaurants, and I was happily stuffing my face with any food I could lay my hands on. I was so ravenous that I'd already devoured a bacon cheeseburger with a double order of fries and a chocolate milkshake. Josie had ordered a steak while Grandma Rosa and Nicoletta both ate club sandwiches.

When we'd first ordered, Nicoletta had wasted no time in trying the waitress's patience. "I tell you I want this." She'd grunted and pointed at the menu.

The waitress had looked pained. "Ma'am, that's the children's menu. You have to be ten or under to get the hamburger patty special."

Grandma Rosa had placed a hand on Nicoletta's arm and spoke. "Bring her the turkey club sandwich, please."

"I cannot eat all this!" Nicoletta complained.

Grandma Rosa looked over at me and nodded. "Sally will help you."

Good grief. "Hey, give me a break. I haven't eaten all day."

Josie grinned as I swiped her coleslaw. "Girl, it's like you have a tapeworm. What's going on?"

"She too fat," Nicoletta grunted.

I inhaled the rest of my milkshake and gave her an evil eye. "I'm *not* fat." *I'm just eating for two.*

"Sally is not fat," Grandma Rosa agreed. "She never eats when she is upset about something. So it is nice to see her happy."

I'd never thought of that reasoning before, but she was right. Even here in Vegas with the sweltering heat and nasty

Nicoletta Gavelli seated across from me, I was happy. Blissfully happy and counting my blessings.

Nicoletta emptied the sugar packets from the caddy on the table into her massive-sized, black leather purse. She added the jam and jelly samples to her haul. For a moment, I waited to see if she was going to swipe the silverware as well. "Enough with food," she grunted. "I need to go to casino now and win big. We go to the MGM and find Violet. We walk there."

"In this heat?" Josie cried out.

Nicoletta tossed her head. "It good for Sally. She need the exercise."

I sucked in a deep breath and fought the urge to wrap my hands around the elderly woman's neck. *Be nice, Sal. She's been sick.* Nicoletta would be singing a different tune when she discovered why I was eating everything in sight. Until then, I decided to ignore her snark and reminded myself that things could always be worse. Heck, what if I was Gianna? Maybe that was the real reason my poor sister looked so haggard. The thought of Nicoletta living with her and Johnny—even for a few days—would wear anyone out.

My phone buzzed from my pocket, and I glanced down at the name on the screen. Brian. *Uh-oh.* It was highly unlikely that he was calling to ask about the weather in Vegas. I waved at Grandma Rosa and Nicoletta. "You two go ahead. We'll catch up." After they were out the front doors, I stayed behind in the lobby with Josie by my side. "Hey, what's up?"

"Are you in Vegas yet?" he wanted to know.

"Yes, we arrived a couple of hours ago. Is everything okay?"

He ignored my question by asking another. "Have you seen Violet Fiato?"

"No. We went to her house when we arrived, but she wasn't home. I talked with a maintenance guy who said he thinks she works evenings. We're going to the MGM Grand right now to see if we can find her. If not, we'll head back over to her house in the morning."

Brian cleared his throat. "Her sister, Anna, got picked up for speeding today. When one of my co-workers pulled her over, he gave her a sobriety test. Her blood alcohol content was .22.

That's almost three times the legal limit."

"Holy cow." I brought a hand to my mouth and stared at Josie, who shot me a puzzled look. "We saw her the other night after the wake, and it was obvious she'd had a few then. At the time I thought maybe she'd knocked back a couple because of the stress associated with her mother's death."

"Yeah, well, I'm guessing there's more to it than that," Brian said. "When she was brought into the station, she became totally uncooperative. She went berserk when the cuffs were placed on her wrists and then blurted out to the arresting officer that it was all her mother's fault. Allegra had ruined her life, and she hoped her mother rotted in hell. Then she said something really weird."

"Because what she said so far sounds totally sane and rational."

Brian heaved a long sigh. "My, someone's feeling sarcastic."

"It's been a long day," I said wearily. "Any day spent with Nicoletta Gavelli seems to drag on forever."

"True that," Josie agreed.

Brian laughed on the other end. "Anyhow, Anna wanted to know why she was being harassed for having one little beer when the rest of her family was getting away with murder. Then she mumbled something about her sister having a dirty little secret and maybe that's why she ran her mother over."

A mammoth-sized chill spread through me. "That's insane. Violet couldn't have done it. She wasn't even in town that day."

"Wrong," Brian said. "We found a plane ticket in Violet's name. She flew into Buffalo Niagara Airport the day before the hit-and-run then flew out the next evening, a couple hours after her mother's death. The Vegas police will definitely be questioning her, but I'll be interested in hearing what you find out as well."

"This is sick," I muttered. "Then again, I'm not sure what Anna's saying can be trusted either. Is she in jail?"

"Her brother, Enzo, bailed her out," Brian said. "She'll be back in court in a couple of weeks. Remember to let me know if you track Violet down. And Sally?"

"Yes?"

There was a moment's hesitation on the other end. "Please be careful."

I relayed everything to Josie as we walked out of the Tropicana. We spotted Grandma Rosa and Nicoletta about two blocks ahead of us on the Strip and quickened our pace to catch up with them. While we walked along, I snapped pictures of the various hotels around us. The trip was worth it just for the hotels, I decided.

"That family gives me the creeps," Josie admitted. "Did you ever meet a more insane one?"

I snapped a shot of the Statue of Liberty outside the New York-New York Hotel. "Well, if you recall, Colin's family had a few issues as well. And as we're both aware, my parents aren't exactly normal either."

"True enough," she admitted. "But your parents wouldn't hurt a fly. They're the friendly type of crazies. Speaking of which, where do you think they took off to?"

It was approaching seven o'clock in the evening, and a welcome breeze had started to filter through the air. I wiped away the sweat gathering on my forehead. Thankfully the MGM Hotel wasn't much farther. Grandma Rosa and Nicoletta were still a few paces ahead of us. Nicoletta was talking earnestly, waving her hands in the air, and my grandmother was nodding in response. "Who knows. It probably has something to do with that literary agent my father's been stalking."

Josie shook her head. "Okay, so your parents would never hurt anyone, but they're not exactly the sharpest crayons in the box either. Is there any reason to be worried they might end up arrested?"

This made me chuckle. "Hey, you never know with them."

The front doors of the MGM brought us right into the casino, which was larger and brighter than the one inside the Tropicana. The smell of cigarette smoke immediately hit my nostrils, and nausea built in my stomach. This was probably the combination of several things—overindulging at dinner and the heat, plus cigarette smoke always made me sick.

"You ask about Violet," Nicoletta ordered. "Check out

all the tables."

"Mrs. Gavelli, do you know how many dealer tables there are in here?" I asked in disbelief.

"Never mind," she grunted. "We ask too. Come, Rosa."

My grandmother looked over at us and rolled her eyes toward the ceiling. I almost fell over because that was something she never did. My grandmother had the patience of a saint. It just went to show that everyone had their limits, especially as far as Nicoletta Gavelli was concerned.

"Why didn't you tell her what Brian said about Anna?" Josie asked.

"Because I don't think it's a good idea." Heck, her wrath might shake the entire casino. "If she flies off the handle when we find Violet, she might scare her away before we can learn anything useful."

"That's good thinking," Josie admitted. "Nicoletta has even less tact than I do, so you might be on to something there. Come on. I'm feeling lucky and see penny machines with my name on them."

She slid into a chair at the end of a row of machines. This particular one had a giant lobster featured on the screen. In fascination, I watched as she withdrew a twenty-dollar bill from her wallet and inserted it into the machine.

"This looks like a fun one." Josie glanced up at me. "Aren't you going to play?"

"No. I'm not any good at gambling." What I didn't add was that I worked too hard for my money and had no desire to feed it into one of these useless machines. To each his own. If they made Josie happy, so be it.

Josie selected the maximum bet. "See, that's the way to win." She gave a proud toss of her head. "If you want to hit the jackpot, you have to play the max. My mother-in-law taught me that. We once went to a casino back home, and she was playing this game with cans of Spam that—"

I barked out a laugh, interrupting her explanation. "Cans of Spam? What will they think of next?"

"Anyhow." Josie punched the button again. "Linda didn't want to take any more money out on her credit card, and I didn't have cash on me. So she decided to play the money out for the last round. And what do you think happened? She had five cans of Spam come up right in a row, without having the maximum bet. So instead of winning $3200 dollars, she won a lousy hundred bucks."

"Well, I'd never play that game," I remarked. "I hate Spam."

Josie gave me a look like *I* had a giant can of Spam sitting on top of *my* head. She became distracted when three lobsters came up in a row on the machine. "Ooh, I got the bonus round!"

I watched with interest as a fisherman in a yellow raincoat appeared in the water, and Josie received four tries at picking a lobster pot. We both waited as he lifted fish out of them, and Josie's point total kept increasing on the screen with each pot. She ended up winning thirty dollars.

"This is awesome," she squealed with excitement.

"Okay, quit now while you're ahead," I urged.

"Are you nuts?" she asked. "This means I'm going to hit an even bigger jackpot."

Yeah, okay. "All right, fine. I'm going to check a few tables to see if I spot Violet."

"Sure." Josie was clearly disinterested and went back to obsessing about lobsters. "Good luck."

It appeared that I was on my own for a while. "You too." I walked through the casino, waving away the smoke with my hands. *Ugh.* We should have gone in the smoke-free section, but she'd told me on the plane that no one ever won there. Hey, what did I know? There were several craps tables, and I stopped for a moment to watch a woman spin a roulette wheel. She had an enormous pile of chips in front of her, and when it landed on a red number, everyone around her screamed. The dealer pushed another tower of chips toward her.

I wandered farther throughout the casino, past a bar where people were drinking and watching a baseball game. The Yankees and the Red Sox were playing in Fenway Park. There was no one anywhere who resembled Violet. I found a table where a dealer was alone, counting cards, and approached him. "Hi. Could I ask you a question?"

"Sorry, miss, this table is closed for the evening."

"Oh, that's not why I'm here." I took the picture out of my purse. "I was wondering if you knew this woman. Her name is Violet, and she works here as a dealer."

He took the picture from my outstretched hands, studied it carefully, then let out a low whistle. "Never seen her before. But let me assure you that if I had, I'd have asked her out by now." He gave me a sly wink. "I kind of have a way with women."

I couldn't help thinking that Al, as his nametag identified him, looked a little bit like one of the lobsters in Josie's game, with his bald head, red flushed skin, and enormous hands enhanced by fingernails in desperate need of a trim. "Uh, sure. I'll bet you do."

He leaned across the table. "I get off work in five minutes. How about a drink, babe?"

Ew. "Thanks for the offer, but I'll pass."

Al shrugged. "Your loss."

Good grief. What was with this place? I wandered over in the direction of the ladies' room and pulled out my phone. It was almost nine o'clock, midnight in New York. Mike must surely be home by now. I had called him when we landed, but he hadn't picked up, so I'd left a voice mail instead. I pushed the button for his number, and he answered on the fourth ring.

"Hi, princess." His voice sounded sleepy.

"Did I wake you?"

Mike yawned noisily into the phone. "That's okay. I'm glad you called. I was sitting here watching the ballgame and must have drifted off."

"Poor baby," I purred into the phone. "How's the renovation going?"

He yawned again. "I think I'll make the deadline. And it's all thanks to Trevor. He's really been a huge help. I may decide to hire him on full-time."

Trevor Parks was new to Colwestern and had answered Mike's newspaper ad for a part-time helper a couple of weeks back. He was about forty, intelligent, and mild mannered. Mike had brought him into the bakery one day last week when they'd stopped in for a midday sugar fix. He was similar to Mike in both height and build, and my husband remarked he did the work of two men.

"That's great. I'm so glad you finally have someone you can rely on."

"Trevor's planning to stay in Colwestern so I should be able to start on expanding your bakery sometime next month."

"There's no rush." I'd wanted to put in a lunch menu for quite a while and increase the main room's seating, but if I was pregnant, that would change things. Maybe it wouldn't be a bad idea to hold off for a year or two. It was going to be tough enough to juggle both the baby and the bakery, and my priority, of course, would be the baby. But I also didn't want to leave any more of the shop's work on Josie's capable shoulders.

He chuckled into the phone. "Well, that's a new one. You've been dying for me to get that expansion done. Why the sudden change?"

"Oh, I don't know." I giggled. "There are some things more important than the bakery, like my handsome husband for one."

His voice became low and husky. "I miss you so much. I can't wait until we go away for our anniversary next weekend."

"Aha. So you have been making plans without me," I teased.

"Guilty as charged. But I know you're going to love it and be surprised big-time. This is one place you probably haven't even thought of—well, not for a while, anyway."

Now he had me intrigued. "It sounds wonderful."

"No, you're wonderful."

Tears came into my eyes, and I was tempted to tell him my news then decided I should wait until I was one hundred percent certain. Besides, I wanted to do it in person. "Go get some sleep, okay?"

Mike yawned again. "How's the investigating going?"

I hesitated. "It's been interesting, to say the least. I'll tell you more about it on Sunday when I get home."

"Okay. Love you, princess."

"Love you too." I clicked off and, after a couple of wrong turns, found the section where Josie had been playing. She was still at the same machine, and I noticed the screen said she had a total of twenty dollars. "Hey, that's not so bad. You've only lost ten dollars since I've been gone."

She gave me a sour look. "I've put in two more twenties since then."

Ouch. "Jeez, don't give all your money away."

"Oh, it's fun," she insisted and knocked on the glass screen. "Come on, bonus round."

"What did you do that for?" I asked, mystified.

Josie shot me an impatient glare. "It's for luck. Jeez, don't you know anything about gambling?"

Apparently not. "Look, I'm tired. Do you want to walk back to the Tropicana with me?"

"Aw, we just got here," she protested. "It's only nine o'clock."

I shifted my purse on my shoulder. "Correction—it's midnight, back home anyway. I want to be over at Violet's by nine in the morning so we can catch her."

"Have a drink with me first," she pleaded. "My treat."

"Aren't they free in the casino?"

She punched the button in frustration. "Oh, come on! Give me ten minutes."

"Okay, fine." I didn't want any alcohol, though. "A Coke sounds good."

"Coming right up," Josie said cheerfully and pointed at a voluptuous-looking, dark-headed waitress who had her back to us. I couldn't believe the skimpy outfits they made the servers wear. The sheer black dress barely covered her rear and had tiny spaghetti straps holding the top in place. The woman handed a beer to a man who was facing me. It was obvious he was staring at the woman's chest instead of the Wheel of Fortune machine he was playing. *Pervert.*

He handed her a five and licked his lips. "Keep it, doll."

I glanced down at the woman's legs. They were shapely in the black fishnet stockings, but just staring at the five-inch stiletto heels she wore was enough to make my feet hurt. Sure, the waitresses probably made great tips here, but who wanted to be ogled like that every day? The guy reminded me of my father in stature and size. Dad was a lot of things, but at least he'd never leer at another woman.

"Excuse me, miss," I called out.

"What can I get you?" The waitress whirled around, and I shrieked.

It was my mother.

CHAPTER ELEVEN

———

Mom was the first one of us to recover from the shock. "Hello, darling! Oh my goodness. What a nice surprise!" She threw her arms around me and kissed my cheek.

Josie turned around from the machine, her jaw almost level with the floor. "Maria?"

Mom gave Josie a hug. "How are the kids doing, dear?"

Finally I found my voice. "Mom! How—where—*what* are you doing here?"

My mother beamed and twirled around in her outfit. "Don't I look great? You wouldn't believe the money I've been making."

I must be hallucinating. There was no other explanation. What had the restaurant put in my chocolate shake? I reached out to grab her by the arm and pulled her closer. "Why are you here? Where's Dad? Is this some fantasy related to his book that you're both acting out?"

She giggled. "Of course not, silly. Your father's here in the casino too. He's at one of the high ante-up poker tables with Steve Steadman."

The name was familiar. "Why do I know that name?"

My mother gave a small sigh of exasperation. "Oh, honey. You've been sniffing too much vanilla in the bakery. Your father said he told you about Steve. He's a literary agent your father wants to reel in—you know, solicit his book to potential publishers. I swear, I don't know what's the matter with both you and your sister these days." She perched her hands on her slim hips and addressed Josie, her back to me. "You tell your kids something, and then it goes right out of their heads five minutes later."

Josie's mouth curved into a smile as she glanced over my mother at me. "This is unreal."

True. It could only happen to me.

"Your mom and Mrs. Gavelli are here with us too," Josie said.

"Really?" Mom scanned the crowded room, her head moving from side to side. "Where are they?"

Josie got to her feet and collected her voucher from the machine. "I'm not exactly sure, but I doubt they went far."

"Steve's been very nice to me when I go over to his table," Mom said. "For some reason, he won't chat with your father about the book. Maybe he's just shy."

Good grief. "Mom, this doesn't explain why you're serving drinks inside a casino in that...outfit." For a lack of more suitable words, I went with that one.

"I'm part of the bait," she said proudly. "We decided I should try to get a job here so I could chat with Mr. Steadman. This was before your father knew that the table Steve was playing at was open to anyone. As it turns out, the casino fired two waitresses today, and the manager took an instant shine to me. He said I could start right away."

"It's kind of like being in *The Twilight Zone*, isn't it?" Josie asked me.

Mom went on. "That Steve is so sweet. He talks to me every time I go over to take drink orders. And he drinks a lot, let me tell you. Steve even asked if I wanted to go to a party with him later—he said it's being held in his room. Your father and I will drop by to chat about the book and have a rum and Coke with him." She handed said drink to Josie and then offered me one.

"Just the Coke part for me, thanks. Uh, Mom, I'm kind of guessing that there is no party in his room. He probably wants *you* to be the party."

She waved her hand and blushed. "Don't be ridiculous, honey. He's so taken with your father. I mean, who wouldn't be?"

Yeah, right. I scanned the room. "Where exactly is this table?"

She gestured with her hand across the room. "See the one that's near the bar? No, over to the left. There he is, playing at the opposite end from Mr. Steadman." As she pointed, my father happened to look over in our direction and gave us a thumbs-up. He was wearing a New York Giants white T-shirt, and even from this distance, I could see a visible stain on its chest. His leg dangled to the side of the table, and I winced at the sight. He was wearing blue shorts of a mesh material, white tube socks that ran halfway up his hairy legs, and black sandals.

"Doesn't he look great?" My mother beamed with pride and then pointed to the other end of the table. "There's Steve."

Josie and I both stared at the man with curiosity. Steve was wearing a beige Stetson and a blue-and-white-striped Oxford shirt with navy slacks. A matching suit coat was draped over the back of his chair. His blondish-brown mustache twitched back and forth as he scanned the cards in his hand. He happened to glance up and looked over in our direction. His tanned face brightened when he saw my mother, and he crooked his little finger at her.

Mom started to push her cart in his direction and gave us a little wave. "We're on the tenth floor here. Come and meet us for dinner tomorrow at five. Bye, sweetheart! Give your grandmother my love!"

"Mom, wait!" But she only waved again as she continued to push the cart effortlessly and efficiently through the crowd. I hated to admit it, but I was impressed. Perhaps my mother had finally found a job she was well suited for. I watched as she went to stand next to Mr. Steadman. He put his arm around her and whispered something in her ear.

Yeah, he's shy all right. "What is she doing?" I squeaked.

Josie watched them with interest. "Don't worry, Sal. Your father won't let anything happen to her. Well, if he gets a book deal out of it, that is."

I was still trying to take this all in. "My father said something about the literary agent living in Nevada, but what are the odds that he…that they…" I couldn't finish the sentence.

Josie slung an arm around my shoulders and echoed my thoughts from earlier. "Yep, it could only happen to you."

"Sally," a voice called from behind us, and we turned to see my grandmother and Nicoletta approaching. Nicoletta waved a large bundle of bills in her hand.

"You won?" Josie choked out. "How much?"

Nicoletta gave us a superior smile. "I win cool grand. I sit down at slot machine, and first time I push button, all the bells go off."

"This is nuts," Josie said in disbelief.

"I am tired," Grandma Rosa said. "Would you like to walk back to the hotel with us?"

Nicoletta fanned herself with the bills. "We go. It always good to leave when ahead."

I cocked an eyebrow at Josie in response. "What did I tell you?"

Her shoulders sagged. "Oh, fine. Whatever."

"Grandma, can you see who that is over there?" I asked, pointing at the poker table.

Grandma Rosa squinted across the room. My father was shouting something as the dealer handed him a stack of chips and had managed to attract the attention of everyone around him.

My grandmother grimaced. "My eyes are old, and they must be playing treats on me."

This was a new one. "Tricks, Grandma."

Grandma Rosa's voice rose an octave, something that hardly ever happened. "Is that your father playing cards? And my very own daughter serving him drinks in that...*outfit*?"

"It is slutty dress," Nicoletta declared.

My grandmother shot her a deathly look. "You watch what you say about my daughter, *pazza*. Maria is no tramp. She just does not think some days. Okay, most days." She turned to me. "I would ask why they are here, but it must have something to do with the ridiculous pile of paper your father calls a book."

"You guessed it," I said.

Grandma Rosa shook her head. "That man. He is another one who does not think some days. Perhaps that is why they get on so well. I will call Maria in the morning. Let us go now. The smoke in here is making me ill."

As we made our way out of the casino, I glanced back in my parents' direction one last time. Steve Steadman had his arm around my mother's waist as she stood between him and my father, who had managed to move a seat closer to the agent. Like a cat, he was getting ready to pounce. I didn't appreciate the way this Steve character was eyeing my mother, but I still felt kind of sorry for the man. He had no idea who he was up against.

We walked back to our hotel. The strip was crowded even though it was almost ten o'clock. Like New York City, Vegas never seemed to sleep. The air was still warm and moist, and I missed Mike as I snapped more pictures of the surrounding hotels lit up against the night sky. He'd have been fascinated with the designs and would have wanted to know more about their structure.

A man was stationed on each side of the Strip, handing out some type of fliers to passersby. One of them pressed a card into my hand and Josie's before we could object. Nicoletta took one and immediately gasped out loud.

"What you give me this for? You some kind of sicko?" she shrieked at the man. As we all watched, she walked over to him and pelted his arm with her leather bag. Then she started to cuss at him in Italian.

"Whoa! Take it easy, lady! Did you just get off the boat?" The man backed away from Nicoletta with his hands covering his face, an effort to defend himself.

Grandma Rosa dragged Nicoletta away. "What is the matter with you? You cannot go around hitting people like that."

Nicoletta waved the card in my grandmother's face. "He give me dirty picture of woman. I sue."

"It's part of his job," Josie laughed. "There are escort services all over the place here. You'll be lucky if he doesn't try to sue *you* for hitting him. What you did can be construed as assault."

"Bah," Mrs. Gavelli snorted. "He no sue me. He will burn in hell first. For shame!" she yelled back at the bewildered man.

My grandmother gave Nicoletta a pointed look as we entered the Tropicana. "The devil comes in many different forms."

"What that mean?" Nicoletta punched the button for the elevator and turned to look at Josie and me. "You two come, or you going to party all night?"

Josie waved them on. "I want to grab some coffee first." There was a complimentary pot set up in the lobby, and she walked toward it.

I gave my grandmother a kiss as she and Nicoletta got into the elevator. "What time should we meet for breakfast?"

"I let you know," Nicoletta called out.

"Good night, *cara mia*. Sleep well." Grandma Rosa stood behind Nicoletta in the elevator, smiling and nodding at me. At the last second, she raised her index finger and pressed it against her white hair in a circular motion then gestured toward Nicoletta. I started to giggle as the door closed.

Josie had her coffee in one hand and was studying the card she'd received on the strip. I poured myself some decaffeinated tea from another carafe. "That woman makes me so tired."

Josie didn't respond.

"What's wrong?" I asked.

"These cards," Josie said. "They don't all have the same woman on them. Mine's different from yours. Take a look."

"Do I have to?" I joked but reached for it anyway. I studied the scantily dressed woman with a huge chest that was all but popping out of the extremely low-cut, shimmering silver dress she wore. She was gorgeous, with ebony-colored hair curling around her shoulders and enormous, almond-shaped dark eyes.

Josie peered over my shoulder as I studied the card. "So what do you think?"

"Oh my God. It's Violet."

CHAPTER TWELVE

───────

"I still can't believe it," I told Josie the next morning as we got ready to leave our hotel room. "Violet moved out here to become a...lady of the evening? An escort?"

Josie snickered. "It would certainly explain the expensive house and what Anna said about her having a secret. Some of those women make a ton of money. But why did she leave New York? There's got to be some other reason."

"I'm not positive about the dates, but it sounds like she left right before her father died in Italy. However, I'm not sure if or how it connects to her mother's murder." I blew out a sigh. "I'd love to be able to tell my grandmother what's going on, but maybe Mrs. Gavelli shouldn't know. If only there was a way we could go to see Violet without her tagging along."

Josie glanced at her watch. "It's eight o'clock. If we sneak out now, we might be able to avoid her, but then she'll follow with your grandmother, and all hell will break loose."

I picked up the hotel phone by my bed. "Let me see what I can do."

Fortunately, my grandmother answered. "Good morning, *cara mia*. Are you ready for breakfast?"

"Um," I hedged. "Where's Mrs. Gavelli?"

"Nicoletta is in the bathroom. She is complaining that the restaurant food made her ill last night, but I believe it is the chemotherapy affecting her stomach."

"Didn't she get done with that about a year ago? The cancer's not back, is it?"

"No," my grandmother said. "She is still in remission, but her doctor told her it may upset her stomach for a very long time, perhaps even the rest of her life. She should be fine in a day or two. I have seen this happen to her before."

My heart filled with pity for the elderly woman. Yes, she was mean, sarcastic, and her mouth knew no filter, but she'd also suffered a great deal in her lifetime. Her only child had died and left her a grandson to raise. Now a close friend—never mind how rotten the other woman was—had been struck and killed by a car on purpose. Plus, she still struggled daily with her fight against bone cancer. It made me realize how fortunate I was.

"I feel really bad for saying this, but it might be better if Josie and I tried to talk to Violet alone. If we can even find her, that is. Remember those cards we were handed on the strip last night? I'm pretty sure Violet was on one of them."

My grandmother clucked her tongue in apparent disapproval. "I was afraid something like this would happen. From what Nicoletta told me, Violet took off very suddenly from New York earlier this year. Nicoletta said she'd landed a good-paying job here, but I figured there must be more going on."

"It's interesting that Violet lived in New York and not New Jersey like the rest of her family," I mused. "What did she do for a living there?"

"I do not know," Grandma Rosa said. "I will tell you that all of the Fiato family lived in New Jersey at one time, Lena and her parents included. Lena met her husband when she came to New York to intern at his law firm. Perhaps Violet was close with Lena and decided to drag along too."

I giggled. "That's tag along, Grandma. It might be a good idea to have another chat with Lena when we get home. Is it okay with you if Josie and I go ahead to Violet's by ourselves? Or would you like us to stay here with you and Mrs. Gavelli?"

"It is not necessary," she assured me. "We must find out who did this to Allegra. Lord knows that I love Nicoletta, but even if she felt well enough to go, she would only make things more difficult. She is like your mama and papa."

"In what way?' I asked, puzzled.

She sighed into the phone. "She is a nutsy cookie too."

Well, at least they were all consistent. "Speaking of Mom and Dad, have you heard from them?" I was curious what had happened at the poker table with the cowboy-like literary agent.

Grandma Rosa gave a loud harrumph. "Yes, I called her earlier. She said they were sleeping in this morning. They want us to meet them for dinner tonight at their hotel's restaurant at five o'clock. She said they have some big news to share. With your mama and papa, that might mean anything from purchasing another casket to moving to Vegas."

"Oh, boy."

"Some days I think that you and Gianna are the adults, while she and your papa are the children," she said evenly. "Does that make sense?"

Unfortunately, it did. "Totally. Something seems to be bothering Gianna. Do you know what it is?"

There was silence for a beat on the other end. "Gianna has not told me anything, but yes, I too suspect that something is wrong."

"It has to be Johnny," I said. "I hope they don't decide to break up. She promised to tell me more when we get home."

Grandma Rosa hesitated again. "All right, then. Call me when you get back from Violet's. *Ciao, bella.*" She abruptly clicked off.

My grandmother's behavior had me concerned as well. Perhaps she didn't know exactly what was bothering Gianna, but she at least had a good idea. Maybe Gianna was sick—that thought filled me with terror. Or maybe she'd lied to me— Johnny *had* proposed and she'd refused him. Whatever the case, leaving her to tend to my bakery when she had enough problems of her own consumed me with guilt.

Josie waved a hand in front of my face. "Sal, did you hear what I said?"

"Oh, sorry." I placed the phone back in its cradle. "Mrs. Gavelli isn't feeling well, so we're going without her."

"Well, I'm sorry about that," Josie said as we locked the door and proceeded down the hallway to the elevator. "But let's be honest. The woman is not exactly tactful. She'd call Violet a cheap tramp or something, and then we'd all be thrown out on our ear."

"That's pretty much what I was thinking too."

We grabbed a quick continental breakfast and then hailed a cab. The sun was already overhead in a brilliant blue sky, and it appeared that we were in for another scorcher of a day.

"I don't know how the heck people stand the heat out here," Josie complained. "Plus, what will we do if Violet isn't there? Wait around for her to show in this godforsaken sauna of a city?"

"We might have to," I said grimly. "This is probably the last chance we'll have to find her. Our plane leaves at eleven o'clock tomorrow morning, so we'll need to be at the airport around nine."

"Ugh, that's right." Josie groaned out loud. "That means home around eight tomorrow night if we're lucky, then back to work bright and early the next day. This was too short of a vacation."

I leaned back in the seat and closed my eyes. "Well, at least you have a lenient boss, ha-ha. A wonderful friend who— oh, I don't know—might let you come in an hour or so later on Monday morning."

"Oh, really?" Josie laughed. "What's the catch?"

I opened my eyes and looked at her. "A trade-off. I was hoping to leave a little early on Monday, maybe about four o'clock, if you don't mind."

"You're the one in charge," Josie said. "So why would I mind? Hey, what's really going on that you're not telling me? Dinner and romance with the hubs?"

My cheeks burned. "Maybe." I still hadn't decided if I'd tell him the news Monday night or wait for our anniversary. It would still be considered an anniversary present, even if it was six days early.

"Sal," Josie whispered. "Did you find out? Are you pregnant? Is that what this is all about?"

I put a finger to my lips, embarrassed for the cabbie to hear. "I don't know anything for certain yet, but I'm cautiously optimistic."

A tear formed in the corner of Josie's eye, and she wiped it away. "Ohmigod, Sal. I'm so excited for you—for both of you. I know how long you've waited for this moment."

"Mike has to be the first one to know officially, so not a word to anyone," I cautioned.

Josie's lower lip trembled. "Oh, this will be so great. Your baby and Jeremy will only be three years apart. I can't wait to throw you a baby shower. Oh, my gosh. What if you have twins?"

"Will you stop?" I couldn't keep the grin off my face. "This will be a dream come true, Jos. I'll have everything I've ever wanted."

The cabbie pulled up to the same security booth as yesterday. I leaned forward from the back seat to speak with the guard, a blonde woman this time. "Hi, we're here to see Violet Fiato, please."

The woman peered in the cab's window at me. "Is she expecting you?"

"No," I said honestly. "But we're friends of her mother. It's about her…inheritance." Okay, a teeny white lie.

The woman's cheeks were tinged pink against her alabaster skin. "Names?"

Violet didn't know who we were—at least I didn't think so. Since Nicoletta wasn't with us, why would she have reason to let us in or even want to? "My name is Sally Donovan. Please tell her my grandmother is Rosa Belgacci."

"One moment," the woman said tersely then slid the window back into place. It was only nine thirty in the morning, but if Violet slept during the day and worked nights, this might be the best time to pay a visit, before she went to bed.

The window slid open again. "She'd like to know exactly what this is regarding."

Great. *Think, Sal, think.* "Uh, like I said, it's about her inheritance. Her sister, Anna, sent me. It's urgent that I speak with her." I was surely going to hell for all these lies.

The woman stared at us with apprehension and closed the window—this time, slamming it shut. Her mouth moved rapidly behind the glass as she held the phone to her ear, and then she slid the window open again. She spoke directly to the driver, purposely ignoring me this time. "It's number eleven twenty-two. Second home on the left."

"Nice attitude," Josie called loudly as we drove away.

"Shh," I warned. "Must you always cause trouble?"

She gave me a sly wink. "I think you already know the

answer to that question."

The driver drove through the opened gate and veered to the left. Josie and I both stared with interest as he pulled up in front of Violet's house. The facade was a light blue stone design, single structure, set on a half-acre sized lot. Despite the heat, the lawn was green and lush, perfectly manicured with white and pink rosebushes adorning it and a row of small evergreens in front of the porch. It was twice the size of my house.

"Very spacious for one person," Josie commented.

It didn't look as if Violet needed her mother's money after all. Maybe she hadn't come to the wake because she just didn't care enough. "Would you wait for us?" I asked the driver. "We shouldn't be more than half an hour."

The driver, a blond man who looked barely out of his teens, nodded. "Sure thing. Take your time."

"Yeah, what does he care," Josie mumbled under her breath as we climbed the front stairs to Violet's porch. "He's getting paid for sitting there."

Before I could ring the bell, the glass-paneled door was opened from the other side by a woman in a blue silk bathrobe. Even though the fine curly mass of dark hair was concealed under a towel and she held a lit cigarette in one hand, it was definitely Violet.

She didn't waste time with pleasantries. "What do you want? Why has Anna sent you?"

"I'm Sally Donovan, and this is my friend, Josie Sullivan. Anna didn't send us. Your mother Allegra was our tenant for a short time in New York. Her friend, Nicoletta Gavelli, is here in Vegas with us."

She shrugged. "Yeah, I know that old lady. Mom was living with her when she passed. But it still doesn't explain what you want."

"We'd like to talk to you about your mother for a few minutes, if that's possible," I said calmly.

She blew out a long, exasperated breath and pushed the door open. "Fine. Let's get it over with. Leave your shoes by the door, please."

Josie and I both reached down to remove our sandals. I stepped onto the thick, plush carpeting that massaged my feet and immediately understood why she'd made the request. Everything inside the house was white and pristine, from the carpet and the leather furniture to the stark walls. The tables and wet bar were glass with gold-plated trimming. French doors led to a wood grain deck, where an in-ground pool, hot tub, and pool house were in plain view. There was abstract art in silver frames on every wall, while an ominous grandfather clock ticked away the minutes. To me, this looked like a staged home. Either Violet was never around or she had a full-time housekeeper.

A white Persian cat was sitting on the leather couch, his large blue eyes regarding us with distrust. When I reached down to pet him, he opened his mouth and rewarded me with a giant hiss. *Okay, then.* Since I was rather fond of my hand, I removed it from his reach.

Violet scooped the cheerful guy up into her arms and sat down in the matching leather armchair across from the couch. She gestured to the spot where the cat had been sitting. "Make yourselves comfortable."

Josie stared at the couch and then gingerly brushed a clump of white cat hair to the floor before she sat down.

"Sorry about that." Violet stroked the kitty's head as he purred with the intensity of a V-8 engine. "Gus sheds everywhere. I had him groomed last week, but it doesn't help much. My housekeeper is always grumbling about picking up cat hair, but hey, she gets paid well enough to deal with it. Now, what's this about my mother?"

"You do know that she left you money," I began.

She gave an arrogant toss of her head. "I don't need her money and certainly never asked for any. She only left it to me out of guilt."

Allegra felt guilty? It seemed out of character for her. "I don't understand."

Violet's dark eyes met mine. "It's quite simple, really. My mother is ashamed of me."

"Because you're an escort?" Josie blurted out.

"Nice going," I muttered.

Violet's mouth dropped open. "Who told you? Not my mother, that's for sure. She was horrified by my profession. That's the real reason she wouldn't come out here to live. Anna must have told you. They're the only ones in the family who know."

"Your face was on a card that was handed to us on the Strip last night," I said.

Her shoulders sagged. She placed Gus on the arm of the chair beside her, then leaned back against the cushions heavily. "Oh, I forgot about that stupid photo. I posed for one when I first came out here."

"We were hoping you might be able to shed some light on your mother's death," I explained.

Violet shrugged. "I don't know anything. My mother left me money in hopes that I'd go back to my life before this." Her voice turned bitter. "She never cared about any of us. She and my father went back to Italy as soon as I turned eighteen. We were pretty much disowned from that point on. Mother and I would talk occasionally, but Anna and Enzo hardly ever spoke to her." She smiled wryly. "When she found out what I was doing here, she was furious."

"How did your mother find out?" I asked.

Violet shifted in her seat and continued to stroke Gus's fur as he closed his eyes in obvious content. "I had to tell her when I thought there was a chance she might come and live with me. And you know what she did? She called me a filthy tramp. My own mother! From there she went on, saying how I was a disgrace—not to mention my ex-boyfriend. She was furious when she discovered who I was dating."

"Someone she didn't approve of?" I was curious myself about the mystery man.

"You could say that." Violet stared out the window. "Look, I didn't wish my mother dead, but I'm not shedding any tears over it, that's for sure."

"I don't think anyone in your family even has tear ducts," Josie blurted out.

She pinned Josie was a cold, dark stare. "Don't judge. You didn't know her—not really, anyway. Mother never should have had kids. She worshipped my father and the ground he walked on, but after he died, she was lost. She needed to find someone else to suck the life out of."

What a cheerful thought and, from what I'd seen,

shockingly accurate.

It was as if Violet had read my mind. "Look, she only cared about my father and herself. I didn't want Mother here but knew that my brother and sister wouldn't take her. When she said she was going to live with Nicoletta Gavelli and not her cheap tramp of a daughter—hey, that suited me fine. What do I care what she thinks of me? She certainly didn't care what we thought of her."

She reached across Gus to extinguish her cigarette in a glass ashtray. "I have to quit. Nasty habit. Plus, I don't want it to affect Gus." She planted an affectionate kiss on the top of his head while the cat let out a tiny mew in return. "Everyone thought that she didn't come here because of the climate. Baloney. She was ashamed of what I did."

"What were you doing in New York?" I asked.

She took a long sip out of the drink in front of her, which looked and smelled like a gin and tonic. I rarely drank and couldn't imagine guzzling down a cocktail so early in the morning. "A lowly receptionist job, but there were certain benefits. Like screwing the boss, for example."

"Charming," Josie said affably.

Violet placed her glass down on the table. "Again with the judgment? You must lead a perfect life, sugar. I thought I was in love with him once but got over that quick. He was like my mother—too self-absorbed and possessive."

Sounds like a great guy.

"He was only concerned with his own needs," Violet went on. "Too damn clingy for my taste, but he did buy me nice presents. Jewelry, dresses, furs, you name it. He was a powerful man, and that's what first attracted me to him. You might think otherwise, but I'm very selective about the men I, uh…fraternize with. They're all successful businessmen like him, and pay me very well, I might add. No strings attached. In less than a year, I've already bought myself a house and a sweet-looking car. What more do I really need? I'm happy and away from my loony family."

Call me crazy, but there was a haunted look in Violet's eyes that cried out to me and said otherwise. I also suspected she was hiding something. Maybe it had to do with her former lover or her dysfunctional family, but whatever the reason, I pitied her.

"Now, if you're all done with this inquisition—or intervention, whatever you want to call it—I need to sleep." She shot Josie a surly look. "I work long hours and need my rest. I can't have myself looking haggard tonight. My clients don't like that." She rose from the chair and draped Gus over her shoulder like he was an expensive fur.

I held up a hand. "One more thing. Do you have any idea of who might have wanted to kill your mother?"

Violet stared at me, puzzled. "What do you mean? She was the victim of a hit-and-run."

So she hadn't heard. I didn't see the harm in telling her since Anna and Enzo already knew the truth and I was surprised they hadn't shared it with her. "It appears that your mother was deliberately run down. Allegra's death has been ruled a homicide."

Her face turned as white as powdered sugar. "Are you serious? Why am I just hearing about this now—and from *you*, of all people?"

"Nicoletta tried to call you," Josie said, "and so did your family. It seems you never answer your phone."

Violet shrugged. "I have no use for any of my relatives. I never got along well with my brother and sister. They've always been jealous of me. Besides, my life is here now." She hesitated for a moment. "Do the police have any idea who did this? Maybe they should take a good hard look at Enzo and Anna."

Wow. Talk about your sibling love. "We heard you were in New York that day—the same day your mother was killed."

Violet swallowed hard and looked away. "Yeah, that's right. I was there to see someone—and not a member of my family. It was my way of saying good-bye to the past, forever."

"Did you happen to see your mother when you visited this"—I took a wild stab in the dark—"man?"

She narrowed her eyes at me. "Yes, it was a man and extremely personal. I didn't even tell my family I was in town. I was in New York for less than forty-eight hours. How do you know, anyhow?" Then recognition dawned on her face. "Oh. The police must have checked the airline records."

I didn't respond to her comment. "If you know

something about her death, you'd be doing us a favor by coming clean. Mrs. Gavelli—err, Nicoletta is very upset about what happened to your mother, and it's affecting my grandmother as well. We only want to help."

"Yeah, like I believe that one. Look, I don't know who killed my mother, but I will tell you this. She had plenty of people who hated her guts, and it was her own damn fault because of the way she treated them." A shadow passed over Violet's face. "Now that I think about it, she did say something weird the last time I talked to her. It was as if she knew that her life might be in danger."

Now we were getting somewhere. "What exactly did she tell you?"

She drew her eyebrows together, and her delicate mouth pursed into a frown. "Something about a locket of hers and that she did it for me. She really wasn't making much sense." Violet gave a low laugh. "To tell you the truth, I wondered if she might have been drinking. She loved a snort every now and then. What really shocked me is when Mother said that she loved me. This was a first. My mother had *never* said those words to me before."

Josie and I exchanged a knowing glance. Allegra must have been referring to the necklace that had been left to Grandma Rosa. "This locket. Have you ever seen it before?"

She nodded. "If it's the one I remember, it was gold with a skull and crossbones. My father gave it to her years ago. Mother wasn't the type of person you gave a diamond to. She liked that creepy kind of stuff instead. There was a compartment inside to put things. You know, where you're supposed to carry around pictures of your child? Except she always carried a picture of my father instead."

"Was it valuable?" Josie asked.

Violet shrugged. "I don't think so. They didn't have any money back then. Mother treasured it, though, all the same." She snapped her fingers suddenly. "That's it. She said something about it holding the key to my fortune."

"What do you think she meant by that?" I asked.

She laughed. "Who knows. Leave it to Mother to say something weird like that. Maybe it had to do with her love of fortune cookies. On the rare occasions we got Chinese food when I was a kid, she'd always steal everyone's cookies."

"Guess not much has changed since then," Josie muttered.

I shot her a warning look. "Well, thanks for your time. We know you have things to do, so—"

The smile disappeared from Violet's face. "You think I'm just some cheap tramp, don't you?"

"I'm not here to judge you," I said calmly. "I only want to find out what happened to your mother."

It was as if she hadn't heard me. "Look, I entertain men for the evening. Sometimes they hire me if they need a date for a high society event or for a night on the town. Hey, if they only want to spend a few hours talking, that's okay by me too. As long as I get paid."

Josie snorted back a laugh. "Okay, sure. Hey Violet, it's none of our business what—"

"You're damn right it's none of your business," she snarled. "I've got everything I ever wanted. A nice car, house, and money. In a couple of years, I might retire and open my own art gallery."

"You like to paint?" I asked.

Her face brightened at my words. "Yes, it's so relaxing. I don't plan to work as an escort for the rest of my life, you know."

I examined her face closely. "Well, as long as you're happy, that's all that counts."

"Of course I'm happy." Violet shot me a look of defiance. "I have everything I could possibly ever want right at my fingertips."

When we didn't respond, I swore that Violet's lower lip trembled for the briefest of seconds. She reached down to stroke Gus's head. "Everything," she repeated.

CHAPTER THIRTEEN

———

"Okay." Josie let her slim legs dangle elegantly in the turquoise blue water as we perched on the side of the hotel pool. "It's becoming obvious that this locket—or shall I say, this *missing* locket—might help us to find out who killed Allegra. How this is possible, I have no clue. Do you have any idea what the old lady might have done with it and why she would leave it to your grandmother of all people?"

"None whatsoever." It was late afternoon, and we were meeting my parents at the grill-type restaurant inside the New York-New York for an early dinner. Josie wanted to walk back to the Tropicana afterward and try out her beloved penny machines one last time before we called it a night. My after-dinner plans included some television and turning in early. Yes, I was a boring date.

Vegas was okay, I decided, but not exactly my slice of cheesecake. Still, it might be a nice place for my husband and me to visit when it wasn't so hot that I resembled one of my cookies during the baking process.

The temperature was in the high nineties, a bit cool for this time of year in Nevada. Still, I was broiling like a fish as I wiped sweat off my brow. "It feels like some type of riddle to me. Like Allegra wanted my grandmother to be the one to figure it out."

Josie's toes, painted a hot pink, kicked water across the pool. She looked fantastic in a new white bikini she'd bought at one of the gift shops yesterday. "Allegra only met your grandmother a few months ago, right?"

I slid my body into the deliciously cool water until it came up to my shoulders. "Yes, but you know that doesn't mean anything. Everyone is always taken with her. She has a certain pull—an irresistible charm."

"Plus she's never judgmental, gives sound advice, and makes the world's best cheesecake, along with every other type of food."

No arguments there. "Okay, there's that too."

"Do you think Violet's wrong and the locket's some type of antique?" Josie asked. "So if Allegra wanted Violet to stop living such a shameful life, why not leave it to her in the first place?"

"The locket must be worth something, then." A light switch flicked on in my brain. "Maybe that's what the killer or killers are looking for and why they trashed my apartment and Mrs. Gavelli's house."

Josie sipped her Long Island Iced Tea thoughtfully. "Unless there's something *inside* the locket."

This was like being in the middle of a maze and unable to figure a way out. A locket left to my grandmother by someone she barely knew *might* hold an important item, but we had to find it first. "Violet could be lying. She wouldn't tell us why she was in New York the same day Allegra died. It's too much of a coincidence as far as I'm concerned."

Josie crunched on a piece of ice. "But why kill Allegra over the locket if you can't find it? What good would that do?"

"Hi, girls!" We turned around to see my mother approaching. She was wearing a fire engine red bikini with matching stiletto sandals. She gestured toward the door of the restaurant. "Go on inside. Daddy's hungry."

Josie and I got out of the water and pulled our cover-ups on over our bikinis. It wasn't a fancy restaurant by any stretch— only your average burger and sandwich joint—so what we had on was suitable. My father had originally suggested we eat poolside, but I'd begged for air conditioning. The heat, like everything else on this planet, never seemed to bother him or my mother.

Dad rose from a table by the window and waved to us, menu in hand. I gave a little involuntary shudder when I saw today's outfit. It consisted of a white tank top and a knee-length pair of gray swim trunks that had "Father Death" inscribed on the lower left leg of the material. I sighed. "He's wearing his name brand swim trunks again."

"Good God," Josie muttered. "Did he have those made to impress the literary agent?"

I shook my head. "No, a woman who designs swimwear sent them to him for free. All she wanted in return was a shout-out on his blog."

"This is nuts," Josie declared as we approached him. My mother was still outside, chatting with the waiter behind the bar as he fixed her a piña colada. She seemed oblivious to the red-blooded males around the pool who were all gawking at her. I breathed a sigh of relief when she put her cover-up on. It's a bit hard to take when your mother looks better in a bikini than you do.

My father patted the chair next to him. "Come here, baby girl. Let me get a good look at you." He draped an arm around my shoulders and planted a kiss on the top of my head. "See, marriage agrees with you. You were too skinny before, but you've rounded out nicely now."

"Gee, thanks, Dad."

My mother sat down across from us next to Josie. She giggled and gave me a sly wink. "I had a dream last night and bet you can't guess what it was about."

"Oh, I don't know—you were working as a waitress in a casino?"

Her laugh sounded like the tinkling bells on my bakery shop door. "No, silly." She pinned me with her large dark eyes. "I dreamed that someone I loved was pregnant."

Josie kicked me under the table.

My heart stuttered in my chest. Cripes. My parents were about to ruin this for me. If I told them I thought I was expecting, my mother would be on the phone sobbing to my husband within seconds. "Well, Mom, when I am, you'll be one of the first to know."

She sighed. "Oh, pooh. You take all the fun out of it." She glanced up as the waiter approached. "You girls order whatever you want. It's on us."

After the waiter had taken our order and left, my mother propped her elbows on the table. "So you girls never did tell us what you're doing here. Were you following us?"

"Nicoletta wanted to come here and talk to Allegra's daughter, Violet," Josie explained. "She thought Violet might know something about her mother being murdered."

"That poor woman." Mom clucked her tongue against the roof of her mouth. "What a horrible way to go."

My father snorted as he slurped the rest of his chocolate shake. "Ah, she had it coming. That woman made Satan look tame."

"Domenic!" my mother cried. "That's no way to speak about the dead."

"Baloney." He dipped a tortilla chip into salsa. "No one liked her. I even heard the neighbors threatening her last week."

"The Gardners?" Josie asked with interest.

"Sure," he said. "They're my homies. We hang together all the time."

Oh, brother. It appeared my mother wasn't the only one who thought she was forever a teenager. "What did they say about her?"

He crunched on the chip. "Well, they didn't like Allegra, that was for sure. She called the cops on them one night. She said they were smoking pot while their baby was sleeping upstairs. The old broad even called them unfit parents."

Josie's blue eyes grew round. "Were they really smoking pot?"

My father waved his hand dismissively. "Carl's got a legit reason. He has glaucoma and only uses it for medicinal purposes."

"But it's not legal to smoke marijuana in New York yet," I protested.

He grimaced. "Yeah, well, thanks to her meddling, Carl got arrested and charged with possession. Man, was he ticked off at the old broad. I heard Rachel went over to Nicoletta's house and had words with Allegra too."

"That must have gone over well," I murmured.

My father stuffed another chip into his mouth. "You're not kidding. Carl told her if she ever went near his house again he was going to flatten her body with his car."

I winced. What an unfortunate choice of words to use.

"They're not violent people, right?" I was looking for some type of reassurance.

Dad shrugged. "I don't think so, but who really knows for sure? People are nuts these days. Everyone gets offended by everything. Sure, the Gardners are a nice couple. They just didn't happen to be fond of Allegra."

"Huh." Josie smirked. "Who was?"

My mother looked out the window. "Where's Ma? Aren't she and Nicoletta joining us?"

I shook my head. "Mrs. Gavelli still isn't feeling well, and Grandma didn't want to leave her. I offered to bring them back something to eat, but she said they'd order room service if they got hungry."

"Speaking of a devil," my father grunted. "That woman's been a thorn in my side since she moved into our neighborhood 30 years ago."

My mother put her hand on his. "Oh, she's all right, darling. It's that Allegra who managed to rub everyone the wrong way. Remember the man who was parked in front of Nicoletta's house last week? He was screaming terrible things at Allegra. It looked like what's his name—that assemblyman. No, wait, I think he's a senator."

Josie and I exchanged a startled glance. "Do you mean Martin Ambrose?" I asked.

My mother spooned some whipped cream from her drink into her mouth. "That's the one. He's a nice-looking man but kind of cocky if you ask me. Of course, he pales in comparison to your father."

"Doesn't everybody?" My father puffed out his chest and blew her an air kiss. Then he promptly dropped a large spot of salsa on his tank top.

I struggled not to roll my eyes and instead focused on what my mother said. Why would Martin Ambrose have visited Allegra? Something told me it wasn't a social call. "Was Lena with him?"

"Who?" my mother asked. "Oh, you mean his wife—Allegra's niece, right? I don't know her. But in answer to your question, no. He was alone."

The more I discovered about Allegra, the more confused

I became. Maybe I would try to give Lena a call later. My grandmother had her cell phone number. Would she be willing to shed some light on her husband's relationship with Allegra?

The waiter brought my father another milkshake, and he clinked it against our glasses. "So I propose a toast. To your father, the most creative genius in the world."

"What exactly are we toasting?" Josie asked.

Dad sucked half of the drink through his straw before he responded. "We are celebrating my newest venture into the publishing world."

Our dinners arrived at that moment. After the waiter had departed, I asked the 64-million-dollar question. "Did you sign with Mr. Steadman?"

My father's jaw hardened. "Nah, he was a bust. He read the first chapter last night when we went up to his room for drinks. It turns out he was more interested in your mother than my book."

My mother drained her glass and nodded emphatically. "The man was a pig. He only had one thing on his mind, and it wasn't your father's book. So we told him what he could do with his unliterary-like intentions. I am *not* a slab of meat."

Dad grinned as he dug into his double bacon cheeseburger. "That's true, hot stuff. You're much healthier for me than this burger."

Ew. "Um, can we talk about something else?" I asked.

Mom tossed her head. "He did give us a few useful tips about self-publishing, so I'm enrolling in a local class next week. It explains how to list your book on Amazon and all those other cute ebook sites. We're going to form our own publishing company, and guess what we're going to call it?"

The possibilities were endless with them. "No idea."

"Bellissimo Books. Isn't that clever?" Mom beamed at my father. "Daddy thought of it."

I considered this for a moment. To my surprise, it wasn't half bad. "I like it."

"Just wait and see, baby girl," my father said. "In less than a year, you'll be hosting my first book signing at your bakery. Mark my words."

Josie almost choked on her sandwich.

* * *

After we got back to our room and had checked on Grandma Rosa and Nicoletta, Josie went down to the casino while I placed a call to Lena. It took a second for her to remember who I was.

"My apologies," she said. There was a murmur of voices in the background. "Sorry. I have some friends over for drinks and a dinner party tonight. What can I do for you, Sally?"

"I was wondering if the locket that was left to my grandmother had been found yet."

Lena was silent for a moment. "Oh! I almost forgot about that. No, it hasn't turned up. If it's any consolation, I don't believe it was valuable."

"We don't care about that. Your aunt might have hidden something inside it, so perhaps that's what the person who broke into Nicoletta's house and my apartment was looking for."

"I guess that's possible," Lena conceded. "I wish I could help but have no idea where it is. Let me know if you do find it, okay? I have to keep a record of everything."

"Of course, but I did have another reason for calling." I decided to keep my parents' names out of the conversation. "I was told by some of the neighbors that your husband and Allegra were heard shouting at each other last week."

Lena sighed heavily into the phone. "Well, it's no secret that they didn't like each other."

This admission surprised me. "Why is that?"

"Let's be honest, okay? There weren't many people who liked Aunt Allegra. She was always bugging Martin about things that he had no time for. God knows he tried to tolerate the woman for my sake, but she made it difficult. Aunt Allegra was like a wasp who kept flying around your face and wasn't afraid to sting you."

I hated to admit it, but her analogy was spot-on.

"The neighbors across the street should be locked up, there were too many potholes in the road, blah blah. Martin is *not* the Highway Department. He is a New York State senator, for God's sake! Why would she bother him about such trivial stuff? Aunt Allegra even called him to say that you—" Lena stopped suddenly.

Uh-oh. "Go on," I urged.

"Sally, I really don't think you want to hear this."

I braced myself for the unknown. "Just go ahead and say it, Lena."

She blew out a sigh. "Aunt Allegra asked Martin about how to deal with a dishonest landlord."

"What?" I shrieked into the phone.

"She told Martin that you guys had been stealing her equipment and were trying to evict her, even though she'd paid her rent and was a model tenant."

I couldn't believe what I was hearing. "Stealing what? Her candy pans upstairs? She's the one who was stealing from me!"

"For what it's worth, I believe you," Lena said. "Want my take on it? I think she was looking for a way to take your building away from you. The day that she died—after you guys had the fight? It made me wonder if she'd planned to get you so angry you might push her, and then she could sue."

My rage had quickly increased from a simmer to a full-fledged boil, and I fought to stay calm. "I'm sorry your aunt is dead, Lena, but this is too much for me to absorb. I can't believe anyone would be that rotten." Or maybe I just didn't want to.

"You've heard the saying about the wolf in sheep's clothing, right?" Lena asked. "Well, that was a pretty accurate description of Aunt Allegra."

CHAPTER FOURTEEN

———

Our flight home was quiet and uneventful. Nicoletta still wasn't feeling well and slept for most of the trip. Josie also took a nap, while my grandmother crocheted, probably overjoyed for the blissful silence. I tried to read a book I'd brought but couldn't concentrate. It was difficult to keep from bouncing in my seat. Tomorrow I would discover for certain if I was pregnant. If the test was positive, how the heck would I manage to keep the secret for six more days until our actual wedding anniversary?

Our flight arrived ahead of schedule by ten minutes, and we wasted no time in collecting our luggage and Josie's minivan from long-term parking. We dropped my grandmother and Nicoletta off at my parents' house first. Mom and Dad weren't scheduled to return home for a couple more days, and once again, I found myself concerned for the elderly women's safety.

"We will be fine," Grandma Rosa assured me as she and I both helped Nicoletta out of the van. "No one knows we are here."

I kissed her cheek. "Promise me you'll call if you need anything."

She nodded. "Yes, I will do this. Now go home to your husband."

We waited until they were inside the house, and then Josie backed her van out of the driveway. Across the street, Carl Gardner was watering his lawn as the sun was starting to sink behind the clouds. He waved when the van drove past him.

"Back up the van," I said to Josie.

Puzzled at first, she then nodded in sudden understanding. "Ah. You want to talk to him."

"Only for a minute. Do you mind?"

"No, it's all right. I'll go with you."

She backed the van up to the curb in front of the Gardner residence, and Carl watched with interest as we approached. He looked about my age and was tall with a burly frame, sandy blond hair, and ruddy cheeks. Eyes as black as tar smiled at us from behind the thick designer bifocals he wore.

"Hi, Sally," he said and then extended his hand to Josie. "Carl Gardner."

She smiled back. "Josie Sullivan. I work with Sally."

He turned the hose off and set it aside. "What can I do for you ladies?"

Okay, Sal. Start with dear old dad and slowly work your way in. "My father said he's been spending a lot of time over here with you and Rachel. I wanted to make sure he wasn't…ah…overdoing it."

His face creased into a broad grin. "Not at all. We like having him around. He's quite the character."

That was one word to describe him. "I'm sure you heard about Allegra Fiato by now."

Carl's face sobered. "Yeah, that's awful. Did they catch the creep who mowed her down yet? I haven't seen Nicoletta in a few days. She's not my favorite person, I'll admit, but I hope nothing's happened to her as well. Why do people have to drive so fast? Driving isn't an entitlement. I try to be extra careful, what with my vision problems and all."

"No, they haven't found the person yet." He didn't need to know that Allegra's death was no accident. We couldn't afford to trust anyone. "Mrs. Gavelli—err, Nicoletta is fine. Sorry about your eyesight."

He took his glasses off and polished them on the bottom of his shirt. "Glaucoma. It runs in my family. It usually hits people who are older, but the pressure in my eye has been terrible for quite some time now. The doctor started me on medication a few months back."

Here was the opening I was looking for. "It must be terrible to deal with—especially the pain. I understand you had a run-in with Allegra about your glaucoma, so to speak."

A muscle ticked in Carl's jaw. "Yeah. She was nosing around our house one evening, and I told her to get lost."

"She saw you smoking a joint and called the cops, right?" Josie asked.

The dark, piercing glare that he shot her made me want to flee his doorstep in a hurry. "Are you here for information or to lecture me?" Carl seethed.

Yikes. "My father mentioned that Allegra reported you to the cops."

"That's true enough. I got arrested for possession, thanks to that witch. She blabbed to the police that I was endangering the life of my child. Rachel was furious and went over to tell her to mind her own business. Then she had the audacity to push my wife! Well, that was the last straw. No one's going to treat my family like that. I went over there myself, and she wouldn't open the door. All talk, no action. Anyhow, why are you asking? Do you think I'm the one who ran her over?" He gave a bitter laugh.

Josie and I laughed too, but mine sounded a bit shaky to my own ears. "Of course not. She was our tenant remember, so naturally we're very upset about this."

"We are?" Josie asked. "Oh, right. We are."

"Sure," Carl said in a disbelieving tone. "Her daughter asked me where the shop was. They wanted to see her business while they were in town. She made candy, right?"

Josie snickered. "Well, she said it was a candy shop. Turns out she—"

I held up a hand and fervently wished my friend would stop talking. "When did you see Allegra's daughter? At the service?"

Carl shook his head. "Nope. Last Saturday, the day she died."

Shell-shocked, Josie and I both stared at him. "Are you sure?"

He paused a moment to think. "Yep, it was definitely Saturday, midmorning, because I had just gone down to the mailbox to get the paper. Enzo and Andrea, right?"

"Anna," Josie corrected.

Carl snapped his fingers. "Yeah, they were looking for Allegra and didn't know which house belonged to Nicoletta since there's no number on her mailbox. So they came here and asked me if I could point them in the right direction."

Holy cow. Anna, Enzo, and Violet had all been in town the day their mother died. What the heck was going on?

"Rachel had taken the baby to her mother's house for a visit," Carl explained. "I showed them which house belonged to Nicoletta, and out of politeness, I asked about the business. Your grandmother stopped over the day before and told me that Allegra had a new shop. By the way, Rosa's the complete opposite of those two old birds. She brought me a cheesecake last week because your father told her it was my birthday."

Oh, I needed to have more birthdays. "My grandmother's cheesecake is the best."

Carl smiled. "She's a wonderful woman. Anyhow, I told Rosa I didn't especially like the new neighbor, and she said the candy store was going to be in the apartment over your bakery. I gave Anna and Enzo directions when they stopped by."

If Enzo and Anna had come into the bakery that day, I didn't remember seeing them. Had they been lying in wait for their mother and then plowed her over when she ran outside? No, that was insane. Or was it?

When we were at Lena's office for the reading of the will, she'd commented how the children already knew what they'd be receiving. Maybe they'd come here to confront their mother. But why kill her if they weren't getting anything?

Carl broke into my thoughts. "I stood here and watched as Enzo and Anna walked across the street and knocked on Nicoletta's door. No one answered. Then they started shouting at each other, got back into the car, and drove away."

"Any idea what they said?" I asked.

He shook his head. "Guess my eyes aren't the only thing that don't work so well these days. The daughter was holding a manila envelope when they came to my door. Sorry I can't tell you anything else." He pinned me with those dark eyes that resembled icicles again. "Rosa mentioned once that you've solved a few murder mysteries."

What was he getting at? "Uh, a couple," I hedged. "I guess I just have bad luck. I'm always in the wrong place at the wrong time."

Josie joined in the laugh with me, but Carl didn't even crack a smile. "I still don't understand why you're asking me all these questions since I didn't murder Allegra," he said.

So he did know her death was deliberate. But how? "Uh, it was a hit-and-run. You said so yourself."

"Right," Carl mocked. "That's why you were so interested to learn that her daughter and son were in town the day she died. I don't appreciate being questioned like I'm a criminal. It's probably best if you both left now."

"What the heck was all that about?" Josie said as we walked back to her van. "That guy's like a faucet—hot one second then ice cold. It makes me think he's hiding something."

My thoughts exactly. "If Carl wants us to believe he's innocent, he's not doing a very good job going about it." I fastened my seat belt and pulled out my phone.

Josie started the engine. "Who are you calling?"

I held up a finger as my grandmother picked up on the other end.

"Hello, *cara mia*. I see that you are across the street. Yes, we are still fine."

"Grandma, can you ask Nicoletta a question for me, please? Does she remember seeing Anna and Enzo at the bakery last Saturday—the same day Allegra was killed?"

"One moment." There was quiet for at least a minute as my grandmother's calm voice and Nicoletta's shrill one could both be heard in the background. Finally, my grandmother came back on the line. "She did not see them. Allegra never mentioned that she was expecting them for a visit either. Are you sure they were in town that day?"

"Yes," I said as Josie stopped at a red light. "We were talking to your neighbor Carl. He said they came to his door that morning. I'm surprised you didn't see them."

My grandmother sounded indignant. "What—do you think I have nothing better to do than stare out the window all day? I am not a fussy body, *cara mia*."

I scrunched up my forehead in confusion. "Do you mean busybody?"

"That works too. I am not sure why they would have come into town that day. Perhaps they knew about the candy store and were curious to see it."

Uneasiness washed over me like a monsoon. Maybe they

had another reason for coming to town. "Violet was reported to be in New York that same day as well. Nicoletta didn't see her either?"

"I do not believe so, but let me ask." She put me on hold for another minute, and I cringed when I heard Nicoletta shouting at my grandmother this time. "No, she did not see Violet either. No more questions for now. She gets cranky if I bother her when the Kardashian ladies are on."

I blinked at the phone. "Nicoletta likes to watch the Kardashians?"

Josie's mouth twitched at the corners. "That's about the last thing I expected to hear."

"Yes," said Grandma Rosa. "She says they are all tramps, but she never misses an episode. She is nutsy cookie too. *Ciao, bella*." My grandmother clicked off.

"This is strange," I said as Josie pulled into my street. "All three children were in town the day their mother died, but it appears they never saw Allegra—at least we don't think so. And let's not forget that my parents' neighbors hated Allegra's guts too. Are we forgetting anyone?"

"Lena's husband," Josie answered promptly. "He had a fight with her, remember. And I'll bet you dollars to cookies that Lena wasn't telling you the entire truth."

"Doughnuts," I said.

"Not in our case. But to be honest, is there anyone who actually *liked* the woman?" Josie pulled into my driveway, and Spike could be heard barking through my half-opened window.

I leaned over to give her a hug. "Well, I'm forgetting about Allegra for the rest of the night. I just want to be alone with my man and not think about anything else."

"I'm with you." Josie grinned. "I've even started to miss Rob. You said you're opening in the morning, right?"

A tingle ran through me as I remembered about tomorrow. "Yes, as long as you don't mind me taking off early."

"Only if I can be the second person to know the results," Josie said.

"What results?"

We both jumped. Mike reached over and opened my door for me. I hoped he hadn't heard too much. Hastily, I got out of the car. "Oh, a new recipe Josie's trying out." I gave her my best evil eye. "Thanks for driving."

Josie grinned at the both of us. "Anytime. You lovebirds have fun catching up tonight." She backed out of the driveway, and the van sped away.

As soon as we were inside and Mike had deposited my duffel bag on the floor, he locked the door and then wrapped his arms around my waist, his mouth closing over mine. "God, how I've missed you," he murmured as he kissed me.

I sighed contentedly when we finally came up for air. "I missed you too."

He surprised me then by lifting me off my feet and into his arms. If I'd gained any weight in the last few weeks, at least he didn't groan with exertion.

"Where are we going?" I giggled and threw my arms around his neck.

His answer was to place his hot, wet mouth over mine again, and I lost my senses. Slot machines, Persian cats, and my mother in fishnet stockings were all but forgotten as he kicked the door open to our bedroom. "I think you already know the answer to that question, Betsy Drew." He grinned at me.

"It's Nancy."

"As your grandmother would say, 'whatever.'"

CHAPTER FIFTEEN

———

Business was slow at the bakery on Monday, so I managed to slip out the door a few minutes before four o'clock arrived. Josie had tried to persuade me take the test upstairs in the apartment and shout down the results to her, but I wanted to go home and make Mike a nice dinner first. I could follow recipes in the bakery with no problem, and of course I knew many by heart. When it came to cooking an actual meal though, my experience was sorely lacking. Since my marriage I'd made a valiant effort to prepare one home-cooked meal a week.

I stopped off at the butcher shop and picked up some center-cut pork chops. From there, I continued on to a local produce stand for fresh potatoes and broccoli. Maybe next summer I'd attempt to start my own vegetable garden—if I had time with the baby. Then I did a mental head slap. How would I still run the bakery *and* take care of an infant? Maybe we'd be able to hire some part-time help in the shop, or the child could sleep upstairs in the now empty apartment. I'd run back and forth between my baby and business all day. It would be exhausting but worth it. I'd figure something out.

After I'd started preparations for dinner, I gave Spike fresh water and food and went into the bathroom. My heart pounded as I opened the box that held the two tests. Hey, it never hurt to be prepared, in case one was defective. I put a hand over my chest to steady myself. This wasn't the first time I'd taken a home pregnancy test. The last time I'd used one, it had been a couple of days early, but I was too excited to wait any longer. The negative result had been a crushing blow. I'd even shed a few tears. Today I was confident that I'd see different results. My time had finally arrived—the day I'd longed for.

As I waited impatiently for three minutes to tick by, I remembered another time, years ago when married to Colin, that I'd suspected I was pregnant. The test had been negative, and even though I'd known it was for the best, it had still saddened me. Colin had been outraged when I'd told him about the possibility and flat out accused me of getting pregnant on purpose. I flinched when I thought of the cruel things he'd said to me at the time. *No. Don't let the past ruin this moment. Mike wants a child as much as you do. The time is finally right.*

A chill of excitement spread down my spine as I looked down to read the plus sign in the tiny window, but all that awaited me was one line. Puzzled, I brought the applicator close to my face and looked again.

The test was negative.

I sucked in a deep breath. No. There had to be a simple explanation. The test was defective. *It had to be.* I was definitely pregnant. What else could explain the queasiness, my incessant appetite, plus the fact that I was constantly tired? Disappointment flooded my body, and tears began to sting the corners of my eyes. *No. It must be defective.* What a relief that I had bought two tests just in case something like this happened.

With a defiant air, I tore the paper off the spare test. I'd read stories about women who received negative results but turned out to be pregnant anyway. After I washed my hands and began the three-minute countdown, my phone buzzed from the top of the bathroom counter. In annoyance, I stared down at it, wondering who would dare interrupt this crucial time in my life. *Josie.* Uh-oh. Something might be wrong at the shop. I swiped my finger across her name. "Hey, what's up?"

"Did you take it yet?" she whispered.

"No," I lied while struggling to control the irritation in my voice. "Is that why you called?"

"Only part of the reason, and I'm sorry to bug you," she said. "I know it's an important day but I wanted to tell you that Enzo Fiato stopped by right after you left."

Why would Allegra's son come into my bakery? "What did he want?"

Josie snickered. "You, of course. It's seems Enzo has a little crush on you."

"Okay, I don't want to deal with this right now, Jos."

"I know," she said simply. "But he was acting kind of strange. He said something about he and Anna heading back to Jersey tomorrow. Then he left his number, in case you wanted to make a date. Enzo said it would be one night you never forgot."

My stomach rumbled at her words. "This is making me nauseous."

"Oh, I'll bet it's not Enzo making you nauseous," she laughed. "That's good old morning sickness—which, by the way, does not occur only in the morning. I had morning, afternoon, *and* evening sickness when I was pregnant with my Danny. But the stretch marks are the worst. Why, I still can't get rid of—"

"Okay, I get it. Is that all?" My three minutes were almost up.

Josie's tone was low. "No. Guess what kind of car Enzo was driving?"

"I give up. What kind?"

Her voice held a hint of annoyance. "Jeez, Nancy Drew, try to stay with me, okay? A Camaro, of course."

We have a winner. "Was it red?"

"No, white. But he could have painted it."

"I suppose so. Did you get the plate?"

She giggled. "Yep. I'm actually pretty proud that I thought of it."

"Okay, pat yourself on the back later. If it's not too busy in the shop, can you call Brian and have him run it?"

"No problem, partner. Should I have him call and let you know what he finds out?"

I hesitated. Tonight was supposed to have been a special evening for Mike and me, and I didn't want any interruptions. However, things were not going according to plan. "Uh, okay. I'm not sure if I'll be able to pick up, but he can always leave me a message."

"All righty, then." Josie's tone became cheerful. "And I suspect he'll be leaving a message because something tells me you and your hubby will be doing some serious all-night celebrating."

My time was up. "See you later." I clicked off while she was still talking, said a silent prayer, and then stared down at the window.

Negative.

A sob escaped from my throat. In anguish, I gripped the bathroom sink between my hands with a strong urge to rip it out of the wall and fling it across the room. Since I wasn't strong enough to do that, I picked up the test and hurled it against the wall. It landed in the tub. I picked it up, deposited the piece of plastic under the heel of my sandal, and then pressed down until I heard a satisfying crunch. After I dumped it in the garbage, I sank down onto the cool tile flooring and buried my face in my hands. Then I burst into tears.

What a fool I was. One of my grandmother's favorite sayings when I was growing up had been, "Never count your ducks before they're hatched." I'd wanted to be pregnant so badly that I must have feigned all the symptoms. There would be no special present to my husband on our anniversary. In fact, I hadn't even bought him a material one yet. What did it even matter anymore? Everything was ruined.

I sat there for a long time and sobbed. Yes, I was feeling sorry for myself but thought I had a right to. Why did this have to be so difficult for me? Why was life so unfair? All I wanted was a baby. I would have gladly cut off a limb if it guaranteed me one. The questions kept running through my head. *What's wrong with me? Why can't I get pregnant?*

Wearily, I sat there and wiped at my eyes with a tissue. Spike tottered over to make sure I was okay. I patted him absently on the head, and he left the room. He was most likely tired of my crying jags too. God knows this hadn't been the first for me.

I stood and washed my face in the sink then looked at my reflection in the mirror for a long time. Yes, I had a good life. A wonderful husband whom I loved more than anything. My business was thriving. I had good, albeit slightly abnormal, parents plus a grandmother who was amazing. My baby sister and Josie would do anything for me. I was blessed and had so much more than other people. So why wasn't it enough?

Spike barked, and there was a sharp tap on my front door. I glanced down at my watch. Five fifteen. Mike wasn't expected until at least six, and he had his own key. The tap sounded again. Whoever it was wouldn't go away. I clenched my teeth together in annoyance. *Okay, you can do this, Sal. Just get rid of them.*

I glanced out the peephole and saw my sister standing there. With a sigh, I opened the front door.

She gave me a faint, troubled smile, which faded when her eyes met mine. "Are you all right?"

"Fine," I said hastily. "What's up?"

The color rose slightly in her cheeks. "Look, I can come back later if it's not a good time. I stopped at the bakery, but Josie said you'd gone home early—"

"Did she say why?" I interrupted.

Gianna gave me a puzzled look. "No, I—Sal, what's wrong? You're scaring me. You look like you're angry at the world."

I was but didn't want to get into it now. Gianna would have been sympathetic and full of sound advice, but the subject was too fresh and painful. "I'm fine, just tired. Come on in. Want some coffee?"

She shook her head. "Um, I was hoping you had a little while to talk. I won't stay more than a few minutes."

"Hey, you're always welcome in our house for as long as you want to stay."

Gianna sat down at the kitchen table while I turned on my Keurig. Well, at least I didn't have to drink decaf coffee anymore. That was a perk, right? I swallowed hard as tears threatened to make another appearance.

Gianna sniffed at the air. "What are you making? It smells wonderful."

"Pork chops." I bit into my lower lip, trying to stop the flux of tears again. Damn it. This wouldn't do. I had to pull myself together. I filled a cup for myself and then joined her at the table. "You sure you don't want some?"

She twisted a paper napkin between her hands. "No, thanks. How was your trip? Did Violet give you any information about her mother and who might have run her down?"

"A little," I confessed. "What do you know about Senator Ambrose?"

She wrinkled her brow. "Not that much. Why—what's

he done?"

"I'm not sure. But Mom and Dad—who we managed to run into in Vegas, by the way—saw him at Mrs. Gavelli's house last week. He was arguing with Allegra."

Her eyes widened. "Really? Well, of course I know all about his law firm and that his wife has an office there too. He didn't practice for very long himself. I've also heard that Lena took the bar exam six times before she passed."

"How do you know this?"

She shrugged. "Lawyers talk just like everybody else. Martin is up for reelection this year, and his personal life has always seemed super squeaky clean, which automatically makes me suspicious. Politicians usually have at least one skeleton in their closet. Why were Mom and Dad out there? Mortuary convention?"

I drained my coffee cup. "Stalking a literary agent."

Gianna rolled her eyes toward the ceiling. "Why am I not surprised?" She folded her hands on the table and stared down at its surface.

I studied her for a moment. Something was still bothering Gianna. She'd tried to tell me what was wrong before we'd left on Friday, but there hadn't been enough time. I reached for her hand. It was ice cold, and I almost drew back in alarm. "You haven't been yourself for days. What's going on?"

Her voice trembled. "Nothing."

"Come on. You know you can always talk to me."

She hesitated as her eyes met mine. "There's obviously something bothering you as well. You don't need to hear my problems in addition to whatever else is going on, Sal."

I still didn't have the heart to tell her about the test. "Never mind. I want to know what's upsetting you."

Instead of replying, she released my hand, folded her arms on top of the table, then sank her head into them. Her entire body shook as she burst into tears.

Startled, I wrapped my arm around her thin shoulders. Her outburst terrified me. "Gi, please tell me what's going on. Are you sick?"

She stared up at me with a tear-stained face. "No. I'm pregnant."

CHAPTER SIXTEEN

———

Bewildered, I stared at my sister in silence. This had to be some type of joke. Finally, I laughed. "Come on, you're making that up." Had Josie told her about my test and they were playing a cruel prank on me? No, they'd never do something like that.

Gianna sat back in the chair and wiped at her eyes with a napkin. "Yeah, I wish. I took a test the other day, and the doctor confirmed it this afternoon. I'm six weeks along."

The room started to spin. No, it couldn't be. The pregnancy gods must have gotten us mixed up. *I* wanted the baby, not Gianna. How could this be possible?

"But…" Words failed me. "You—you and Johnny—were trying for a baby?"

Gianna barked out a laugh. "Hardly. You could say that it was a piece of bad luck. I don't leave things to chance, Sal. I always take precautions. But as they say, nothing is one hundred percent foolproof."

I tried to swallow the lump in my throat, but it wouldn't go down. "What did Johnny say?"

Her red-rimmed eyes regarded me with misery. "He doesn't know yet, but there's no doubt in my mind that he'll be thrilled. *If* I tell him."

"What do you mean 'if'?" Perplexed, I stared at her. "He's the father—*of course* you're going to tell him!"

Gianna's jaw set in a determined lock. She stared straight ahead as if she had tunnel vision and refused to look at me. "I don't know if I'm going to have this baby."

Horrified, I watched her for some type of reaction, but there was none. My sister suddenly seemed cold and aloof.

"What are you saying? You'd never do something like that." A baby was a gift. She couldn't just get rid of it like it was yesterday's newspaper. This was my niece or nephew she was talking about. Didn't she realize how lucky she was? "Please tell me you're not serious."

Gianna exhaled sharply and focused on me with a mournful gaze. "I knew you wouldn't understand. You want a child so badly that you can't comprehend why everyone else doesn't feel the same way. I'm not ready for kids, Sal. Johnny wants them, but I didn't make him any promises when we moved in together. In fact, I warned him it might never happen. I felt it was important for our relationship to put my cards on the table at the very beginning."

"You're just like Colin." The name popped out of my mouth before I could stop it. *Oh no.* What had I done? I longed to take it back, but one look at my sister's face told me that the damage had already been done.

Gianna's chocolate brown eyes turned to steel. "Really? You're comparing me to your cheating, lying ex-husband now?"

"Of course not. No, I didn't mean it that way." Resentment started to burn inside me like a flame. *Why can't it be me instead of her?*

Gianna stood and shifted her purse over her shoulder. Her lips were drawn together tightly in a stubborn manner. "It was obviously a mistake to tell you. Next thing I know, you and Mike will be offering to raise this baby for us."

Fighting for self-control, I bit so hard into my lower lip that I tasted blood. "But you have to tell Johnny. It's his child too!"

"It's my body," she said calmly. "This is my decision. And I'd better not find out that you breathed a word of this to him, or I'll never forgive you."

As her eyes clouded over with anguish, I felt about as big as a pin. "No—of course not," I stammered. "I mean, you have to—"

"I thought I could count on your help," she said in a choked-up voice. "You've always been so supportive of me. But it's obvious you can't look past your own hurt now."

Tears crept into the corners of my eyes. "You don't

understand." I should have told her about the test then—how all my hopes and dreams had vanished in three minutes flat. For some reason, I decided not to.

She grabbed her car keys and started for the front door. "Thanks for all the help. It's appreciated more than you know." The bitterness in her tone was apparent.

"Gianna, wait. Please don't leave like this!" I hurried after her and grabbed her arm, but she shook my hand off. Weeping, she ran down the front steps to her car while I stood on the porch watching in shocked silence. She backed out of the driveway with her tires screeching and at such a furious pace that she almost hit Mike as he pulled in.

Oh, no. What had I done? She was right, of course. This was none of my business. I should have been supportive of her and whatever she decided. My heart hurt over what had just transpired between us. Gianna had a tough decision to make, and I hadn't made things any easier for her.

I'd never been jealous of my sister before. She'd always been prettier and smarter, more outgoing than me. She could polish off an entire cheesecake in one sitting and not gain an ounce. These things had never bothered me because I loved her so much. From the moment my mother had laid her in my arms when I was three years old, I'd adored Gianna and always tried to watch out for her. I'd proudly announced to everyone that day that I would always take care of my baby sister. My parents had recorded the moment on a VHS tape they still had around somewhere. Why couldn't I have offered her a few lousy words of encouragement instead of sounding so judgmental?

Because now, after all these years and for the first time ever, I wanted to *be* her.

The smell of smoke permeated my nostrils, and I ran back into the kitchen. I grabbed a potholder and lifted out the pork chops, which were now black around the edges. I turned on the wall fan before the smoke alarm went off. The top crust on the potatoes was a charcoal color as well. Yes, it was a banner day for me. I couldn't even make a decent dinner for my husband. Dejected, I set both items on top of the stove, hung my head, and silently cried.

The screen door opened, and I heard Mike's footsteps in

the living room, his work boots reverberating against the wooden floor. I knew he was behind me but didn't turn around from the stove.

"What's the matter with Gianna?" Mike asked. "She barreled out of the driveway like her car was on fire."

"Nothing." It was the only word I could manage to choke out without crying again.

He put his arms around my waist and buried his lips in my neck. He smelled of sweat and hard work with a hint of his spicy cologne mixed in. "Mmm. Look at my princess, working hard on my dinner." He stared down at the pork chops over my shoulder, his rock-hard chest pressed against my back. His body started to shake with laughter. "They're not supposed to be that color, right?"

"No. I forgot they were in the oven," I said hoarsely.

He kissed me again and chuckled. "Well, I didn't exactly marry you for your cooking skills, so no worries there. We'll order a pizza."

I didn't reply.

Mike slid his hands up inside my shirt. They were warm and gentle as he caressed my skin. "Better yet, why don't we skip dinner for now and go straight to dessert?" His voice was low with a sexy undertone as he kissed my neck again.

I still didn't turn around, praying for some self-control before I did something really stupid, like break the pan over his head in a sudden fit of rage. What was the matter with me?

It must have finally registered with him that something was wrong. "Princess?" He gently turned me around to face him and ran a finger down the side of my face. "You've been crying. What happened?"

"Nothing." I tried to move away, but he refused to let me go.

Mike lifted my chin until our gazes met, and I stared into his dark blue, mesmerizing eyes, which were filled with concern. "Talk to me, baby."

Oh, wrong word to use. I started to sob. "Gianna's pregnant."

His jaw immediately dropped, and a broad smile spread across his handsome face. "Wow, that's fantastic! I'll bet

Johnny's thrilled."

Didn't he understand? His words only caused another pang in my chest. Mike obviously had no idea how much his simple statement hurt me, otherwise he never would have said it. But in my opinion, he *should* have known. *My* husband should have been the one to be thrilled. *I* should have been the one to say those beautiful words to him as we lay in bed with our arms around each other. *We're going to have a baby, honey.*

I stared down at the floor. "He doesn't know yet, so please don't say anything to him. I probably shouldn't have even told you."

"Sure, okay." He wove his fingers through my hair. "Well, don't worry. My lips are sealed. Gee, I wonder if they'll have a boy or a girl? I'll bet Johnny wants a boy."

Anger rose from the pit of my stomach, and for the first time in my life, I wished he would stop talking. My behavior was unreasonable and not sane—I knew this. For some odd reason I wanted Mike to be as upset as I was. Shouldn't we both be angry at the injustices of the world?

"Gianna is less than thrilled. It wasn't exactly planned."

"Oh, she'll come around." He smiled down at me, the love shining through his mesmerizing eyes, but his next words were my undoing. "Holy cow, your mother is going to be so excited. When they tell her, she'll freak out and—"

He didn't finish the sentence because I burst into tears. "Don't." I held up my hand as sobs racked my body. "Please stop."

"Sal." Mike's voice was gentle but firm. His hands went around my waist as I continued to cry. "What's got you so upset?"

"Isn't it obvious?" I snapped. "How can you even ask me that?"

His face dawned with sudden understanding. "Come on. You're not actually jealous of Gianna? That's not like you."

I pushed his hands away and walked over to stand in front of the sink, where I stared out the window into our small, fenced-in yard. Spike was busy digging a hole under the elm tree. He seemed to be having a good time. An anguished wail rose from my throat. "What's wrong with me? Why couldn't it be me? Gianna doesn't even want a baby."

"There's nothing wrong with you." He pressed up against me and wrapped his strong arms around me as I continued to stare miserably out the window. The sun had sunk lower amongst an array of blue and pink streaks in the sky. "It's going to happen, sweetheart. We've only been trying for a year." He turned me around again to face him and gave me that sexy, lopsided grin of his. "But we've sure had fun, right?"

This was when I lost it completely. "You don't get it, do you? You say that you want a baby, but it really doesn't mean that much to you. As long as there's an excuse to fool around, that's what really matters."

He narrowed his eyes. "That's crazy, and you know it. Where is this coming from?"

I was so upset I couldn't see straight. "It isn't fair." I sounded like a pathetic five-year-old who'd dropped her ice cream cone on the sidewalk. "What if I can't get pregnant? Did you ever stop and think about that?"

His face sobered. "Sal, it wouldn't make any difference to me. I'll always love you, whether we have ten kids or none."

"But it makes a difference to me." Large, hot tears gushed down my cheeks, and I made no attempt to stop them this time. "My sister isn't even sure she wants kids. They took precautions, while we never do. Why can't I have the one thing I've always wanted?"

"Sweetheart, please." His voice broke. "I can't stand to see you like this."

With a sniffle, I wiped my eyes and drew a long, ragged breath. "I want to go see a fertility specialist. Maybe they'll be able to tell us what's wrong."

A muscle ticked in Mike's jaw. "Sal, you know I'm not comfortable with those places. God knows what they'd make me do. I've heard about stuff with ice cubes and—I. No, I don't want to do that. At least not yet."

I blew my nose on a napkin. "You're only thinking about yourself. I can't believe you'd be so selfish. Maybe you're like my sister and you don't really want a child either." I tried to walk past him, but he grabbed me by the arm and whirled me around to face him, placing both his hands on my shoulders. His confused look had turned to one of disbelief—and anger.

"You need to stop obsessing over this, okay?" he said. "If for some reason we can't have kids, you've got to learn to accept it. There's always adoption, you know. What's wrong with giving a child who's already on this earth a loving home?"

"Nothing." What he said made total sense. In defense, I wrapped my arms around my stomach—my potentially barren stomach—and had to force myself not to cry again. "I'd love any child, whether it came from me or not. I don't care what color it is, what sex, what its ethnicity is. But I want to experience everything that an expectant mother does. I want to feel my baby kick, be able to nurse him or her, experience morning sickness. Hell, I don't even care about stretch marks!"

Poor Mike's face was baffled. "What do stretch marks have to do with anything?"

"You don't care," I sobbed. "It's not the same for a man."

"Listen to me!" Mike exploded. He cradled my face between his hands. "I hate seeing what this is doing to you. I *do* care. I love you more than anything in this world. I want children—*our* children—but I don't want to end up fighting with you over this. What are you really telling me? That our marriage isn't strong enough to survive if we can't have kids by natural childbirth?"

His words only made me cry harder. "No, it's not that. I love you and can't imagine my life without you in it. But I always thought we'd have kids. I want—I *need* a baby to love. Is that too much to ask?"

Mike's shoulders sagged. I hated the devastated look in his eyes and knew that was my fault as well. I'd succeeded in building a wall between us. He was trying to break it down, but I wouldn't let him. Was I being unreasonable? Maybe, but I couldn't help myself. For a year I'd been telling myself that it would happen and not to worry. But today's results had devastated me. I'd honestly thought I was pregnant. It was as if someone had sucker punched me in the stomach, and I was still trying to recover from the blow. All I wanted to do was curl up in a ball somewhere and feel sorry for myself.

"Sal." He put his arms back around my waist. "Let's wait a little longer before we start running all those tests and putting ourselves through that torture, okay? We could even fill out an adoption application in the meantime. You know what they say. People end up adopting a child, and then—bam! They get pregnant on their own. This isn't the end of the world."

No, but it was a good portion of my world. Shaking my head, I removed his hands from my waist. I didn't want to hear him or be touched right now. "Don't. I need to think this through." I grabbed my purse and car keys from the counter.

"Whoa. Where are you going?" he asked.

"I think it's better if I stay somewhere else tonight."

If I thought Mike was going to let me leave without a fight, I was sorely mistaken. He followed me out to the living room and reached the screen door before me, blocking my path. "Running away isn't going to solve anything. Where the hell are you going? To your parents'?"

"No, they're not back from Vegas yet. Besides, I wouldn't want to involve them or Grandma Rosa in our fight."

"What fight? How did we even get to this point?" he asked in obvious exasperation. "I only wanted some intimate time alone with my beautiful wife."

"I'm going to the bakery. I'll spend the night in the apartment upstairs."

"Damn it, Sal, don't do this!" he pleaded. "Stay here and talk to me. We can work this out."

I removed his hand from the screen and let myself out the door. I turned to stare into his eyes—eyes I'd always adored, ones so breathtakingly beautiful it hurt me to see them in such pain. But I was hurting too. "Please don't follow me. I need to be alone for a while."

Without waiting for his response, I turned and hurried to my car. As I started the engine, I let myself glance over at the front door one more time. Mike stood on the porch, hands in his jeans pockets, watching me. He made no attempt to stop me this time. Maybe I had secretly hoped he would.

My mind was not functioning properly. I was too upset to realize how much I was hurting him too. The memory of his face, haunted and pained, was burned into my brain. Mike looked like he'd suddenly lost his best friend. I loved him more than anything, so why did I want him to suffer too?

Well played, Sal.

CHAPTER SEVENTEEN

————

When I arrived at the bakery, I was relieved to see that Josie's minivan was gone. There were days when she stayed well past our closing time of six o'clock. The woman was dedicated through and through. As much as I loved her, I didn't want to talk to anyone right now.

I had created this disaster. In less than an hour, I'd started a fight with both my sister and my husband. Because I couldn't get pregnant, I'd decided to take it out on them. This was my problem, and I needed to solve it alone.

My heart was heavy as I entered the shop and turned the alarm off. I climbed the stairs to the empty apartment where Allegra had busied herself for those scant few days—making candy and stealing fortune cookies and recipes from me. The glass display case was still there, along with a few of Allegra's personal items. The couch and a small television were the only furniture in the lone bedroom. Heck, maybe I'd lose myself in mindless *Seinfeld* reruns for a while.

My phone buzzed from my jeans pocket. It was probably Mike asking me to come home. With a sigh, I pulled it out and glanced at the screen. My parents' landline. Worried that something might be wrong with my grandmother or Nicoletta, I swiped the screen with my finger. "Grandma, is everything all right?"

"That is what I would like to know." Her voice was calm, but I sensed a certain edge to her tone. "What has happened between you and your sister?"

I shut my eyes. *Oh, good grief.* I hadn't thought Gianna might go to my grandmother, especially since Nicoletta was with her. "She—she's there? Where's Mrs. Gavelli?" Then I placed a hand over my mouth. Maybe Gianna hadn't told my grandmother about her pregnancy. Not that it mattered. She'd probably already guessed what was wrong.

"Nicoletta has been asleep for most of the evening. She was running a slight fever earlier. She did not even know Gianna was here." There was a slight pause, and I sensed a lecture coming on. "What have you done, *cara mia*?"

The lump in my throat grew so large that I feared it might choke me. "I—I can't say."

"You do not have to," she said in a matter-of-fact tone. "I suspected your sister was pregnant, and she confirmed it when she was here. No one else knows yet—only you and me."

"Grandma," I began.

She didn't let me finish. "I know you are upset, my dear. You have dreamed of a child for so many years. But your sister is devastated right now. Gianna needs your support, not your judgment."

I started to weep. "You don't understand. I thought *I* was pregnant."

"You did not think I was aware of this?" she asked. "When you asked for decaf coffee the other day, I knew how your mind was working. Oh, how I hoped you were, but something told me that was not the case."

I blew out a sigh. How I longed to have her intuition. She must have been born with it. "Gianna's not sure she wants to keep the baby. Do you know how this makes me feel?"

"That is not your business," she said curtly. "It is for Gianna to decide. I hope she will decide to tell Johnny, but again, that is not for me to say. Your sister is worried about the pregnancy, but she seemed even more upset about the words she exchanged with you. You have hurt her, *cara mia*."

Her words were a crushing blow. "I didn't mean to," I cried out. "This is hard for me."

"Yes," she agreed. "I know how it must hurt. I love both of you and never want to see either one of you in pain. It makes my heart sad to see two sisters who love each other so deeply fighting like this."

"It was right after I took the test." My voice sounded defensive. "I was upset."

Grandma Rosa sighed into the phone. "Yes, I know. But still, I am very disappointed in you, *cara mia*. Please get some sleep, and we will talk tomorrow."

She clicked off without saying another word.

If she had stabbed me in the heart with a butcher's knife, I doubted it could have hurt any worse. Grief and pain blended together in my chest. I put the phone down and wailed like a wounded animal.

Next to Mike, Grandma Rosa was the other love of my life. She'd done so much for me since I was a child—in some ways, even more than my parents had. The last thing I ever wanted to do was disappoint her. How had I managed to make such a mess of everything? My world was slowly crumbling to pieces around me, and I didn't know how to stop it.

I lay down on the couch but knew sleep wouldn't come. Emotions of heartache, sadness, and anger raced through my veins in a competition to see who would win. Anger seemed to be edging ahead.

I punched the throw pillow, and something crackled from underneath it. I lifted the pillow and found a plastic bag filled with fortune cookies. I stared at it in silence for a moment then started to laugh bitterly. Good old Allegra. Stealing fortune cookies from me and hiding them around her apartment—*my apartment*, in fact. The bag was open slightly, and as a result, the cookies were as hard as rocks. I held the bag between my hands for a minute, thinking of the message I'd received less than a week ago.

A new blessing will be born to your family soon.

Oh, the message had been correct all right. But it had been meant for another family member, not me. *Poor little Sally. No baby for you.* As tears ran down my face again, voices babbled and collided in my head—mocking me for my stupidity, for screwing things up with the people I loved, for making everyone so unhappy. In agony, I covered my ears, but the sound refused to be drowned out.

Anger flared in the bottom of my stomach. With renewed strength, I picked up the fortune cookies and hurled the bag at Allegra's motto on the wall. The motto fell off the hanger and onto the floor. I was left staring at a small gaping hole in the wall.

At first, I didn't comprehend what I was seeing. Allegra had succeeded in doing permanent damage to the wall—one more thing for Mike to fix. She was still finding ways to torment me, even after her death. I walked over to examine the hole, which was barely big enough for me to reach my hand inside. That was when I saw the plastic bag. More fortune cookies? I stretched my fingers forward and pulled it out. Something gold in color glimmered and caught the overhead light. When I realized what it was, I sucked in a deep breath.

The locket that had been left to Grandma Rosa in Allegra's will.

With trembling fingers, I ran my fingers over the metal. This was by no means an expensive piece of jewelry. There were scratch marks on the surface, and the paint was chipped. A skull and crossbones design had been intertwined on the face of it. If Josie was here, she'd have made a sassy comment about Allegra being the devil and this being an appropriate piece of jewelry for her to wear.

I shook the locket, and something rattled on the inside. I found the clasp, pried it open, and an object fell to the floor. I picked up a small silver key and studied it carefully. There was a number on one side—1010—with the letters *CB* underneath it. Colwestern Bank? My heart hammered against my chest. This might be for a security box.

My earlier grief and disappointment were briefly forgotten as I continued to stare at the key in awe, my mind doing cartwheels with possibilities. What did Allegra have in the security box? Was there something inside that might lead me to her killer?

My phone buzzed from the couch where I'd left it, and I glanced down. It must be fate. Brian's name was displayed on the screen. "Hey," I said hoarsely.

There was silence for a moment. "You okay, Sally?"

"Sure, fine." Brian didn't need to know about my temper tantrum. "Actually, I was just about to call you."

"Josie phoned me earlier with the license plate on the Camaro that Enzo Fiato was driving. She said to call you with the information. Is she there with you now?"

"No. What did you find out?"

"Sorry to say, but it's not the same car that hit Allegra."

This with another disappointment. "Are you sure?"

"Positive," Brian said. "Enzo's Camaro is from the late nineties, while the one that hit Allegra was made in the eighties. I'm guessing the vehicle that struck her was probably a show car, perhaps even owned by a collector. I checked out Enzo's Camaro at the hotel where he's staying. The vehicle is pretty much on its last leg. Quick thinking on Josie's part, though."

I blew out a breath. "Um, I need a favor."

Brian sighed heavily into the phone. "Why is it that I immediately start to cringe whenever you say those words?"

Despite everything that had happened today, his words made me smile. "I found a key—I think it might be to a safe deposit box for Allegra's personal items. You could have the bank open it for you, right?"

"Well, I'd have to get an order, but yes, it can be done. What do you think is inside?"

I rubbed my fingers over the skull and crossbones. "I'm not positive. Either money or, hopefully, something that will tell us who killed Allegra and why."

He made a loud harrumphing noise. "I suppose this means you want to be there when it's opened?"

"Well," I hedged, "if you want me to hand over the key, yes, that's pretty much a given. And"—I couldn't believe I was saying this—"if it's something that might help me figure out who killed her, perhaps I could hold on to the items for a day or so?"

"Forget it," he growled. "That's not how it works."

"Can't you make an exception this time?" I pleaded.

Brian cursed under his breath. "What you're asking me to do is illegal, Sally."

I'd gone too far this time. "Sorry, forget I asked. But will you call me in the morning after you've gotten the order?"

He was silent for several seconds. "Sally, I…"

"Yes?"

Brian hesitated on the other end. "Nothing. I'll call you when it's all set up. Do you want me to stop by the bakery and pick you up?"

"That would be great. Thanks, Brian."

After he'd disconnected, I sat there staring down at the phone in my hands. A text had come in from Mike during our conversation. The words, like everything else today, managed to tear at my heart.

Please come home, princess. It's lonely here without you.

I stared down at the message for a long time. Running away solved nothing, and I had to face the facts here. If we couldn't have children, Mike and I would have to deal with it together. Our marriage was a partnership. Did I want to risk destroying our love over this? No. As long as we had each other, we could survive anything. That much I already knew. Despite my attempt to come to terms with this alone, I needed him with me.

With the necklace in my purse, I hurried down the stairs, set the alarm, and locked the door behind me. As I sped off in my car, I realized this was only the beginning of an attempt to solve my problems. I still had to talk to my grandmother and needed to hug my sister and make things right between us. But for now, I only wanted my husband. When I thought back on the ten years we'd been apart because of one stupid mistake, I didn't know how I'd ever survived without him. Those days were long gone. We'd wasted enough time.

Although I hadn't texted back, I sensed that Mike would be waiting for me. When I drove up to our house, I spotted the silhouette of his figure on the front porch, leaning against the building and outlined in darkness. It was as if he'd never moved from the spot two hours earlier. A lamp glowed from inside our front window, welcoming me home.

I shut the car door and sprinted toward the porch as if my life depended on it. Neither of us said a word as we embraced. We held each other for a long time, my head against his chest as I listened to the steady rhythm of his heart. Finally, I lifted my face and stared up into his. "I'm so sorry. Forgive me?"

He kissed me and tenderly brushed a strand of hair back from my face. "There's nothing to forgive, Sal." His voice was gruff. "I'm the one who's sorry. Sorry that I didn't understand your pain. But I promise you, we'll get through this together. All I want is to make you happy."

Tears dripped down my cheeks, and he wiped them

away with the pad of his thumb. "You do. Every day of my life."

CHAPTER EIGHTEEN

———

The next morning after Mike had left for work, I called Gianna's cell, but it went straight to her voice mail. I knew she was in court today and that Johnny had arrived home last night, so maybe she wasn't intentionally avoiding me. I decided not to leave a message since I preferred to speak with her directly.

Business was slow in the shop, and I caught Josie glancing at me worriedly several times. I'd relayed the story of the locket but conveniently left out the part about the pregnancy test. Finally, she dared to broach the dreaded subject. "I'm guessing things didn't go as planned last night," she said.

"That's an understatement." My voice was raw with emotion.

"Do you want to talk about it?" she asked gently.

I shook my head. "Thanks for the offer, but not right now."

She came around to my side of the block table where I was scooping out cookie dough onto a tray and gave me a quick hug but said nothing further. For this, I was truly grateful. Josie knew I'd tell her everything in my own good time.

The morning dragged on until Brian called at noon. "I've got the court order to open the safe deposit box," he said. "Are you free now?"

I put my hand over the phone and went into the back room, where Josie was baking chocolate chip cookies. The warm air smelled of rich chocolate and sugar. "Do you mind if I take off for a little while and run to the bank with Brian?"

Her slim mouth formed into a pout. "Bummer. I want to see what's in the box too!"

"I promise to fill you in as soon as I get back."

While waiting for Brian, I decided to call my grandmother. I held my breath when she answered.

Grandma Rosa greeted me in her usual way. "Hello, *cara mia.*"

"I'm so sorry for the way I acted—it was wrong—please forgive me," I blurted out all in one breath.

She sighed heavily into the phone. "You do not need to apologize to me. But please talk to your sister—she is the one who needs to hear those words."

"I haven't been able to reach her. Is she okay?"

"Johnny came home last night," Grandma Rosa said. "I have not spoken to her since. She said she had a long day ahead of her in court today."

"Oh, right. I'll stop over and see her tonight." A lump lodged in my throat, making talking difficult. "Please don't be angry at me."

"I am not angry with you, *cara mia.* You are in pain but need to look past your own hurt right now and help your sister. She is very confused about what to do."

I blew out a deep breath. "Yes, I promise. I'll do anything I can to help. Does...does Mrs. Gavelli know yet?"

"No. That would only make things worse. It is my opinion that Nicoletta would be thrilled to learn she has a great-grandchild on the way, but she would need some time to get used to the news. She is old-fashioned and would only cause more problems for them." Her voice sounded wistful. "I do hope Gianna decides to tell Johnny, but that is not for me to say."

At least my grandmother had been smart enough not to judge Gianna, unlike myself. "Maybe she'll let me take her out to dinner. Where are you? At Nicoletta's? "

"No, I am at home. Johnny is with Nicoletta at her house. I believe he plans to bring her back to his place tonight. It is not what Gianna needs, but again, this is not my business."

"I can't imagine what she's going through." How could I? I'd never been pregnant and wanted children so badly that it was hard for me to look at the situation and be objective. Still, I loved my sister and vowed to support whatever decision she made.

"I have made you a new tablecloth for the bakery," Grandma Rosa announced out of the blue. "Your other one is ripped at the corners. I will drop it off before my poker game at Lucia's house."

"Oh, is she hosting this time?" My grandmother and a few of her friends, including Nicoletta, played cards once a week or whenever their schedules allowed. They also rotated locations.

Grandma Rosa sniffed into the phone. "I do not like to play at her house. I think she hides cards under her table because she always wins. They would all like some of your fortune cookies, so I will pick them up when I drop off the tablecloth."

"Of course." Relief flooded through me, and I was happy she didn't seem to be upset any longer. Two down, one to go. "I'll leave some on the table in the back room. We may close up a little early tonight—it's been dead anyway. Plus, I want to see Gianna. Do you still have the key to the bakery, and do you need the alarm code?"

She sounded surprised. "Well, of course I still have it. I am old but not abstract minded, *cara mia*."

I had to think about this one for a minute. "Do you mean absentminded?"

"Yes, I like that too." She paused for a few seconds. "Have you found out anything else about Allegra's death?"

"Not yet," I said. "I did find your locket hidden in the upstairs apartment last night. Guess what? There was a safe deposit key inside. Please don't say anything to Mrs. Gavelli about it for now."

Grandma Rosa clucked her tongue. "That explains it, then. Allegra was leaving a clue for us to follow. Perhaps it will lead to her killer. Call me when you know more."

"I will." The weight on my chest had started to dissipate. "I'm so glad you're not angry with me anymore."

"I never said I was angry with you, my beauty, only disappointed. I know how much you long for a child, and it saddens me that you are going through this. You must have faith that it will happen eventually. Your sister needs our love and support right now. I adore both my granddaughters and only want their happiness. She is your flesh and blood. Be good to each other, and always support one another. *Capisce*?"

"Yes, I promise." I sniffled into the phone as she clicked off.

Josie came into the front room with a tray of butter cookies for the case. "Everything okay?"

"It's all good." I couldn't get into further details with Josie about the conversation without divulging the news that Gianna was pregnant. Knowing my sister as I did, she wouldn't want me to say anything until she'd decided what she was going to do with the baby. My heart still hurt when I thought about it, but like Grandma had said, it wasn't my decision to make.

Fortunately, I was spared from further conversation by Brian's cruiser pulling up to the curb. I tossed my apron and cap on the counter. "I won't be long."

Josie crossed her fingers and held them above her head. "Good luck. Hope you find something that will help."

"Me too."

I got into the front seat with Brian, and we took off. Except for a brief nod to me, he stared straight ahead, and the ride was eerily quiet. When we stopped for a red light, I glanced sideways at him. "Something wrong?"

The color rose in his neck. "No."

"How's Ally doing?"

The light turned green, and Brian's jaw tightened as the car moved forward. "Ally's fine. She...she's kind of been hinting around about an engagement ring."

"Oh." That didn't seem unusual to me since they'd been dating for a year. "Need some help picking one out?"

Brian pulled into Colwestern Bank's parking lot and then turned to look at me. There was something masked in those brilliant green eyes of his—a hint of sadness carefully hidden behind them. "I'm not quite sure I'm ready for marriage. I mean, I definitely want to have a family someday." He blew out a breath and looked away. "I love Ally, but I'm not sure that I'm *in* love with her. Does that make sense?"

"Yes, totally." It was how I'd secretly felt about Colin when we'd married, although I didn't bother to explain that now.

Brian stared at me so intently that my skin started to heat from his gaze. It was almost as if I had a premonition of what he was going to say and desperately prayed that I was wrong.

"There's still someone else I can't completely get out of my head."

Oh, God. My heart sank at Brian's words. I'd thought for sure that his feelings for me had died long ago. My cheeks burned with discomfort, but I forced myself to look straight into his forlorn face while struggling to keep my composure. "Well, perhaps you should try a little harder, then."

Brian nodded without speaking, and we both got out of his vehicle. My level of discomfort soared like the blazing sun above us. I loved Brian as a friend, but nothing more. He had always been good to me, and there were undoubtedly many times he could have slapped handcuffs on my wrists for obstructing justice. There was only one man I had ever truly loved, and that would not change. Brian was aware of this, but I also knew from my previous marriage that feelings didn't always obey the law. Sadly enough, it was Ally, not Brian, whom I felt more compassion for right now.

Brian asked for the bank manager, a Mr. Wallace, and then showed him the search warrant he'd obtained. He explained that the contents might divulge suspects of a recent homicide. Since Brian was the law, his sworn statement was all that was needed. We were shown into a small room at the rear of the building that held a round, wooden conference table and plush, red velvet chairs. We sat down next to each other and waited for Mr. Wallace to return. He reappeared a couple of minutes later carrying a long, narrow box between his hands. He placed it on the table in front of Brian.

Mr. Wallace raised his eyebrows at me in somewhat of a curious manner then returned his attention to Brian. "Please let me know if I can assist you in any other way, Officer."

"Thanks for your help," Brian said.

After Mr. Wallace had left the room, I placed the key in Brian's outstretched hand. "I thought he'd have to stay while you opened it."

He shook his head and grinned. "Nope. There could be evidence in there that I don't want him to see."

"Well, he didn't like it that I was here with you."

His eyes rested on my face for a moment. He was careful to look away as he fumbled with the lock. "It doesn't matter what he likes. I'm allowed to have anyone I want in here with me. It's one of the perks of my job."

Brian lifted the lid as I leaned over his arm. My heart started to pound in excitement and then stopped when I noticed a lone manila envelope inside. I wasn't sure what I'd expected to find. Jewelry? Money? A stash of fortune cookies?

Brian opened the envelope and took out a handful of pictures. His jaw immediately dropped. "Holy blackmail, Batman."

The photo he handed me was of a man and woman in bed together. I couldn't see the woman's face from the particular angle, but the man's was in full view. He was good-looking, late forties or so, his dark hair peppered with gray, and a scruff of a beard surrounded his mouth. It was apparent from the shot that his body was well toned and muscular. I stared at the man's face critically. "He looks familiar."

Brian raised his eyebrows in surprise. "You don't know who it is?"

I shook my head.

"It's Senator Ambrose."

Holy crap. I put a hand to my mouth in horror as Brian showed me the next photo. I couldn't see the woman's face in this shot either, but it was definitely not Lena. This woman's hair was longer, darker, and she had one of those perfect bodies that I would have killed for. Bad choice of words.

"Oh, my God. Why would Allegra have these photos? Did she know about Martin's affair and was blackmailing him?" Poor Lena. "Was she going to tell her niece?"

"It looks that way." He turned the photo over and glanced at the stamp on the back. "This picture is only four months old." Brian stared grimly at the next photo, and then his face reddened with discomfort. Hastily, he passed it to me, and my cheeks flamed as well. Both lovers were clearly naked in this photo, displaying more than I was interested in seeing. God, this was embarrassing. "Can he be arrested?"

Brian gave me a strange look. "On what grounds?"

"He must be the one who killed Allegra."

"This isn't any proof," Brian said. "Maybe Allegra *was* blackmailing him, but we don't know that for certain. All it proves is that the guy—this so-called high-power political figure—is a sleaze and was cheating on his wife. Personally, I always wondered about him. He seemed too good to be true—I figured there had to be a dark side to him."

I racked my brain, trying to decide what to do next. "If Martin knows someone else has the pictures, maybe he'll come clean."

"No." Brian's tone was firm. "It's dangerous. Besides, I have to confiscate these pictures, so don't even think about it."

Of all the rotten luck. What good would the pictures do me if the police had them?

Brian's cell buzzed. He glanced down at the screen and frowned. "It's my boss. Hang on. I've got to take this."

"Sure, no problem." I watched as he walked to the other side of the room, his back to me. I reached into my jeans pocket and then realized I'd left my phone on the bakery counter. *Head thunk.* Some detective I was. How could I get copies of the photos now?

I thumbed through the rest of the photos. There were eight of them total, and I wondered who had taken them. Allegra? No, unless she had a powerful camera *and* was a Peeping Tom. That was too creepy to imagine. Maybe she had paid a photographer to shoot them. Out of all the photos, there was only one that gave a clear shot of the woman's face, and I stared at it intently.

She was lovely, an exquisite beauty. Her dark curly hair was past her shoulders and framed her perfect, heart-shaped face. The woman's eyes were huge and exotic looking, almond-shaped with long lashes, and her dark red lips were full and pouty. My entire body went rigid as recognition set in.

The woman was Violet.

CHAPTER NINETEEN

Brian was still talking to his boss, so I didn't think he'd seen the photo in my hand. I wasn't even sure he knew what Violet looked like.

One little photograph... It wouldn't be missed, right? Plus, it might help me get some answers. What was Brian going to do with them anyway? He'd only keep the photos for evidence. Martin was a sleaze, but this wasn't anything he could be arrested for...yet. There was no actual proof that he'd been the one to mow Allegra down. Lena said he'd been in New York City that day, but what if he'd managed to get back into Colwestern unnoticed?

Brian nodded and wrote something on a small pad of paper. I scooped the photo up and slipped it into my purse before he said good-bye and turned around. Our eyes met, and for a moment, I thought I was busted. He reattached the phone to his belt and came over to the table, then picked up the photographs.

"Sorry, Sally," he said. "I'm sure you'd like to be able to take a few of these, but I have to give the judge a return."

"What's a return?"

"A document that states what was removed from the safe deposit box." He placed the pictures back into the envelope and shut the lid on the box.

"Are you going to talk to the senator?" I asked.

Brian cocked a well-defined eyebrow at me. "I can have a chat with him, but don't expect too much. He'll most likely claim that he has no idea how Allegra got the photos. We don't know for certain that she was blackmailing him, either."

My grandmother wanted me to help find out who did this to Allegra. She hated seeing Nicoletta so distraught over her death. Perhaps this was affecting Nicoletta's remission as well. I loved my grandmother and would do anything she asked of me. It still hurt to think how I'd disappointed her. Maybe I felt I had to redeem myself in her eyes. What harm would it do if *I* asked the senator a few questions?

Brian must have guessed what direction my mind was running in as we left the bank. "Don't even think about it, Sally. If you go see Martin Ambrose, I will *not* be happy."

I flashed him a sly smile. "So what else is new?"

His mouth twitched at the corners. "Please let us handle it, okay? We'll talk to him, and I promise to let you know everything we find out."

He pulled his car over to the curb in front of the bakery.

"Want to come in for coffee and one of your favorite chocolate chip cookies? Josie made a fresh batch this morning." I'd never known him to refuse one before.

His bright green gaze observed me thoughtfully for a moment. "I would, but my boss needs me back at the station. Raincheck?"

"Sure. Thanks for letting me tag along."

Brian gave me one last long look, and the cruiser sped away.

The bells on the front door of my shop jingled away merrily as they announced my entrance. Josie was chatting with a woman at one of the tables. There was a large photo album spread open between them that held pictures of cakes and cookies Josie had designed for special occasions. She'd even made my wedding cake, a one-of-a-kind cookies and cream sensation. As far as I was concerned, she could bake anything she wanted to, and it didn't have to profit the bakery. The cakes helped Josie and her family out financially, and without her, I wouldn't even have a business.

The woman at the table turned around when she heard the bells and smiled up at me. "Hi, Sally."

Lena. Crap. Why did I always have the worst luck? How could I look this woman in the face after what I'd discovered about her husband? "Uh, hi, Lena."

"Lena wants me to make a cake for her husband's birthday," Josie explained. The bakery phone rang from the back room, and she rose to her feet. "Let me grab that. I forgot to charge my cell and think it's my kid calling. Well, one of them," she laughed. "Excuse me for a second?"

"Of course." Lena stretched her long legs out in front of her under the table and then smiled coyly at me. "Sit down, Sally. Tell me all about your trip to Vegas."

Talk about your uncomfortable moments. "Sure." Reluctantly, I sat in Josie's vacant seat.

Lena sipped from the paper cup of coffee in front of her. "Did you get a chance to see Violet while you were there?"

Well, not quite like your husband did. "Yes, we saw her."

"Did she offer any useful information?" Lena asked. "Did she know why someone might have wanted Allegra dead?"

I sidestepped her question. "Lena, the day that Allegra got run down—did Martin happen to be in town?"

She shot me a puzzled look. "No. I thought I told you he was in New York City. As a matter of fact, he just got back yesterday. Why do you ask?"

I couldn't bear to show Lena the photo. It would be a huge shock to her system. Perhaps it might be easier for Lena if I just told her instead. When I'd walked in on Colin in bed with my high school nemesis, I'd been frozen with shock. Although I had managed to forgive him since his death, I'd also discovered that it didn't matter how many years had passed—I'd never erase the mental image from my brain. Maybe I hoped to spare her some of the pain I'd experienced. Lena obviously adored Martin, and this was going to turn her entire world upside down.

"I…think that I know why Allegra was killed. She was blackmailing someone," I said slowly.

Lena narrowed her eyes. "What are you trying to say? You think my aunt was blackmailing Martin?"

I didn't respond, and as it turned out, there was no need to. As usual, my face had given me away.

Her nostrils flared in anger, and she hastily rose to her feet. "Why would you even think that? What proof could you possibly have?"

What a mess. I didn't want to be the one to tell her that her husband was unfaithful, and with her cousin of all people.

Would she confront Martin and secretly be grateful for the news? Doubtful. Or maybe she'd refuse to believe it and live in denial? I was guessing the latter. With a deep breath, I took the plunge. "Lena, I found photographs of Martin with...another woman."

"Liar," she rasped out and then turned her face away. "Martin loves me. He'd never cheat."

Yep, denial. "There's no reason for me to lie to you, Lena."

Her face turned the color of flames. "Where are these so-called pictures? Give them to me right now."

It probably wasn't a good idea to tell her the police had them. "I don't have them with me at the moment."

"*Right.*" A small smile played on her lips. "What are you really after? Money from us? A job for your husband in Martin's firm? God, you're despicable." She picked up her handbag and started toward the front door.

"Lena, wait!" I called urgently. She whirled around, one hand on the door. "Please believe me. I'm not lying and can even tell you who the woman is."

She glared at me with contempt. "Who?"

"Violet."

Lena stood there motionless for several seconds. Her face looked as if it had been carved out of stone. Finally, she spoke. "Where are the pictures so I can see for myself?"

I couldn't blame her for asking. Heck, if I was in her place, I'd want to know for certain too. "I can't give them to you, Lena, because Martin is a suspect in Allegra's murder."

She barked out a laugh. "That's insane. Martin wouldn't hurt a fly. It must be someone who looks like him. Now give me those pictures. Don't you dare hand them over to the police."

Man, she really was in denial. "I can't give them to you, Lena. I'm sorry."

"Oh, you haven't begun to be sorry," she breathed in a venomous tone. "You're going to be so, so sorry that you ever tangled with us." She pushed on the door so furiously that it whipped around and slammed into the building. The bells on the door clanged loudly in my head as I watched her rush across the street to her BMW.

Josie came running up behind me. "What the hell

happened?"

"Brian and I found pictures in Allegra's lockbox of Martin and Violet—in, uh, some compromising positions."

"Oh, my God." Josie muttered an expletive under her breath. "Are you serious?"

"Afraid so." I pulled out the business card that Lena had given me when we were in her office last week.

"Who are you calling?"

I put a finger to my lips. "Yes, is Senator Ambrose in?"

"Sal! What are you—"

Annoyed, I waved my hand furiously at Josie. "Okay, yes. No message. Thanks."

Josie thrust her lower lip out at me. "Okay. What have you got up your sleeve, partner?"

I put the *Closed* sign on the door. "It's after four o'clock, and Tuesday is always slow anyway. How about we close early and go pay a little visit to our favorite senator? His secretary said he's in the office this afternoon."

The freckles stood out on Josie's face. "He's an important political figure. We can't exactly walk right in."

I grabbed my purse off the table and headed for the back door. "Come on. Something tells me he'll see us. Especially when I tell him that it involves certain photographs."

"We can't just leave now," Josie protested. "Mrs. Hershey is coming to pick up her cookie order at five o'clock."

"Shoot." There was no way I wanted to confront this guy alone, and who knew how much longer he might be there. "I think I have a solution." I whipped out my phone again, pressed a button, and Grandma Rosa answered on the first ring.

"*Cara mia*, do you and Mike want to come for dinner?" she asked.

"Thanks, Grandma, but Mike's working late," I said. "Josie and I are closing up early. We have a little more snooping to do into Allegra's death. Would you be able to come by and wait for a customer to pick up her cookie basket? It's in the back room, and she'll be here at five. It's for Mrs. Hershey."

"Of course. I was coming over anyway to get the fortune cookies. You need to get to the bottom of this my dear, for Nicoletta at least. I will wait for Mrs. Hershey and leave the tablecloth on the counter."

"Wonderful—thank you so much, Grandma."

"All set?" Josie asked as I clicked off.

We stepped into the alley, and I glanced around. "Yeah. For the record, I don't think we'll be there long." Martin was certain to throw us out. "Where's your van?"

"In the shop," Josie replied. "I need new brakes. Rob dropped me off this morning."

I dug into my purse for keys. "Well, when we get done, I'll take you home."

"Perfect," she said and got into the passenger seat. "I was going to have my mother-in-law pick me up. Danny's got a baseball game tonight. Now I'll be able to ride over with everyone else."

After I was settled behind the wheel, I took the picture out and showed it to Josie. She blew out a long breath. "Wow. That might ruin his entire career if it leaks out."

"And Lena's meal ticket," I added. "Maybe she's afraid of losing it. Why else would she deny it?"

"Some women just can't face the truth," Josie remarked.

I started the engine. "Well, I guess I can't blame her. It's pretty pathetic when your husband is sleeping with your own cousin. That's even worse than your husband sleeping with your high school nemesis."

"If *my* husband ever cheats, I'll stick his head in the oven and bake a batch of cookies around it," Josie declared. "But hey, that's just me." She watched as I struggled to shift the vehicle into gear. "What's wrong?"

We started to slowly move forward. "I can't believe I'm having problems with this car already. It slipped from park into drive, and that's the third time this week. Mike thinks there's a problem with the transmission. I've got to have it looked at tomorrow."

"This sure isn't our week for vehicles," Josie mused. "Okay, I can pick you up in the morning if you want, and then we'll drop your car at the repair shop. Now, getting back to Lena. If she knew Brian had the photographs, she would have sung another tune. Hey, why are you going that way? I thought Martin's office was in Buffalo?"

"He's at his law firm today—that's where I called. Even though he doesn't practice, it seems that he likes to hang out there most days."

Ten minutes later we arrived at the building and rode the glass-paneled elevator up to the 13th floor, which seemed to be devoted entirely to Martin. A blonde woman in a tight, short red dress was sitting at a desk in front of a double set of doors. Martin's name was embossed in block, gold letters on them. The blonde looked young enough to be in high school. She glanced up at us and put away the nail file she'd been using.

"Hi, we were wondering if we could see Senator Ambrose for a minute," I said.

She batted long fake eyelashes at us and spoke in a high-pitched, squeaky voice. "Do you have an appointment?"

I shook my head. "Please tell him that we're friends of Allegra and Violet Fiato."

"Sal," Josie whispered nervously in my ear as the blonde trotted into Martin's office. "I'm feeling a little weird about this. It's kind of like playing in deep water when you can't swim. What if this backfires on us? He's a freaking senator, for crying out loud."

"I don't care." Even though Mike and I had made up and Grandma Rosa was no longer upset with me, I was still angry at the cruel hand fate had dealt me yesterday. I wasn't thinking straight and personally didn't give a damn about the photographs. But I'd promised my grandmother I'd help, and there was no way I was going to let her down again.

The blonde reappeared and held the door open for us. "Senator Ambrose has a few minutes between meetings and said that he'll see you now."

"Thank you." We walked inside, and she closed the doors behind us.

Martin's impressive quarters made Lena's suave office pale in comparison. His office had a layout similar to a high-rise apartment's. The open floor plan held a wet bar, living and dining area, and a small kitchen that looked to be stocked with all the amenities. There was even a treadmill and exercise bicycle stationed in front of a 70-inch, high-definition television. Abstract paintings covered the paneled walls above the built-in mahogany bookcases.

I knew from newspaper articles I'd read that Martin was close to fifty in age. He had a solid, toned build to his body and was extremely good-looking. His short black hair was sprinkled with silver throughout, his face tanned and lean. His piercing gray eyes were cold as he observed us.

He nodded at the two plush chairs in front of his desk. "Please sit down," he said curtly.

Uneasiness settled into my bones as Martin continued to watch our every move. Josie stood very still, waiting to see what I was going to do first.

I shook my head at the man. "Thanks, but we're fine standing."

"All right, let's cut to the chase. Where are the pictures?" Martin snapped.

CHAPTER TWENTY

———

My mouth fell open in amazement. Lena had told him *already*? Why would she protect a man who was cheating on her? "Ah, I don't have them with me."

Martin swiftly rose to his feet and came around the desk. He shot Josie a distasteful look, and then his gaze shifted to me. His eyes narrowed in contempt. "What do you really want? Money?"

There was no reason to beat around the bush, and I had hoped to gauge his reaction with my next words anyway. "You killed Allegra. You ran her over so that she'd stay quiet about the photos."

He threw his head back and laughed. "I wasn't even in town the day the woman died. Besides, it was an accident, right? Still, I'll admit I was delighted to hear the news. God, how I hated that old hag."

"It wasn't an accident," I said evenly. "There's proof to attest to that as well."

A muscle ticked in Martin's jaw. "As I already stated, I don't know anything about that. Now it's probably best that you and your friend leave, unless you prefer to have security escort you out."

"Why did Lena tell you about the pictures?" Josie asked.

Veins bulged in his thick neck. "Don't mention my wife again," he hissed and took a step toward her. I wasted no time inserting my body between theirs.

Josie clutched at my arm. "Come on Sal—let's go."

"Yeah, Sal," he mocked. "Get out while you still have a chance."

This man was a powerful force and not one to be taken

lightly, but I didn't care anymore. What was happening to me? I wasn't sure where my bravery—or perhaps stupidity—had come from, but I was tired of people pushing my loved ones and me around. Martin thought that because of his political position, he had the right to intimidate whomever he pleased. After everything that had happened in the last couple of days, something inside me had changed. I was determined to fight for justice and see Allegra's killer pay. It was time to take a stand.

"Did you hear what I said?" Martin asked. Without waiting for an answer, he sauntered behind his desk, picked up the phone, and gave us one last defiant look.

"Sal," Josie pleaded as she tried to pull me toward the door. "He means it."

It wouldn't help for Josie and me to wind up behind bars. The most logical thing was to call Brian—who would be furious that I'd come here—and let the police take over. "Fine. We're leaving."

Martin folded his arms over his chest and stared down his nose at us. "A wise decision, ladies. And don't come back—unless you actually have something to back up your claim."

I didn't respond as Josie pushed me out the door. When she turned to shut it, I was treated to one last view of Martin, standing behind his desk and glaring back at me in return. Those cold, calculating eyes continued to follow me in my mind as we rode downstairs in the elevator.

"Holy crap." Josie wiped her hand across her forehead. "That guy gave me the willies. He's always sweet as sugar when you see him on TV."

"Politicians are trained to be that way," I murmured.

"So what now? We call Brian, and hopefully this guy is arrested for murder?" Josie asked as I beeped my car door open and we got inside. "Hey, what's wrong with you?"

"I'm not sure," I confessed. "Something here doesn't add up. Why would Allegra blackmail him when her own daughter was involved? Why didn't she just destroy the pictures instead?"

Josie shrugged her slim shoulders. "That is kind of weird. But the old woman didn't care about anyone, her kids included. You are going to call Brian, right?"

"Yes, as soon as I drop you off. Then I'm going to let

this go for a while. I want to see if Gianna's available for dinner, then spend a quiet evening alone with my husband."

She reached over to squeeze my hand. "Sal, I'm so sorry about the test."

I refused to look at her as I pulled into her driveway. "Thanks. I appreciate that."

Josie unfastened her seat belt and reached over to envelope me in a tight hug. "You need to keep the faith, honey. One of these days it will be positive. Probably when you least expect it." She smiled wryly. "It happens like that for a lot of us."

She meant well, but her words brought all the pain back from last night. I took a moment to steady my voice. "I got really upset. Mike and I had an argument, and even Gianna and I had words. It's a good thing you didn't call me back, or I probably would have bitten your head off too."

Josie gave me a sympathetic smile. "It's okay. God knows I've snapped at you enough times. Hey, that's what friends are for. Remember, you don't have to keep this all bottled up inside of you."

That got a laugh out of me. "Oh, I didn't, believe me."

"Think good thoughts, honey," she said and opened the car door. "I'm always available if you need to talk, any time of day or night. Got it?"

How lucky I was to have her for a friend. "Same here."

The front door of Josie's house opened, and a menagerie of boys in various sizes tumbled out, accompanied by Rob. They were all loaded down with snacks, water bottles, and baseball equipment.

"I'd better let you go so that you can get to Danny's game. Good luck."

"Thanks. Call me later and let me know what Brian says?"

"Will do. Have fun with the gang."

I watched Josie rush toward them and start organizing everything and everyone into Rob's car. The kids turned to wave at me. I smiled and waved back but was aware of a dull ache spreading across my chest.

Damn it. Now I was jealous of my best friend too? But this was nothing new. I'd always envied her those beautiful kids.

Sadness started to overwhelm me again. Would that ever be Mike and me someday? In desperation, I shook it off. This solved nothing. I drove down the street and tried to collect my thoughts. No sense in crying over spilled chocolate chips again. I had to think positive—someday I would have a child to love.

My phone buzzed as I waited at a traffic light. I glanced down to where it rested in the console and saw Brian's name pop up on the screen. The light turned green, and I quickly pulled over to the side of the road to pick up. "Hey."

"Sally." Brian's voice was grim. "We found the Camaro that hit Mrs. Fiato."

I clutched the phone tightly between my hands. "Is it licensed to the senator?"

"No," he said, "but it is licensed to a colleague of his by the name of Richard Gallagher. He's an attorney who works at Martin's firm, and he collects classic cars. The interesting part is that Richard only got back into town today. He's been in Aruba on his honeymoon for the past two weeks."

My eyebrows drew together at his words. "I don't understand. Did someone else use Richard's car, or is he lying?"

"He's not lying," Brian said. "His plane records check out. When questioned, he claimed he left the car in the parking garage of Ambrose's law firm while he was gone. Employees park there for free. He left a spare set of keys with Martin's secretary in case the vehicle needed to be moved during his absence."

My brain started to work overtime. "So anyone in the office could have taken those keys."

"If they knew they were there, yes," Brian agreed.

It had to have been the senator. He must have returned to town, taken the car, and run Allegra down. "So maybe he never went to New York City that day? Or he returned and then went back?"

"Ambrose was definitely in New York City, but it is possible he left a day later. We haven't been able to find any eyewitnesses who saw him the day Allegra was hit. There were no plane records either, although he could have taken the train."

"He must have pretended to go but actually left a day later," I mused, "or right after he ran Allegra down."

Brian's tone became terse. "By the way, Little Miss Snoop. We went to Martin's office to have a chat with him, but his secretary said he left abruptly. Coincidentally, it was right after two attractive females—a brunette and a redhead—stopped by to see him, unannounced. He told his secretary he was ill and had to go home."

Crap. I was busted.

Brian breathed so noisily on the other end of the line that I was afraid he might hyperventilate. "You don't happen to know *who* his visitors were, do you, Sally?"

There was no point in even attempting to lie to him. "Oh, fine. It was Josie and me."

Brian cursed in a loud voice—something he didn't usually do—and the word made me cringe. "What's the matter with you, Sally! You guys could have screwed everything up."

"Look, I'm sorry. Lena was at the bakery this afternoon when you dropped me off. She was ordering a cake for Martin's birthday and asked about our trip to Vegas. One thing kind of led to another. She was furious when I told her about the pictures, and now she wants them. I don't know if or what she told Martin, but he seemed to know exactly what had happened when we got to his office."

"Why would she do that?" Brian asked, sounding puzzled. "It doesn't make sense."

"No idea. I suppose Allegra could have told him, too. My parents saw them arguing shortly before she died. That entire family sounds pretty messed up if you ask me. Maybe Lena doesn't care about the cheating part and is afraid Martin will leave her high and dry. Or she could be desperately in love with him."

Brian snickered. "Or just desperate, from the sound of things. Look, we're going to put an APB out on him and bring him into the station for questioning. Please stay out of trouble now, okay? This is a powerful man we're talking about, and powerful can also mean dangerous. Which leads me to something else."

Uh-oh. I knew what was coming. "What's that?"

"I know there's a photo missing. How stupid do you think I am? You have at least one in your possession, and that's tampering with police evidence, Sally. I should throw you in jail."

I sucked in a deep breath. Yes, I'd known Brian would be mad, and no, I certainly didn't think he was stupid. "You're right, and I'm sorry. I haven't been thinking very rationally the past couple of days. Believe me, I'd like nothing better than to disengage myself from this whole mess. I promised my grandmother I'd help, but to be honest, I almost wish I'd never agreed. You can stop by my house if you want the picture, or I'm happy to bring it to you."

There was silence for several seconds. "I'm sorry. Who are you, and what have you done with Sally Donovan?"

In spite of everything, I laughed. "It wasn't my intention to make things more difficult for you, honest. I promise to take a step back."

"Well, I'd appreciate that. For my part, I promise to keep you updated on anything we might find out. Now go home and do something that's not related to snooping. Make cookies, play with the dog, watch a chick flick, whatever. You're wearing me out." He clicked off before I could say another word.

As I started to put the car back into drive, my phone pinged with an incoming text. Puzzled, I stared down at it, not comprehending the words at first. It was from a private number with no name attached, and there were only four words on the screen.

Your granny needs you.

Another message instantly appeared on the screen, and my insides filled with dread as I read it.

Come to the bakery and bring the pictures. Make sure you're alone. If you call the police or anyone else, I'll kill your grandmother.

My entire body started to shake. No, this couldn't be. *It's just a hoax—some type of sick joke. Grandma Rosa's safe at home—oh, dear Lord.* She was going to the bakery to wait for Mrs. Hershey. In desperation, I fumbled with the phone and started typing my parents' number in by hand. As I pressed the digits, my phone pinged with another incoming text.

Enter through the alley. You'll be searched, and if I find weapons or your phone, both of you will die. You can watch me kill her first. Follow directions, and I'll let Granny go upon your arrival.

I opened my mouth to scream, but no sound came out. Sweat trickled down the small of my back. Breathing heavily, I continued to stare at the text, unsure what to do next.

Another message popped up. *Are you there? Do you understand? Type back Y, or we will have a problem.*

Before I could follow through, my phone pinged again. Damn it! This person was torturing me and most likely enjoying it too.

This time there was no message. A lone picture was attached of a woman lying on her side on a floor that I recognized as the blue vinyl tile of my bakery. The woman's eyes were closed, as if she was sleeping. It was definitely my grandmother.

A sob escaped from my throat. *No, no, no! This can't be happening. Dear God, please let her be all right.*

At that moment I realized who was responsible for hurting my grandmother and had also killed Allegra. I wasn't positive about the motive yet, although I had a good idea. But I was convinced I knew the identity of the killer.

With shaking fingers, I typed and then had to retype my message. *Y. Please don't hurt her. I'll do whatever you say.*

I pressed *Send*, and the response came back within seconds.

You have ten minutes to get here.

I was just around the corner from Josie's street and didn't see how I could make it by then. My heart pounded as I typed another message. *It will take me closer to fifteen.*

Ten minutes or she dies. You'd better drive fast.

Cold, stark fear flooded my body. Sadly, there were no choices for me. Sure, I could call Mike or Brian, but there was no way I would compromise my grandmother's safety.

I no longer cared about the lousy photographs. Yes, I was sorry that Allegra had died because of them, but this was my grandmother we were talking about. I loved this woman more than life itself. She had done so much for me in my thirty years on this earth. If she lost her life because of me, I'd never forgive myself, and it would haunt me for the rest of mine.

I couldn't even remember the drive or how fast I went. Several drivers honked at me, and there were flashes of red on a few traffic lights, but I didn't lessen my speed. The journey seemed to have no end.

What would I do if a cop chased me? Suppose they followed me to the bakery and the psycho inside killed Grandma Rosa before I arrived? There was a chance that neither one of us would make it out of this alive, but I had to do what I could to save her.

I drove into the alley behind the bakery and shut the engine off. My legs shook like Jell-O as I got out of the car. With trepidation I started to move forward, knowing without a doubt that the monster was watching me from behind the door. It was open a small crack. I'd left my phone, purse, and all keys, except the one to the bakery, in the car as instructed. There was nothing on me that I could use to defend myself. Hot tears stung the back of my eyes, and with frustration, I wiped them away. This wouldn't do. I'd stared death in the face before, but it might beat me this time. As long as Grandma Rosa was okay, that was all that mattered.

As I approached the door, I spotted the barrel of a revolver poking out from the other side and someone said, "Hands in the air."

My earlier suspicion was confirmed when I heard the voice. Having no choice, I obeyed the command. The senator's powerful empire might crumble around him if the pictures got out, but there was someone else who had just as much, if not more, to lose.

The door opened farther, allowing me entrance. As soon as I had stepped into the kitchen area, it shut and locked behind me. I turned to stare into the face of Allegra's killer. "Don't do this," I begged.

There was no answer as Grandma's captor patted me down with one hand while the other was wrapped around the revolver, pointed strategically at my head.

"Please," I whispered, "let my grandmother go, Lena."

CHAPTER TWENTY-ONE

———

Grandma Rosa lay on the floor, motionless. She was pale and lifeless, and I feared the worst.

"What did you do to her?" I screamed and rushed to my grandmother's side. Thankfully she was breathing, but it was faint and sporadic. I dropped to my knees besides her and shook her gently. "Grandma, please wake up." Then I noticed the bloody bump on the back of her head and brought a hand to my mouth in horror. Something inside me snapped when I turned to face Lena. "What kind of a person hits an elderly woman?"

"Relax, she's fine," Lean scoffed. "I'd been casing the joint, waiting for you to come back so that I could make you talk. Imagine my surprise when Granny showed up instead. After a woman walked out with a large tray of cookies, I said to myself, hey, this is even better. Now I can use Granny as bait to lure Sally here. So I left my car down the street and snuck into the alley where hers was parked. When she came out the door and tried to lock it, I let her have it. She never saw me, which was even better."

"Monster," I spat out. "If you weren't holding that gun, I'd claw your eyes out."

"Ooh, scary stuff there," she laughed. "She'll wake up in a little while, but by then I'll be gone, and you'll be—oops! Dead. You just sacrificed your life for your granny's. What a noble, selfless thing to do. I mean, you've got your entire life to look forward to while she's got what—a handful of years left?" Lena shook her head in disbelief. "Damn. You certainly didn't come from *my* family."

I placed a protective hand on Grandma Rosa's shoulder. "That's what happens when you truly love someone. You care more about their happiness than your own. But I suspect you don't know anything about that."

"Careful," she warned, "you don't want to get on my bad side today."

She actually had a good side? "My grandmother doesn't have a mean bone in her body. How could you do such a thing?"

She waved a hand as if bored with me already. "Never mind. Where are the pictures?"

Despite how worried I'd been on the drive about my grandmother, I'd tried to concoct a plan that would at least insure her safety. I knew my life was already hanging by a fingernail but wasn't taking any chances with hers. "They're out in the car, but I'm not giving them to you while my grandmother's still at risk."

"Give me those pictures now," she hissed through clenched teeth.

I held up a hand. "Let me finish. You let me lock my grandmother inside the bakery, and I'll leave the key on the table so you can't get back in. When we're in the car, I'll give you the envelope, and then you can do whatever"—I swallowed hard—"whatever you have to with me."

She shot me an irritated look. "I told you that I won't hurt her."

"You already have. And sorry to say, but I don't exactly believe in promises that killers make."

"Oh, fine," Lena huffed, "but if you're bluffing or try anything stupid, you're going to be very sorry."

As she pushed me toward the back door, I was already sorry. Sorry that I had gotten my grandmother and me mixed up into this mess. Unfortunately, it was too late now. Lena was going to shoot me and dump my body somewhere, and there still might not be any way to pin the two murders on her. If Grandma Rosa hadn't seen her approach, there was no way anyone could be positive Lena was at fault. Perhaps Martin would take the blame, unless Brian managed to put it all together like I had. At least then I wouldn't have died in vain.

After scanning the alley in both directions, Lena forced me into my car from the passenger side. "Move over. You're driving." She pushed me into the seat and got in next to me, pointing the gun at my head. "Hand over the pictures *now*. If you don't have them, I swear to God I'll put a bullet through your head."

In an effort to stay calm, I slowly pulled down the visor and handed her the envelope inside. She kept the gun pointed at me as she opened it with her other hand. Then she muttered a four-letter expletive. "Where are the rest?"

"The police have them."

"They what!" Lena's eyeballs bulged as she screeched. "What the hell have you done?"

"Allegra had them in a safe deposit box. I found the key, and the police had to go with me to open it. They confiscated the rest."

She swore again. "I don't believe this. You lied to me!"

How ironic. A killer was upset at *me* for lying. "I didn't lie to you. I said I had pictures, but I didn't tell you how many."

"Turn left!" she screamed. "I have to think about what to do next. You've ruined everything! Okay, we'll go to my house. No one's there. You're going to help me figure out how to get the rest of the photos back. I'll hide your car in the garage for now. Maybe I'll tie you up and smack you around for pulling such a dumb stunt."

Gee, my idea of a good time. "You stole the keys to Richard's car so you could run Allegra down."

"Hey, I got it fixed while he was on his honeymoon," she said, sounding slightly defensive. "I know a great mechanic outside of town who never asks questions. No one was ever the wiser. Turn right here."

I had more questions, and if they weren't asked now, I might never know what had transpired. "What was Allegra planning to do with the pictures?"

Lena shrugged. "Probably nothing. She just didn't want to take a chance they'd leak out. The battle-axe thought I'd keep paying her money—a win-win situation for her. But Auntie's greed got the best of her. God, I hate people who just take and take, you know?"

I rolled my eyes at this one. "Totally."

A smile formed at the corners of her mouth. "Aunt Allegra needed to know that things don't always work out the way you plan. Not in my book anyhow. I realized after a while that she never intended to give the pictures back to me. I was a fool—handing out money to her with no return. And if I stopped paying, what did she care? She had her dough, she had the photos. But I *needed* those pictures—for leverage."

"Leverage for what?" I asked.

She scowled at me. "Do I look stupid? Everyone thinks Martin is some squeaky-clean politician. Well, let me tell you, that's a joke. He started cheating on me right after our wedding. Maybe your marriage is based on love and trust, but I know better. After his last election there were rumors going around the law firm that he was into prostitutes, and if he wasn't careful, it might hurt his chances of becoming reelected. He needed a wife to make his image look better."

Lena paused for breath. "I was an intern at his firm, and we hooked up one night. Man, I was dumb enough back then to think that I was in love with him. I used to get so turned on by him. I mean, the man reeked of charisma and power, you know?" Lena breathed in deeply, as if she could actually smell the traits. "Soon afterward, he proposed marriage, and we concocted this story that he was my mentor, blah blah, and that was how we'd fallen deeply and passionately in love."

Lena smiled—almost sadly I thought. The gun was positioned inches from my head as I swallowed back a lump of panic in my throat. "He told me the marriage would be no strings attached and mandated I sign a prenup," she said. "In return, he'd help me pass the bar and give me a job at his firm. A nice offer, but it wasn't enough for me. I wanted—no, I *needed* more. Martin's lifestyle is so much better than mine ever was. My parents didn't have two nickels to rub together. So I thought I could live with the cheating. When I found out about Violet though, I saw an opportunity to get more."

"Was Violet in love with him?"

She shook her head. "If you ask me, Violet moved to Vegas to get away from him. When Martin wants something, he gets annoying and ridiculous, like a baby crying for the moon. He had friends in town last year who run an escort service in Vegas. One of them slipped Violet a card, and Martin was furious about it. I think Violet liked the idea of getting under his skin because he was smothering her. She told Martin that their fling was over, but he still wouldn't accept it."

"He told you all this?" I couldn't fathom a married couple talking about the husband's affair, especially with his wife's cousin.

"Not everything. What I didn't know I figured out. Plus I always checked his cell phone after he went to bed. For such a smart guy, he could be pretty stupid about leaving it on. He'd been begging her for months to come for a visit and even sent her a first-class ticket. Imagine his surprise when she finally accepted his offer then returned all the jewelry he'd given her during their affair." Lena's nostrils flared. "There was even a bracelet that he'd originally bought for me! Martin's such a piece of crap. Take a right here."

My mind was desperately searching for a way to get away from her. Crash the car? Try to grab the gun? If Lena got me inside her house, it would be all over. *Think, Sal. Think.*

She giggled. "When I found out that Violet was coming to see Martin, I thought it would be the perfect day to rid the world of Auntie. Anna already had told me that she and Enzo were coming into town to see their mother's shop. So if I could manage to mow her down, there were so many other potential idiots—ahem, I mean people—to pin it on. Sure, the cops in this town move slow, but I knew they'd eventually figure out that Violet was in town the same day."

"Who took the pictures?" Maybe her arm would get tired of holding the gun and she'd let it waver. Somehow, I needed to distract her.

"I hired a private detective to start following Martin around about a year ago," Lena explained. "I knew pictures would come in handy at some point, and sure enough, it didn't take long for Roger to snap them. Then out of the blue, Martin announced to me that after he got reelected, we would agree to divorce amicably. I said yes—if he gave me a partnership in the firm. He said 'no way in hell.' So that was when I broke the news and told him I was ready to go public with the pictures and his affairs, specifically the one with my cousin. Martin had no choice but to agree to my demands. After he put it all in writing and won the election, he could tell everyone that I was the cheater for all I cared."

I was still piecing this together in my mind. Not an easy thing to do when you're driving with a gun positioned next to your head. "How did Allegra get the pictures?"

Lena's smile turned bitter. "She saw a chance to make some cool dough and keep her daughter's name out of the scandal. Yeah, she'd never be Mother of the Year, but Violet was her favorite. Or at least the one child she somewhat cared for. Allegra didn't want to see her baby dragged through the mud. Guess the old bat had feelings after all. Anyhow, one night a couple of months ago, I came home to find Auntie waiting for me in my study. The maid had let her in. Believe it or not, she came over to ask about you. Of course, I didn't even know who you were back then, and now we're such close buds. Amazing, isn't it?"

"She asked about *me*?"

Lena laughed. "Yeah, she said she had a chance to rent an apartment over a bakery to start her candy business. She asked me questions about a tenant's rights, and if I knew of any situations where the landlord had been sued for threatening a tenant with bodily harm. *Hello*, do I look like a real estate attorney? Guess she planned to play you for a chump all along."

I fumed in silence at her words. It was hard to believe anyone could be so rotten to the core.

Lena went on. "I tell you, the old bat was part dragon and part psychic. I had the photos taped to the underside of my desk drawer. Martin would never think to look for them there. Allegra must have been snooping around while she waited for me and found them."

"Allegra already knew about the pictures?" I asked.

"She might have. Martin may have told Violet about them and then she in turn told her mother. Hey, whatever. But Allegra had the audacity to lift them from my study—*in my house*! A couple of days later, I started getting texts and orders to deposit sums of cash into her bank account." Lena shook her head in apparent disgust. "My own aunt. I mean, how could someone do something so despicable? She was my flesh and blood!"

Incredulous, I stared at her. "I can't believe you're saying that. You deliberately ran her over. You planned ahead of time to kill her. That's premeditated murder."

"You don't understand," she said angrily. "I didn't have a choice. I needed those photos. They were my only chance—my only leverage against Martin and the only way to gain the power I need. I crave power like a drug addict craves crack. Like a vampire craves blood. Like a—"

Jeez Louise. "Okay, I get it," I snapped.

"Would you believe that dear old Auntie had the audacity to hit Martin up for money when I stopped paying? *Hello*? Where did she think I was getting the money from to begin with?"

"So that explains why he went to Nicoletta's house to confront Allegra."

Lena let out a giggle reminiscent of a little girl's. "That woman had real nerve, that's for sure. I guess she thought she'd double her funds. Martin and I don't agree on a lot of things these days, but we both like power and how it makes us feel."

"So Martin was in on the scheme to kill her too?" I asked.

"Go straight here." Lena shook her head. "Nope, I take credit for that. Martin didn't know about my plan. When he learned of Aunt Allegra's accident, he called it a stroke of good luck. The devil was interfering in our lives. She had to go."

Somehow I found it difficult to believe that Lena had only married Martin to advance her career and vice versa. How could these people have no respect for the institution of marriage? "You really didn't care that he was sleeping with other women? I mean, with your own *cousin?*"

"Okay, that part bothered me a little," she confessed. "But like I said, we both had our reasons."

I still didn't understand. "He's your husband. I once had a cheating husband. He's dead now, and I've moved on, but the pain never goes away."

She looked at me, confused. "Who cares about that? I only married Martin to get ahead. He married me to help keep his reputation as an honest, standup politician and to get reelected. Everyone loves those sappy stories. You know, the girl who comes from a very modest background. Her poor parents immigrated from Italy, gave birth to a daughter in America, and this girl, with nothing but a dream and drive to succeed, meets the dashing, rich, and powerful senator. People eat that crap up. God, when are they going to wake up and smell the Amaretto?"

We started along the long, paved driveway that sloped gently toward Lena's house. "Stop," she commanded. "I gave the security guard the afternoon off, so I'll have to open the gate myself."

"Oh, okay." I gripped the steering wheel between my hands, waiting for her to get out of the car.

She barked out a laugh. "You really must think I'm dumb. Move it, Nancy Drew. You're coming with me."

I remained sitting there until the cold tip of the gun's barrel connected with my temple.

"I said to move!" she yelled. "Or I can kill you now and stuff your body into the trunk. No biggee. I can always figure out what to do with it later. That's right, toward me now."

Trying to stay calm, I slid across the passenger seat and out the opened door. She pushed me around to the front of vehicle and kept me by her side as she attempted to open the gate. It was heavy wrought iron, and she struggled with the latch.

"Damn thing," she hissed. "I told that stupid idiot to leave it unlocked and opened. God, it's so hard to find good help these days."

She struggled with the latch with one hand, the other pointing the revolver at me. As she continued to curse, my eyes darted around in hopes of an escape. We were too far off the main road. If I tried to run, there was no doubt in my mind she'd shoot me. This was a private estate, and the chance of another car coming onto the property was slim.

Out of the corner of my eye, I spotted movement and realized my car was slowly edging forward. For a split second, I continued to stare at the vehicle, immobilized with fear. If I didn't make a run for it, we'd both end up pinned between the vehicle and the gate. Lena might still try to shoot me, but it was a chance I had to take.

The car crept forward, its motor rumbling. I inched farther away from Lena.

She lifted the latch and clicked the barrel on the gun.

"Move any farther and you're dead, Nancy."

"Look out!" I shouted and dove across the driveway as the car smashed into the gate. Lena screamed as she fired the gun, but the shot went wild. I looked up from my fetal position on the grass, but all I could see were Lena's legs sticking out from underneath the car, in a manner eerily similar to the Wicked Witch of the East from the *Wizard of Oz.*

If Allegra was watching from heaven—or perhaps that other, fiery place—I knew she must be smiling and thinking it was about time her niece got her just desserts.

CHAPTER TWENTY-TWO

———

The sharp clacking of heels against the linoleum floor grew louder by the second. I looked up from the message I was texting to Josie and saw my sister approaching. Her face was a sickly gray color, and she stopped for a moment to catch her breath.

"Is—is she okay?" Gianna asked nervously.

I rose to my feet. "Grandma's fine. She has a concussion, and they want her to stay the night to be on the safe side."

She nodded, not saying anything further as her large, chocolate-colored eyes filled with tears.

I swallowed around the gigantic lump building in my throat and threw my arms around her. "Gi, I'm so sorry."

"No, I'm the one who's sorry," Gianna choked out as she wept into my shoulder. "I didn't know—I mean, what was going on with you. My timing was awful."

I released her and drew back. She had to mean the pregnancy test, but I wanted to be certain first. "What are you talking about?"

Before she could reply, Johnny came over to us and placed a hand on her shoulder. "I'm going to call Gram and fill her in on what's happening with Rosa."

"How is she?" I asked.

"Feeling better," Johnny said. "She's back at her house, and Ronald's with her. I told her to stay there. The last thing we need right now is Gram wandering the halls, shouting for Rosa at the top of her lungs." He glanced around the waiting area. "Is Mike with you?"

"He went down to the cafeteria for some coffee," I said.

"I'll go see if I can catch up with him." Johnny gave

Gianna a light peck on the lips, and I saw a genuine look of affection pass between the two of them, making me wonder if Johnny knew about the baby. He quietly strode out of the waiting room and left us alone.

We both sat down and faced each other while holding hands. "What happened with Lena? Is she going to survive?" Gianna asked.

I nodded. "Brian called and told me she's got two broken legs, a shattered pelvis, and some other injuries. She's actually here in the hospital somewhere, but I'm sure there's a police officer guarding her room." With the injury to her pelvis, it wasn't likely she'd be much of a threat. "Lena confessed to running Allegra down, and she'll be going away for a long time."

Gianna exhaled sharply. "I never would have dreamed it was her. It sounded like Martin had more to lose. Was he involved too?"

"Lena told me no, and Brian said the police don't think so either. Martin swore to them that he had no idea what Lena was planning. She blackmailed him with the photos of him and Violet so that he'd give her a partnership. It was all about power for them but she took it a step too far."

Gianna raised an eyebrow at me. "They were both obsessed. People like that give lawyers a bad name. Remember, I did tell you she failed the bar six times. She was nothing if not persistent, I guess."

I put my phone away in my purse. "The crime was clearly premeditated. Lena knew that Allegra's kids would all be in town that day and figured it would be a great time to get rid of her then blame it on one of them."

Gianna's eyes widened in horror. "She could have killed you. God, Sal, how many times has someone held a gun to your head?"

Yes, it was starting to get a little old. The scary part was that I hadn't been as phased by it as much this time around. Sure, I'd been frightened, but somehow had managed to stay calm during the process. Was I starting to get used to having my life in danger? A disturbing thought. Then again, I'd been more concerned about my grandmother's welfare than my own.

I smiled at my sister. "The woman's missing a few nails

upstairs, as Grandma would say. She killed her own aunt, assaulted our grandmother, and then kidnapped me."

"Some people in this world are just born evil," Gianna agreed. "And you always seem to have a way of finding them."

She had a valid point. "Even if Martin wasn't involved, the police have pictures of him and Violet, and they'll probably go public now. It looks like his reputation will be tarnished after all."

Gianna wearily leaned her head back against the seat. "It's sad to say, but I've never met a totally clean politician. I've always had my doubts about him. What's going on with Mom and Dad? Did you speak to them?"

I shook out my leg, which had started to cramp, in front of me. "They're catching the red-eye back from Vegas tonight and should be home early tomorrow morning. They renewed their vows today, with an Elvis impersonator officiating."

"Give me strength," Gianna muttered. "Can we go see Grandma now?"

"Soon, I hope. I'm waiting for the nurse to come out of her room and give me the go-ahead."

She stared down at the floor. Silence hung heavy in the air between us until she finally spoke. "Sal, about yesterday. I'm so sorry. I had no idea you'd just taken a pregnancy test when I came over."

I drew my eyebrows together in confusion. "Who told you?"

"Josie," Gianna said. "After I got done with work, I thought I'd reach out to her and see how you were doing. I wondered if you might have told her about our…argument. She was at the ballfield and told me to stop by. Josie mentioned what had happened—with your test. I guess she figured I already knew. Then I, in turn, told her about my pregnancy." Her face became grief stricken. "Sal, if I'd known, I never would have told you about the baby yesterday. It was so insensitive of me."

Tears started to well in the corners of my eyes. "You have nothing to be sorry about. This is your baby, and whatever you decide to do, I'll support you. I don't want you to ever feel like there's anything you can't talk to me about."

She squeezed my hand. "I've decided to have the baby."

I reached out to hug her, relieved by the statement. "I'm so glad, Gi."

Gianna blew out a breath. "I know there are choices, but for me, this seems like the right thing to do. It's going to take a while to come to terms with everything, but with Johnny's support, I'll be fine. The baby's due in March. When I finish my maternity leave, Johnny will be done with school for the year, and he can watch the baby the entire summer. Next fall, he may try to find a teaching job at night so that he can stay home with the baby during the day."

Dang, she moved fast. "When did you tell him?"

"This morning," she said, "I couldn't have made any major decisions without his knowledge, Sal. Like you said, it's his baby too. I guess I was in total shock yesterday when we first talked. After I left your house, I went to see Grandma, and that helped."

Guilt overwhelmed me. I was her big sister and still felt like I'd failed her in her hour of need. "What did Johnny say?" Although I was pretty sure I already knew what his reaction would be.

Gianna's eyes glowed with happiness. "Johnny's on cloud nine. He was so happy he even started to cry."

We both paused to wipe our eyes, although probably for different reasons. She couldn't know how often I'd dreamed about Mike having the same reaction when I told him my wonderful news. But this was her moment, not mine. "You're both going to make terrific parents."

"Thanks, Sal. That means more to me than you'll ever know. Fortunately, Nicoletta was sleeping when I broke the news to him but he was so excited that he rushed right upstairs to tell her."

Oh boy. "Do I dare ask how that went over?"

"Better than I expected," Gianna admitted. "She immediately started talking about weddings, and Johnny told her it was our child and we would do what we wanted. Well, she didn't like that one bit, swore at us in Italian, and went home." She laughed. "Now that the threat to her life is over, she'll stay there. I want her involved with the baby, but I could never stand living with her."

"Yeah, I know. Going to Vegas with her was quite an experience."

We were interrupted by the arrival of the nurse, a middle-aged woman in pink scrubs and matching crocs. "You can go in to see your grandmother now," she told me. "Mrs. Belgacci is down the hall in room 566. Turn left at the nurse's station."

"Thank you." I gestured at Gianna. "This is my sister. Can we both go?"

"Of course." She smiled warmly. "Don't stay too long, though. She's tired and needs her rest."

We started down the hallway together. The door to Grandma Rosa's room was partially open, and the television was on, but she wasn't watching it. She was lying in the bed with a large bandage wrapped around her head. Her eyes were closed, but they fluttered open when we entered the room. Gianna and I each pulled up a chair and sat down on either side of the bed.

Grandma Rosa stared up at us and smiled. "I am glad to see that everything is all right between my two beautiful granddaughters."

"Please don't worry about us," I said. "How are you feeling?"

She wiggled her hand back and forth. "My head hurts, and I am tired. Let's face it. I am no summer chicken."

Gianna gave a small chuckle. "You mean spring, Grandma."

"Bah. It is summertime, so it fits." My grandmother watched me thoughtfully. "But I feel a bit like an imbecile, for I did not even know that Lena was behind me in the alley. I always tell my granddaughters to take precautions, and look what happened to me. *Cara mia,* I am so glad you found out the truth. Now Allegra can rest easy."

"What about Enzo and Anna?" Gianna asked.

"Brian told me they were notified about Lena. They've already left for New Jersey." It angered me that they hadn't even stopped to see Nicoletta or so much as inquire about my grandmother's health before leaving.

My grandmother made a *tsk-tsk* sound. "It is too bad that they did not care about their own mother. Then again, it was

Allegra's fault too for the way she treated them. You reap what you sow, and a child must know they are loved." She reached for Gianna's hand. "Johnny knows about the baby?"

Gianna smiled. "Yes, and he's thrilled."

Grandma Rosa nodded in approval. "I knew he would be. Is he here?"

"He went downstairs to the cafeteria with Mike," Gianna replied. "Do you want to see him?"

"For a minute." She closed her eyes. "But I would like to talk to your sister alone first."

Gianna looked wide-eyed from Grandma Rosa to me. "Of course. I'll go find him and Mike and give you guys some space." She patted my shoulder lightly and then left the room.

Grandma Rosa reached for my hand. "I wanted to thank you, my dear. You saved my life."

"There's no need to thank me."

"Yes, there is," she insisted. "I could not move, but I heard what you said to Lena in the bakery. It means more to me than you will ever know. I am very proud of you."

I bit into my lower lip, afraid that I might cry. "Thank you. When you told me that you were disappointed in me yesterday"—I couldn't finish the sentence—"it hurt me so badly because I never want to let you down."

She waved a hand in the air. "Bah. That does not mean I do not love you, *cara mia*. I know how difficult it must have been for you to hear those words from your sister. Sometimes in this life we must put our own personal hurt aside to help others. You are so much stronger than you think. You are a good girl, a good wife, and someday, you will be a wonderful mother."

"But what if it never happens?" I blurted out.

"It *will* happen," she insisted. "You must be there for Gianna first. She will have a beautiful baby, and then it will be your turn. Perhaps it will not happen like you want it to, though. Perhaps you must love a child that was born to another woman. But that part does not matter. You and Mike have enough love between you to care for any child. Remember, without faith there is no hope. Nothing in this life is fair, my dear. You should know this by now."

"Yes." She had me on this one.

"Your day will come, *cara mia*. And when it does, we will all rejoice for you."

"Thank you, Grandma. I needed to hear that." I exhaled a long, steady breath. "Maybe we're not supposed to get everything we want in this life. Sometimes, though, I feel that I want this more than life itself. Does that even make sense?"

She nodded in her understanding way. "Yes. You were meant to be a mother, *cara mia*. I remember as a little girl how every Christmas you asked your parents for a new baby doll. You must have had ten of them and always took such good care of each one. It will happen. Call it my sick sense."

"You mean sixth sense, Grandma."

"I like that too."

CHAPTER TWENTY-THREE

———

Saturday morning dawned sunny and warm, a gorgeous summer day with a cloudless blue sky and the hint of a gentle breeze. Mike and I were all packed and ready to go for our weekend trip. Tomorrow was our anniversary, and we planned to spend two nights in Niagara Falls. The trip was less than an hour each way, and although the waterfalls were beautiful any time of the year, I preferred to visit in the summer—basking in the sun and sand. Gianna had offered to help at the bakery today, and Josie was confident she could handle everything until I returned home Monday afternoon.

My parents had asked us to stop over on our way out of town. Gianna told me that she and Johnny would be there as well. I suspected Gianna was going to tell them about the baby and an impromptu celebration would follow.

"Are you going to be okay with this, sweetheart?" Mike asked anxiously.

"Of course." I gave Spike a hug and shut and locked the door. Johnny had promised to stop by later this morning to pick the dog up and bring him back to his and Gianna's house. They were dog sitting for the weekend and even thinking about getting a puppy themselves. Neither one had ever owned a pet before and thought it would be nice with the baby coming. I didn't mention the fact that Spike was 13 years old, and there was a big difference between a dog his age and a puppy. They'd figure things out for themselves.

I settled in the truck next to Mike and pulled my seat belt around me. "I'm much better now. Wow. Just think. In less than a year, we're going to be an aunt and uncle."

Mike started the engine. "I wonder what it's going to be."

"Well, probably a boy or girl," I teased.

He brought my hand to his lips. "Wise guy. It's kind of a miracle that I don't have an ulcer yet. I hope you're done with these brushes with death for a while—or maybe even forever."

"Me too," I admitted, though sometimes I wondered if it would continue to be my destiny to run into these life-threatening situations. Sure, I didn't go looking for trouble, but it seemed to find me anyway. Thankfully, Grandma Rosa was fine. She'd returned home on Wednesday and was back to her normal self again.

She was waiting for us when we pulled into my parents' driveway. I'd always thought of my grandmother as invincible, but the other day had sadly taught me that no one was. To see her looking so frail had been frightening and forced me to face some unpleasant realities. As she'd often told Gianna and me in the past, we could only control our own destiny to a certain extent. One had to live life to the fullest and make every day count because we never knew when it might be our last.

I stared down at the fortune cookies in my lap that Mrs. Gavelli had requested—okay, demanded—that I bring. So much had happened since I'd read the message about family blessings, and here I was, about to experience one today.

With a smile, I leaped out of the truck and rushed toward my grandmother. Hope and faith. I would continue to live with them every day and not ignore the other blessings in life. And perhaps wish upon a star now and then.

She stretched out her arms to me, and I flew into them while Mike kissed her on the cheek. "Are you feeling okay?" I asked.

Grandma Rosa gave me a surprised look. "Of course. I told you that I am fine. Come inside. Everyone is already in the dining room. You shall have breakfast before you leave on your trip."

We followed her to the cherrywood dining room table where my mother, father, Gianna, and Johnny were gathered. My father had his laptop next to his plate. These days, he never seemed to travel without it. He and my mother were already looking into ways to market his novel and planning to visit a few independent bookstores in the area.

My mother got up from her seat and hurried over to hug me. "Oh darling, isn't it wonderful? You're going to be an aunt, and I'm going to be a grandmother."

Mike placed a protective hand on my shoulder, but it wasn't necessary. I hugged Mom back and looked over her shoulder at Gianna, who was watching me anxiously. I smiled in reassurance at her. "It is wonderful, Mom. I can't wait."

"Sit down before everything gets cold," Dad said as he shoveled a hefty amount of bacon and pancakes into his mouth.

I stared at the food, and my stomach rumbled in response. My grandmother's famous breakfast quiche was among the dishes, which also included homemade biscuits, hash brown potatoes, pancakes, bacon, and sausage.

"Where are you guys going in Niagara Falls? The American or Canadian side?" Gianna asked as she helped herself to a biscuit.

I pointed at Mike. "Ask him. He made all the arrangements. It's apparently some kind of big secret."

Mike polished off a glass of orange juice and reached for the carafe of coffee. "That's right. There's always a method to my madness."

"Well, enjoy. You're supposed to have perfect weather." Gianna reached out a hand to Johnny, and he sandwiched it between both of his.

My father proudly puffed out his chest in the somewhat snug, white Sally's Samples T-shirt that I'd had made for the shop. I'd wanted to give him a larger size, but he'd refused. "I'm going to be the most famous grandparent in the state of New York, and your mother's going to be the best-looking one."

I reached for the chocolate cheesecake my grandmother had placed in front of me and cut a large slice.

She smiled at me. "I knew you would have some."

"Hey, we're on vacation this weekend," I said in my defense. "But you never make chocolate cheesecake. What gives?"

She folded her hands primly on top of the table. "I did not make this one."

I looked over at my mother with surprise, but she only giggled and clapped her hands. "Oh, Sal. You know I don't cook.

Maybe I should learn since I have a grandbaby on the way."

"And I—I be the smartest great-grandmother around," a sharp voice announced from the kitchen.

I jumped, not realizing Nicoletta was there.

She came out of the kitchen with a cup of coffee in her hands. "I make cheesecake," she said to me. "It better than your grandmother's. And *I* will be the best great-grandma around."

"Ahem," my grandmother snorted. "I may have something to say about that."

At least Nicoletta seemed to be taking the baby news in stride, which made me happy for my sister.

"I bet it will be a boy," I said.

"Nah. A girl for sure," Johnny replied.

"Are you going to find out?" my mother asked Gianna.

Gianna nodded. "Probably. I don't like surprises." She winked at me, and I laughed out loud.

"I'm always full of surprises," my father added.

Boy, was that the truth. I placed two pancakes on my plate. "This is wonderful, but I thought you invited us over so we could be here when you told Mom and Dad, Gi? I didn't realize they already knew."

Gianna prodded Johnny in the shoulder. "This was all his idea. What are you up to?"

Johnny looked around the room at all of us and flashed a gleaming white smile, but he seemed a bit uneasy. "Like Mike, I have a method to my madness too." He got out of his chair and dropped to one knee in front of Gianna. She looked startled as he opened a small box and presented her with a magnificent diamond solitaire, its stone winking in the bright lights from my parents' chandelier.

"Oh, my God!" My mother covered her mouth with a hand.

"Oh God," Gianna whispered breathlessly.

My father reached for a slice of cheesecake and then typed something in on his laptop. "This will make a great story for the blog today. Well, if she says yes, that is."

"Hush, fool," Grandma Rosa snarled at him.

Johnny reached for Gianna's hand. "Gianna Muccio, I love you more than anything in this world. I always have. Please say you'll make me the happiest man on the face of this earth and be my wife."

We all held our breath for a moment.

Tears ran down Gianna's cheeks as she threw her arms around his neck. "Yes. Yes, of course I'll marry you."

My mother started to cry, and my father let out a whoop as he shoved a forkful of cheesecake into his mouth. "Here's to an Italian son-in-law!" Then he glanced sheepishly over at Mike. "No offense, son. You're pretty okay, even if you're not Italian."

Mike suppressed a smile as he leaned over to kiss me. I stood up, and he drew me onto his lap, wrapping his arms around me. "There was a time when you would have said something different to me, Domenic. I seem to remember you chasing me down the driveway with a baseball bat on prom night."

My father's mouth twitched into a small smile. "That's true," he agreed. "But, hey, what can I say—I've grown up since then."

* * *

Two hours later, Mike and I checked into our room at the Grand Falls Hotel. I wasn't sure what I had expected to find but was a bit surprised to discover that it was a standard room, although there was a bouquet of roses and a bottle of champagne inside to greet us. Mike and I had been here once before, and that fact was not lost on me.

"Is this the same room?" I asked, placing my bag on the king-size bed.

He grinned at me mischievously. "The very same one. Hard to believe that was thirteen years ago."

Like both of us, the room had changed over the years and the décor had been updated to a more modern one. The one thing that was still the same was the glorious view of the falls. I stepped out onto the small balcony and stared out at the mesmerizing sight before me, watching the foam skim off the top of the water.

It had been a forbidden weekend when we'd run away from our families thirteen years ago, an attempt to express our young love for each other. The only person who'd known about it back then was Josie, who'd also acted as my alibi. At least I thought she'd been the only one. Afterward I'd discovered that my grandmother, who'd fortunately kept the information to herself, had known too. "This is perfect."

Mike slid the glass door closed behind him. "If your father was aware I'd brought you here while we were both still in high school, he probably wouldn't have said those nice things to me earlier this morning."

"Probably not," I laughed. We stood there for a long time, watching the waves and the breathtaking view. The setting was peaceful and serene, and it was as if we were the only two people on the face of the earth.

Mike put his arms around my waist and planted a kiss on my neck. "They weren't sure if this room would be available, but I told the manager I had to have it."

"Did you now?" I placed my hands over his as we watched the mist rising above the water. I thought I could stand here forever. "So pretty. Truly a wonder of the world."

He turned me toward him and kissed me. "Well, you're definitely the number-one wonder in my world, princess. And now that Trevor's accepted my job offer, I'll have time to start on the bakery's renovation this fall. Sound good?"

"It sounds wonderful. Did those recommendations ever come through for him?"

"Yeah, I got a great one from a guy he did construction work for last year. It doesn't even matter, though. Trevor can fix anything, his rate is reasonable, and I really need the help." He wove his hands gently through my hair. "He understands that I can't promise anything long-term, but since he's new in town and limited for opportunities, he was thrilled. I told Trevor we'd have him over to the house for dinner soon. This just feels right, Sal."

"I'm so glad." We stood there for several minutes, my head pressed into his rock-hard chest as I exhaled a long, steady breath. "I really needed this time away—just you and me. Some days I think I'm too obsessed with—" Then I stopped, afraid to ruin the moment.

"I know." Mike's voice was gentle as he rested his face in my hair. "I know how much you want it, sweetheart. But you can't lose faith. We'll always have each other, no matter what happens."

I stared up into his handsome face. "I honestly don't know what I'd do without you."

He laughed. "Well, I certainly don't know what I'd do without you either." He gestured for me to sit down in one of the white, plastic chairs. "I have a present for you."

"But our anniversary isn't until tomorrow," I protested.

Mike's midnight blue eyes gleamed at me, the sun in the background reflecting off of them. He gave me an impish grin that reminded me of a little boy's. "I can't wait any longer. I almost wanted to smack Gavelli this morning. It felt like he was trying to steal my thunder." He dropped to one knee in front of me and presented me with a small package wrapped in silver paper. "For my princess."

I cocked my head to the side and studied him for a moment. "Um, I'm not sure where you've been the past year, Mr. Donovan, but I'm already married. To a pretty hot guy, in fact."

He grinned. "Just open it."

Unable to contain my excitement, I tore off the paper and found a white jewelry box. I lifted the lid, and my breath caught in my throat. There was a beautiful ring inside, surrounded by a satin lining. The ring was a slender gold band with a row of tiny diamonds around it.

Stunned, I sat staring as Mike removed the ring from the box and placed it on the same finger as my wedding and engagement rings. He held fast to my hand, examining and turning it so the light from the sun caught it. "An eternity ring. Do you like it?"

My voice trembled with emotion. "I love it. It's beautiful, sweetheart, but you shouldn't have spent so much money on me." I'd ended up buying him a watch with a small diamond on the face of it, but that probably hadn't cost anywhere near what this exquisite ring had.

He held fast to my hand. "I've been planning this for a while and putting my pennies aside, little by little, so to speak."

I ran my other hand through his hair and leaned forward to kiss him. "This cost more than a few pennies."

"I don't care," Mike said. "You're worth it and so much more." He pointed at the row of tiny diamonds. "See the continuance around the ring? That symbolizes our love—going on forever. It's you and me together for always, my princess. We will have our family, Sal. It's going to happen someday. I want children as much as you do. They don't have to be ours biologically—they'll be a product of our love no matter what. It's your dream to be a mother, and I promise to do whatever's necessary to make that dream come true."

So much for watching the waterfalls since my own had started. "I have my dream already." My voice was hoarse. "I have you. Anything else is a plus."

Mike lifted me to my feet and kissed me passionately. We stood there in silence, for words weren't necessary. He was my biggest blessing, and as long as I had him, everything would work itself out.

"We'll get through this, princess," he said, his reassuring voice next to my ear. "Nothing has ever come easily or quickly for us. Hell, we were apart for ten years but managed to find our way back to each other. You trust me, right?"

"Always."

Mike cupped my face between his hands. "As long as I have you, the world could crumble around us, and it wouldn't make any difference to me."

"Another cookie pun?" I teased.

He kissed me lightly on the mouth. "No, your grandmother's the expert on those."

"On getting them mixed up, you mean."

"Well, she's certainly original," Mike admitted. "Then again, your entire family is. She doesn't come close to your nutsy cookie parents, though."

"You mean cuckoo," I laughed.

He smiled down into my eyes. "I like that too."

RECIPES

———

DOUBLE CHOCOLATE CHILI COOKIES

Ingredients:
1 cup all-purpose flour
2 tablespoons cornstarch
1 cup Dutch-process cocoa powder
1 ½ teaspoons flaky sea salt or kosher salt
¾ teaspoon baking soda
¾ teaspoon baking powder
½ to 1 teaspoon cayenne powder, depending on how spicy you
want the cookies
1 cup packed brown sugar
¾ cup granulated sugar
¾ cup unsalted butter, room temperature
2 teaspoons pure vanilla extract
2 eggs, room temperature
1 ½ cups chocolate chip (your choice of dark, semi-sweet, milk,
or white)
Granulated sugar for rolling

Prep time: Several hours to overnight in order to chill properly.

Whisk flour, cornstarch, cocoa powder, salt, baking soda, baking
powder, and cayenne together in a small bowl. In a standing
mixer fitted with the paddle attachment, cream butter until pale
and fluffy. Beat in sugars until smooth and fluffy, scraping down
the sides of the bowl as needed. Add in vanilla then beat in one
egg at a time until incorporated. Add in half the flour mixture on
low and mix to incorporate before adding the other half. Once
flour is incorporated, stir in the chocolate chips.

Cover and refrigerate dough for several hours or overnight.
Using 1-½ teaspoon scoop, roll dough into a ball. Roll each ball

in granulated sugar before placing on a parchment-lined baking sheet about two inches apart.

Bake at 350 degrees Fahrenheit for 10 to 12 minutes. The tops of the cookies will have a crackled appearance. Let cool for 5 minutes on the baking sheet then remove to a wire rack to finish cooling. Store in an airtight container for up to 5 days.

Makes about 40 to 50 cookies, depending on size.

CHOCOLATE CHEESECAKE

Ingredients:
Crust
1 ½ cups crushed vanilla wafers (or about 35 cookies)
¾ teaspoon cinnamon
3 teaspoons butter or margarine, melted

Filling
1 ½ cups semisweet chocolate chips
½ cup whipping cream
3 packages cream cheese, (24 ounces total), softened
½ cup sugar
½ teaspoon ground cinnamon
1 teaspoon vanilla
3 eggs

Topping
2 cups sweetened whipped cream
Chocolate shavings, if desired for garnish

Heat oven to 350 degrees Fahrenheit. Wrap the outside bottom and sides of an 8-inch springform pan with heavy-duty foil to prevent the cheesecake leaking out. Spray the inside bottom and sides of pan with cooking spray. In a small bowl, mix crust ingredients together, and press into bottom of pan. Bake 8 to 10 minutes or until set and remove from heat. Reduce oven temperature to 300 degrees Fahrenheit. Cool crust 10 minutes. In 2-quart saucepan, melt chocolate chips and whipping cream over medium-low heat; stir until smooth. Remove from heat. In large bowl, beat cream cheese, sugar, ½ teaspoon cinnamon, and the vanilla with electric mixer on medium speed until fluffy. Beat in eggs, one at a time, just until blended. Stir in chocolate mixture. Pour filling over crust. Bake for one hour or until edge of cheesecake is set at least 2 inches from edge of pan, but center of cheesecake still jiggles slightly. Turn oven o☐ and open the oven door a few inches. Let cheesecake remain in the oven for 30 minutes. Run small metal spatula around edge of pan to loosen cheesecake. Cool in pan on cooling rack 30 minutes. Refrigerate at least 6 hours or overnight.

To serve, run small metal spatula around edge of pan; carefully remove foil and ring of pan. Cut cheesecake into slices. Top slices with whipped cream; sprinkle with ½ teaspoon cinnamon. Garnish with chocolate shavings. Cover; refrigerate any remaining cheesecake. Makes about 16 servings.

SNICKERDOODLES

Ingredients
1 cup, plus 2 tablespoons butter
1 ¾ cups sugar, divided
2 large eggs
2 tablespoons milk
2 teaspoons vanilla extract
2 ¾ cups flour
2 teaspoons cream of tartar
1 teaspoon baking soda
¾ teaspoon salt
1 tablespoon cinnamon

Heat oven to 400 degrees Fahrenheit. Using an electric mixer at medium speed, combine 1 ½ cups sugar, butter, eggs, milk, and vanilla in a large bowl until well blended. Combine flour, cream of tartar, baking soda, and salt in medium bowl. Add gradually to butter mixture at low speed. Mix just until blended. Combine remaining ¾ cup sugar and cinnamon in small bowl. Shape dough by hand or with cookie scoop into 1-inch balls. Roll in cinnamon-sugar mixture, and place 2 inches apart on parchment paper. Bake about 7 minutes, and then place on cooling racks to cool completely. Makes between 2 and 3 dozen cookies.

FUDGY DELIGHT COOKIES

Vanilla Cookie:

Ingredients:
4 ½ cups all-purpose flour
4 ½ teaspoons baking powder
¾ teaspoon salt
1 ½ cups (3 sticks) unsalted butter, at room temperature
1 ½ cups sugar
3 large eggs
5 teaspoons vanilla extract

To make the cookies, preheat the oven to 350 degrees Fahrenheit. Line baking sheets with parchment paper. In a medium bowl combine the flour, baking powder, and salt, and whisk together to blend. In the bowl of an electric mixer, combine the butter and sugar, and beat together on medium-high speed until soft and fluffy, about 2-3 minutes. Beat in the eggs one at a time, mixing well after each addition and scraping down the bowl as needed. Blend in the vanilla. With the mixer on low speed, add in the dry ingredients, mixing just until incorporated and evenly mixed. Cover and chill the dough for 1 hour.

When you are ready to bake the cookies, scoop out the dough into the size of a golf ball, or use a 2-tablespoon scoop for them. Flatten the ball slightly, to about half-inch thickness, and place on the prepared baking sheet. Repeat with the remaining dough, spacing the cookies at least 2-3 inches apart. Bake about 10-12 minutes or just until set. Do not overbake. The edges should be no more than very lightly browned. Let cool on the baking sheet for several minutes. Transfer to a wire rack to cool completely. Makes between 3 and 4 dozen cookies, depending on size.

Ingredients for Frosting:
2 cups granulated sugar

1 cup baking cocoa
1 cup milk
½ cup butter or margarine
¼ cup light corn syrup
¼ teaspoon salt
2 ½ to 3 cups powdered sugar
2 teaspoons vanilla extract

In 3-quart saucepan, mix granulated sugar and cocoa. Stir in milk, butter, corn syrup, and salt. Heat to boiling, stirring frequently. Boil 3 minutes, stirring occasionally. Beat in powdered sugar and vanilla extract with spoon until smooth. Fudge will be runny so chill in the fridge for a few hours or until firm and then frost. There will be enough fudge to frost at least 4 dozen cookies.

ABOUT THE AUTHOR

USA Today bestselling author Catherine Bruns lives in Upstate New York with a male dominated household that consists of her very patient husband, three sons, and assorted cats and dogs. She has wanted to be a writer since the age of eight when she wrote her own version of Cinderella (fortunately Disney never sued). Catherine holds a B.A. in English and is a member of Mystery Writers of America and Sisters in Crime.

To learn more about Catherine Bruns, visit her online at:
www.catherinebruns.net

Enjoyed this book? Check out these other fun reads available in print now from Gemma Halliday Publishing:

www.GemmaHallidayPublishing.com

Printed in Great Britain
by Amazon